BURDEN OF A MOUNTAIN MAN

LOGAN MOUNTAIN MAN SERIES - BOOK 4

DONALD L. ROBERTSON

Edited by
PAULINE NOLET

Illustrated by
CHARLENE RADDON

COPYRIGHT

Burden of a Mountain Man

ISBN: 979-8-9912601-5-2

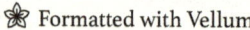 Formatted with Vellum

1

March 2, 1841

Owen Fisher's head jerked up when the stage station door banged open, allowing rain to whip across the floor he had just swept. A beginning frown disappeared when he saw it was a lovely young woman dressed in men's boots, trousers, a coat too large for her, and a soaked slouch hat. She pushed the door closed behind her, whipped off her hat, and beat it against her wet pants. Released, long black hair cascaded over her shoulders.

"How do, mister? You the bull-of-the-woods at this here stage company?" The backwoods twang went with her clothing, but not her striking beauty.

Owen could make out a group of riders in front of his office. In the pouring rain, the men hunched over in their saddles, staring through the rain-swept windows.

"A bit wet outside," Owen replied as he continued to examine the striking features of the woman's face. Dark eyes set deep in a mud-smeared face stared out at him from beneath long black lashes.

She was new in these parts. Her accent hinted of the hill

country back east, Kentucky, maybe Tennessee. In his line of work, he saw many different people and cultures. Independence was the jumping-off point for those seeking new lives in the west.

"I said, you be the man what runs this here lashup?"

"Why, yes," Owen replied, a little flustered that he had been so obviously staring at her. "How may I help you?"

"Lookin' fer a Floyd Logan. Hear tell he be a mountain man."

Before he could answer, two of the men, one obviously older, walked into the station.

The taller, slightly stooped, older man said, "Mary Grace?"

The girl, frustrated, threw an impatient look at the older man. "He ain't answered me yet, Pa. He's just been staring at my upper parts."

The two men, water dripping from their hats and slickers, turned their heads toward Owen. The older fella glared at him. "Mister, are you some kind of freak, staring at my baby girl like that? You know what we do with folks like you back home?"

"No. No, sir." Owen fiercely shook his head. "I . . . I wasn't staring."

The older man impatiently waved Owen's objection away. "We be lookin' fer a Floyd Logan. My girl's done asked you once. Why ain't you been gentlemanly enough to give her an answer?"

The cold gust of air that had accompanied the men chilled the office, but despite the temperature drop, Owen could feel trickles of sweat flowing down his back and under his arms. "I know Mr. Logan. Yes, sir, I sure do. He's well known in this country and west of here."

"So, where can I find him?" the older man asked, his tone and glare carrying an unspoken threat to Owen.

Owen swallowed. "Well, sir, he's way across the high plains. He's in the Rocky Mountains. Probably there by now. He left over a month ago."

"I'm Roscoe Akers, and this here Floyd Logan killed two of my boys. Ain't no man kills a son of mine and goes on breathing.

Where's that young feller what was with him, name of Bobby Sutton?"

Owen swallowed again, feeling relief flood his body. "Why, Mr. Akers, Bobby took his aunt Judith back to Nashville. They left over two weeks ago."

Roscoe slowly turned his head until his cold gray eyes rested on the younger man at his side. "Cooter, I thought you checked all them stages."

Cooter's eyes shifted from his pa's, glancing toward the men outside, then down at his boot, which he scuffed on the rough planking. "I swear we did, Pa. Course, Gent's always been hard to keep in line, him chasing the girls like he does."

Roscoe cursed. "You two git back on yore horses and wait for me. I can handle this." His son Cooter turned immediately, but the girl remained stationary. His frown deepening, he motioned outside with his head.

Her full lips turned into a pout, and wide dark eyes gazed up at Akers. "Pa, it's bone-soaking wet out there, cain't I just wait in here with you 'til we be goin'?"

"Git."

She flinched as if expecting a blow and dashed out the door into the driving rain.

Roscoe turned back to Owen. "Now, Mr. Station Man, you know where in those mountains this here Logan might be?"

"No, sir. I don't have the slightest idea. He ranges all over the Rockies."

The furrows in Roscoe's forehead deepened, and he took a step forward. "I know there's somebody in this here town what can tell me where to find this here mountain man. It'd behoove you to tell me right now, or I just might have to spill yore guts all over this nice pretty counter."

"Mr. Akers, I imagine there are several trappers in the Trail-head. That's the saloon up the street. They could probably give you more information."

Roscoe took another step toward Owen and pulled his long knife from its scabbard on his belt. He began cleaning his dirty fingernails with the razor-sharp tip while staring at Owen. "I'm askin' this one last time, mister. You sure he ain't got no friends here in Independence? I heared he worked for that Hugh Brennan feller what has the wagon business."

The small stream of sweat flowing down Owen's back had turned into a torrent. His shirt was sticking to his back and his sides. "Well . . . yes . . . there is one man he is quite friendly with besides Hugh Brennan."

"Don't keep me waiting, boy. Tell me who it be."

Owen's eyes locked on the big knife. His heart pounded so hard he knew his shirt must be jumping with each beat, and the words fell from his mouth like a racing waterfall. "Salty Dickens. He's a good friend of Floyd's. If he's not at the Brennan barn, you'll find him at the Trailhead, eating dinner."

Roscoe Akers gave a curt nod and slid the shiny blade back into its scabbard. Without a word, he turned and was gone.

"What have I done?" Owen said as he dropped onto the tall stool behind the counter. Never had he been so afraid for his life. He had heard stories of hill people who would kill you over the smallest perceived slight, and he had sent them after Salty. He spoke again to the empty office. "How can I live with myself?" He looked at the Chauncey Jerome eight-day wall clock, which hung on the wall across from the counter. It seemed to stare back at him in disgust. Its hands showed five fifteen. If he went out the back door and ran down to the Brennan barn, he just might catch Salty before he left for the Trailhead. "That's the least I can do." Yanking his coat and hat from the coat tree so hard it crashed to the floor, he bolted for the back door.

～

SALTY DICKENS HAD BEEN on this earth since seventeen sixty-three, and he had the aches and pains that came with his seventy-eight years. But to any of Hugh Brennan's freight or wagon customers, he looked and acted twenty years younger except when he was complaining, and he only complained to his friends. One of whom was old Doc Bessel. Salty thought of him as old, but the doctor was thirty years his junior.

He had closed the barn early today, sending his helper home but staying on to curry four mules. Finished, he blew out the lantern hanging by the door and stepped outside into the pelting rain. "Reckon I deserve an early break today," he said to himself.

Salty slogged across the muddy street, jumping over several small rivers running through the main street. "I'll be glad when this dad-blamed rain stops."

Doc Bessel watched him from the sheltered boardwalk, protected from most of the downpour by the building's overhang.

Salty made a last leap to the boardwalk, mud covering the bottom third of his boots. "What are you goggling at, you old codger?"

The doctor looked him up and down, hunched his shoulders from a gust of chill wind, and said, "I wanted to see what a muddy old, drowned rat looked like. Now I know."

Salty, standing close to the doc to make use of the roof above their heads, removed his soaked hat and beat it against his leg before slapping it back on his full head of white hair. The doctor leaped back to stay out of the spray.

"I swear, Salty, you're worse than an old dog. Just because you're soaked doesn't mean everyone else should be."

"Stop complaining, Doc, and come on down to the Trailhead. I just might buy you a beer."

The doctor pulled his coat closer. "On a night like this, I might need something stronger than a beer to warm me up."

The two men walked toward the Trailhead. Salty watched as a scraggly-looking bunch rode past.

"There goes trouble, if'n I've ever seen it," he said to Doc.

"They do look a little rough."

"More than rough. That's a bunch of backwoods fellers. I'm guessing from either Tennessee or the Kaintucky mountains. Notice they ain't got any wagons or womenfolks. I'm bettin' they're on the prod. Probably after some feller or fellers who wronged 'em some which way."

They watched as the group tied up at the Trailhead.

"You know if the marshal's around?" Doc asked.

"Danged if I know. I've been in the barn all day. Any fellers from the mountains still in town?"

The doctor shook his head. "Don't know. I think most of them rode out with the last wagon train for Santa Fe. I have noticed none arriving today."

Salty nodded. "Just as well. Them not being here'll probably prevent a shootin' or stabbing. Neither them trappers or that bunch of hillbillies'll take anything off the other." Nearing the saloon, he loosened the .36-caliber, five-shot Colt Paterson in his belt. Floyd had given it to him not a month ago. Salty had never liked newfangled things, but after watching Floyd shoot it, he was persuaded. Five shots were always better than one. He slid the Paterson back behind his belt, still thinking of Floyd. *That boy should be back with his family by now. He's growed into a mighty fine feller.*

From behind, running bootsteps banged dully against the rain-soaked boardwalk. Salty wheeled, his hand reaching for the pistol in his belt. Seeing it was Owen Fisher, he relaxed. "Boy, don't you know you could get yourself kilt running up behind a man like that?"

Nodding toward the bunch walking into the Trailhead, Owen gasped, "They're looking for you, Salty."

Salty squinted at the strangers walking into the saloon, too far to recognize any of them. "I swear, Owen, when they rode by, other than recognizing the type of fellers they are, I ain't made out a soul I know."

"You don't, Salty," Owen said. "It's my fault. They came into the office and asked for Floyd Logan. Roscoe Akers, he's the old man, said Floyd killed two of his boys. He pulled out a pig sticker, I swear was over a foot long, and threatened me with it. Scared the sense right out of me. Before I knew it, I had rattled out that you were Floyd's friend and probably at the Trailhead."

Doc Bessel's face grew bleak in the fading light of day. Staring at the station manager, he snapped, "That was a fool thing to do. What were you thinking, man?"

Owen Fisher turned his sad face toward the doc. "I wasn't, Doc. I guess I lost my nerve. All I could see was that big, shiny knife. It happened so fast." He turned back to Salty. "I'm really sorry, Salty."

Salty patted the man on his shoulder. "That's all right, boy. There's many a stronger man than you who's had a case of the nerves. You had the gumption to come tell me. That rates highly with me, and don't you forget it."

Salty pulled the revolver from his belt and checked the loads. Satisfied, he slid it back into its place and turned to Doc Bessel. "With all this talk, I'm gettin' mighty dry. What say we git on to the Trailhead?"

The doctor stared at his friend. "You're not going in there now. You can't be that crazy."

Salty grinned at the doctor. "Doc, I was facin' down the likes of them before yore folks was even born. I'm still kickin'. You comin' with me?"

"Of course I am, you old fool."

"I'm comin' too," Owen said.

For a long moment, Salty looked at the station manager, then nodded. "Come along, then. Seems I ain't the only one buildin' up an almighty thirst."

The three men, bent forward in the wind, trooped steadily

toward the Trailhead. The rain had grown harder. Drops exploded into the mud, joining the flowing water in the street. Salty walked along the outside edge of the boardwalk, the huge drops more than occasionally finding him. He thought, *This here is a fine night. I ain't plannin' on it, but I'm ready. If it's my time, I'll danged sure take a couple of those critters with me.*

They opened the door to the Trailhead and, with Salty leading them, walked dripping into the saloon. The opening of the door attracted all eyes. Salty, with his left hand, unbuttoned his slicker, making sure it would not restrict his weapon. Once finished, he led the way to the table they always used and looked toward Clarence, the bartender. "Howdy, Clarence, we worked up an almighty thirst in that rain. How's about sending Ellie over with three beers?"

"Coming right up."

A few hardy individuals had made it to the Trailhead on this dreary, wet Missouri evening. Besides the Akers clan, who kept eyeing the newcomers, especially Owen, Salty recognized several regulars, who nodded to him when their eyes met. He pulled off his slicker, tossed it on a nail protruding from the wall, pulled out a chair facing the bar, and sat.

Ellie arrived with their three beers as Salty, like an old bear, scratched his back against the back of his chair. He stopped and smiled at the pretty blonde. "Ellie, you're always a pleasurable sight to these old eyes. I ain't figgered out why some young feller hasn't snatched you up. I might do it if'n I was twenty years younger."

Ellie leaned across the table, placed a mug in front of each man, and gave Salty a wide smile, green eyes flashing in the lamplight. "Don't let age stand in your way, Salty."

Salty cackled. "Best be careful, girl. I ain't dead yet."

Ellie winked at him and whirled back toward the bar.

Owen reached for his beer and took a long sip while Doc just shook his head.

At her mention of Salty's name, the Akers crew, who had been leaning against the bar, turned in unison and stared at Salty.

Roscoe said, "You be Salty Dickens?"

Salty took a long draw from his mug, set it down, and said, "Doc, Owen, you hungry?" Both shook their heads no. He called to the bartender, "Clarence, I could sure use a bowl of that stew I smell cookin'."

The bartender nodded. "Comin' right up."

The Akers crew continued to stare at him. Roscoe Akers said, "I asked you a question, mister."

Salty wiped his mouth with his sleeve, let out a long burp after the slug of beer, and stared back at Akers. He watched the man's impatience grow, and just before he was about to speak again, Salty, wrinkles surrounding and almost hiding his hard gray eyes, said, "Who's askin'?"

"I'll tell you who's askin', old man. I'm Roscoe Akers, and this is my brood. I ain't gonna ask you again."

Salty sized up Roscoe. He was a big man, obviously used to hard work and hard living. There wasn't a trace of kindness in the man's chiseled face. A thick black beard with sprinkles of gray hid his chin. Salty thought, *Hard man. If he's after Floyd, he and his boys might be tough to handle, unless I stop him here.*

Salty's right hand was beneath the table's edge, resting on the butt of the Colt. He moved his hand to his knife hilt, slid it around where he could easily reach it, and placed his hand back on the Colt. "Well, Roscoe Akers, you've found your man. I'm Salty Dickens. What's your pleasure?"

"Where's Floyd Logan?" Akers asked.

Salty took a long sip of his beer, wiped his mouth again, and pointed west. "Yonder. Why ya lookin' for him?"

Akers hawked and spat a gob of mucous and tobacco juice across the floor, ignoring the spittoon. "I'll tell you why, old man. 'Cause he murdered two of my boys. They wus good boys. Now

I'm left with only two sons and my girl. I aim to make that killer pay."

Salty eyed the boys. They were all big and looked as mean as their pa. "I'm gonna do you a kindness, Akers. If you ain't wantin' that daughter of yours to lose her last two brothers and her pa, you best beat a path back to the hills you came from. If you head on west, the worst thing that could happen to you is that you'll find him. Once you latch onto Floyd Logan, the onliest thing you'll be thinkin' about is how to turn loose."

Akers, reaching for the knife that had put fear into Owen, started toward Salty, his boys following. "You ain't answered my question, old man. Reckon I'm gonna have to cut it out of you."

The metallic clicks of two hammers being eared back came from behind the bar, stopping all four men in their tracks. They turned around to look toward the sound.

"That's a mighty handy shooter, Clarence," Salty said. "That ten-gauge loaded with buckshot?"

The bartender, holding the shotgun steady on Roscoe Akers, shook his head. "No, sir. With the close-up work I have in here, I load it mostly with pieces of nails. You should see the nasty hole they make in a man's belly."

Roscoe Akers eyed the bartender and the gaping maws of the sawed-off shotgun barrels staring at him. "This ain't none of yore business, bartender. You just put that scattergun down and get somebody a drink. I wouldn't want to have to hurt you."

Clarence waved the muzzle of the shotgun toward the door. "You can cut a trail on out of here, Akers, or whatever your name is. And take your filthy clan with you."

Akers slowly moved his shaggy head around to focus on Salty. "You won't always have the bartender to protect you."

Salty gave Akers a smile that was as cold as the rain slashing down outside. "Sonny, everybody needs protecting now and then. Right now, I'm protecting you by giving you a handy piece of advice. Listen to Clarence, and mosey that brood of yours on out of here, and keep on going until you're back home. There's a lot worse than nails waitin' for you out west."

Salty watched Akers assess the situation and make a conscious decision to withdraw. The man eyed him for a few moments more, turned, and headed for the door, his boys and daughter following.

"Akers," Salty said, "I wasn't joshin'. Floyd Logan's a bad man to tangle with. Most that have ain't around to tell about it."

Without pausing, Akers continued to the door and yanked it open, allowing the cold, gusting wind to race through the saloon. Several lanterns flickered, and the one on Salty's table went out. The door closed, and they were gone.

Owen let out a sigh of relief and a nervous chuckle. "Looks like you scared them, Salty."

Salty, still watching the door, shook his head. "Nope. That ain't a bunch you can throw a scare into. The old man's smart. He knows there's no upside to a tussle with a shotgun." Salty looked around and saw several of the regulars sliding their pistols back behind their belts. He nodded to each one. "Plus, I've friends in here, and Akers knew it. He's a canny coon, he is." After pulling his coat back and moving the Paterson to a more comfortable position, he looked toward the bar. "Clarence, would you quit fiddlin' with that there scattergun and let sweet little Ellie bring me my bowl of stew afore it's too cold to eat?"

Doc took his first sip of beer. "Salty, you'd better be careful. Those men, and that girl, are dangerous, and I think they'll do anything the old man tells them to do. Anything."

2

June 5, 1841

Floyd Logan, his body stretched behind the dark green spread of a mahogany bush, held his .54-caliber Ryland rifle tight to his shoulder. Below, in the shallow mountain valley, he saw movement in a small grove of tall quaking aspen. Moments passed. The mountain man took a deep breath, slowly released half of it, and waited.

A cow elk walked from the aspen thicket. The front sight of the Ryland settled behind the cow's shoulder, and Floyd's trigger finger tensed.

The elk staggered to a halt, lowered its head, and Floyd could see blood dripping from the animal's nostrils. He spotted the tiny remnant of the arrow's fletching where it had driven through the cow's body. He took his finger from the trigger and waited.

The elk's legs trembled as it labored to remain on its feet. With life ebbing from its body, the elk's forelegs bent, and it slowly lowered itself to the valley floor. Silence filled the normally active forest. No squirrel was heard to bark or raven caw.

Knowing the elk's pursuer was waiting for the animal to die,

Floyd lay still beneath the bush. At sixteen, he had arrived in these mountains, and his past eleven years had been spent learning, fighting, and surviving. He could lie silent on this mountainside as long as necessary. He did not know if the hunter of the elk was a friend or enemy, whether he was a lone hunter or a hunting party. His only move was to wait.

The elk stretched her long neck across the fallen leaves of the aspen and rolled slowly on her side. Floyd could see the bloody shaft and head protruding from the opposite side of the cow. He watched the chest rise and lower. Once, twice, three times, then it was motionless. Floyd, eyes moving quickly, examined every boulder and thick pine trunk. He especially watched the shadows within the aspen thicket from which the elk had emerged. Whether friend or foe, it was imperative to see before being seen.

Time passed. Patience could be the difference between life and death. His deep blue eyes caught a movement in the aspen thicket. Appearing like a wraith, a man limped slowly from the shadows of the tall white aspen, arrow notched and ready.

Floyd's body was flooded with relief and surprise. The tall gaunt man's resolute movement toward the elk, his limping from an old leg wound, the deep black hair, now turning gray and pulled back in two braids, all combined to bring quick recognition. It was Wirasuap, a powerful Shoshone shaman from the Snake River tribe. Wirasuap was a long way from home. *What's he doing so far south?* Floyd thought.

Though he knew the man, Floyd remained still. Something told him to wait.

Wirasuap poked the elk with his arrow. When the animal gave no response, the old Indian knelt, with difficulty, by the side of his quarry. He began to sway. Floyd could faintly hear the low chant of thanks and blessing.

Feeling foolish at his excess caution, he tensed his muscles to rise.

A flash of movement from behind a large pine near the aspen

thicket caught his eye. The Ryland rifle snapped snugly into his shoulder, and the sights lined up on an Indian brave streaking past the pine and into the glen toward the shaman, tomahawk raised. Only yards behind him raced two more.

Even as his sight settled on the first brave's chest and his finger tightened, a thought dashed through his mind. *More Apaches. I wish they'd stay south.* The Ryland bucked against his shoulder, and the first brave momentarily disappeared in the smoke.

Floyd knew Wirasuap was old. The last time he had seen him, he was still strong, but Floyd doubted he was strong enough to best a young battle-hardened Apache warrior, and there were at least two left. He dropped the Ryland, for it could fire only a single shot before reloading, and grabbed the repeating Colt ring rifle lying on the ground to his right.

Wirasuap had risen and stared up at Floyd, obviously trying to discern why this mountain man was firing at him, until the second Apache brave let out a whoop. At the sound of the brave's cry, the old shaman twisted around toward the remaining attackers.

As Floyd settled the sights on the second warrior, he could see the old Shoshone bring up his bow. Floyd squeezed the trigger. The Colt roared, sending a .52-caliber ball coursing toward the Apache. It tore through the man's chest. Dead on his feet, the attacker pitched forward and rolled down the slope toward Wirasuap.

Floyd pulled the forward ring of the Colt ring rifle. The movement rotated the cylinder, bringing the next of the eight chambers in line to fire, and cocked the hammer. Before he could settle the sight on the last of the Apache braves, Wirasuap sent a shaft toward the attacking Indian. It struck the man in the neck, passing completely through and embedding in a small pine directly behind the attacker. Blood spurted from the brave's neck. He collapsed, dying along with his companions. Wirasuap gave a whoop, yanked his knife from his belt, and raced toward the last Apache.

Reloading the Ryland, Floyd watched the activity of the old shaman. He was moving around like a man twenty years younger. Invigorated by the adrenaline from the brief battle, he ran, barely limping, from the fallen Apache, scalp in hand, to his arrow deep in the pine. Remembering Floyd, he turned, raised the scalp high, waved it toward him, and whooped. Floyd lifted his now-loaded Ryland in a single wave and examined the countryside for additional Apaches before turning back into the forest. Vigilant, lest he walk into another ambush, he made his way toward his animals.

They were both glad to see him. Buck, a big buckskin, was tied well out of sight of the valley, back in the tall ponderosa pines, along with Browny the mule. When Floyd stepped from behind a tree, both horse and mule were staring at him. Softly, Floyd said, "Good boys. You may be getting older, but those ears are still working." The horse and mule watched Floyd's approach with their solemn brown eyes, almost as if they were listening. Reaching Buck, Floyd slid the Ryland into the scabbard, untied the reins, and swung into the saddle. Keeping the Colt rifle handy, across his legs, he untied Browny's lead from the saddle horn and said, "Let's go, boys. We've got some elk to haul home."

Cresting the lip of the valley, he again surveyed the timber, rocks, and brush for anything out of place. Satisfied for the moment, he dropped down the slope, letting Buck make his way among the boulders and pines. Reaching Wirasuap, Floyd pulled up and swung to the ground, dropping the reins. Opening his saddlebags, he pulled out some pemmican, turned, and extended his right hand to accept the Indian's. They both spoke in Shoshone.

"Igasho comes at the right time," Wirasuap said.

Floyd nodded solemnly. "The Great Spirit guided me to help the great Wirasuap."

The Indian nodded. "Ahh. Yes, it is true. Had you not been here, I would have been dead, and my mission would have died with me."

Floyd extended the pemmican. "Leotie made it. It is good. A mite better cooked, but I'd like to get this animal dressed and be on our way. Those braves may not be the onliest ones around."

"I do not think there are more," the old Indian said while easing down onto a convenient log. "Of course, I knew nothing of them until just now, so what do I know?" He shook his head. "You must forgive me, Flo-yd. My old body demands a moment of rest."

Floyd had begun gutting the animal. Working quickly, he said, "It is not a problem, Shaman. I will have this fine young cow finished quickly, and then we will ride back to the village. I am surprised you are not mounted."

The shaman's face clouded. "I was until five suns ago. A fine horse. He stepped into a badger's hole and broke a foreleg. I have been walking since."

Floyd made quick work of the elk, carefully separating the liver and heart from the viscera. He dropped the two valuable organs into a deerskin sack that Leotie had made and pulled the drawstring tight. Next, he looped the drawstring over the saddle horn and turned to the elk.

He didn't want to overload Browny, but the mule was big, and they didn't have far to go. The elk was young and wouldn't weigh over two hundred pounds. The old shaman couldn't weigh a hundred and twenty-five pounds. That would make three hundred and fifty. Of course, the elk would be dead weight, but again, it wouldn't be far.

The shaman stood and said, "I can help."

Floyd had several lengths of deer-hide rope he had braided. He handed one to the shaman. "The elk is small enough. It'll fit just behind the saddle. As soon as I get him up there, tie him while I hold him, then I'll get this side."

Browny looked back, watched for a moment, and went back to pulling at the long grass. Floyd squatted, grasped the elk in his big hands, and stood, lifting it across the mule's back. They quickly secured the animal.

Floyd felt the wind against his cheek and smelled rain. "We best get a move on. I'd like to make it back before the rain catches us, but I have a question for you."

The shaman looked at Floyd across Browny's saddle.

"Leotie sent me out to kill an elk because she wanted elk liver. She's been craving elk liver for several days. There's a nice herd of deer not far from the village, but deer wouldn't do. She wants elk. I know it is your kill, but would you mind if I have part of the liver?"

The shaman smiled. "You must please your wife. All the liver is yours. Take it with my thanks for saving my life."

Floyd grinned back. "Thanks, she'll appreciate that, and she and the entire village are going to be happy when I bring you home."

Solemnly, Wirasuap nodded. "It will be a great pleasure for me to again see my brothers and sisters."

They mounted and headed down the small valley, both watching for Apaches.

∾

Wirasuap's name spread quickly through the village, drawing every adult, along with the hushed children. The people walked alongside, touching him, smiling up at him, and asking questions about their relatives back at the Snake River, so many miles away.

Pallaton, the chief, and Nina, his wife, stepped from their teepee. Leotie, Floyd's wife, was with them.

Floyd's eyes found her deep, dark brown eyes, which were sometimes so dark they looked black, bringing a smile to his face, and hers. *How could I have been so lucky to find this woman?* he thought. Then his smile broadened. She was finally putting on a little weight. She had always been slim, but he noticed the almost white deer-hide dress she wore was just a little tight. *Why didn't I notice that before?* But his train of thought was interrupted as Chief Pallaton stepped up to greet the shaman.

"My friend," Pallaton said, "what brings you so far south?" His brow wrinkled as he looked around. "And you are by yourself?"

The shaman swung his right leg over the saddle and dropped to the ground. The wince of pain could only be seen in his eyes, but Floyd saw Pallaton had also noticed it.

"I come alone." He placed his left hand on the taller man's right shoulder. "It is good to see you. It has been too long."

"Yes." Pallaton swept his arm across the village. "We often speak of our brothers and sisters west of the mountains. But we can talk of that later." Pallaton glanced at the elk. "I see Igasho has had a successful hunt. We will roast elk and speak of many things."

Floyd spoke up. "Wasn't me who killed this elk, it was the shaman."

Pallaton's eyebrows rose, and for the first time he saw the scalps adorning the saddle horn next to the bag. He stepped forward and examined them. "These are fresh." He lifted them high above his head, speaking so everyone could hear. "Our brother not only brings us meat, but signs of recent battle, close."

Cries and whoops lifted from the braves and women. A shout rose from the crowd. "Tell us the story of your bravery, Wirasuap, our shaman."

The old man shook his head. "Now is not the time. Later, after I have rested, for I am old and have traveled far."

"Come," Pallaton said. Towering above the older man, he offered Wirasuap his arm and led him into his teepee. Nina followed.

Mika, now a tall thirteen, reached Floyd before Leotie. "You had a fight? You are all right?"

Floyd put his hand on his son's shoulder and spoke in English. "Yep. I sure am." He stepped back to Browny's side and lifted the sack from the saddle horn. "Guess what's in here."

A wide grin lit Mika's face. "Liver! At last, we will hear no more about how good a piece of liver would taste."

His last words were punctuated with a playful slap on the back of his head. Still in English, Leotie said, "Be respectful of your mother."

The boy grinned at her. Floyd swept the petite woman into his arms. She pulled her head back and laid her slim hand across the long scar on his left cheek. "You have not been gone *that* long, my husband."

Floyd examined the lovely face with full lips and wide-set eyes. "Any time is a long time away from you."

Her hand moved quickly from his cheek to grab the sack. "Do not speak of longing to me. Give me that liver."

He held on to it for a moment until wrinkles formed across her forehead and her eyes narrowed. "All right," he said, releasing the bag, "here's your liver."

Her face lightened immediately. She threw him a quick smile and dashed toward their teepee.

To her back, he called, "The liver is yours, but the heart is Wirasuap's."

She raised her hand in acknowledgment before disappearing behind the flap of their teepee.

Jeb Campbell, Floyd's best friend, had been watching and waiting. When Leotie left, he stepped up. "Saw those scalps. Looked Apache. Only three?"

Floyd turned serious. "Yes. Good thing I was there. I don't think the shaman could have handled all three of them. Since the Apaches are normally south of here, and Wirasuap came from the northwest, I'm guessing they must have picked up his trail only a short time before they jumped him."

Jeb nodded. "See any sign of others?"

Floyd shook his head. "Nary a thing, though it doesn't make sense for only three of them to have come this far north. I'm guessing they're up here for buffalo."

"There'd have to be an almighty big bunch of them to attack the village. I'm guessin' we don't have to worry much about that. Still, it won't hurt to keep a sharp eye out. You never know about Apaches."

Mika was still with them. "Uncle Jeb, do you think there'll be a fight?"

Jeb grinned at the boy. "Ain't no sense in you gettin' all hot and bothered about a fight. There might be, but I reckon them Apaches are after meat more than anything else. Anyway, you're still a youngster. You ain't a-goin' to be fightin' nobody."

Floyd saw the crestfallen look on his son's face and threw his arm around the boy's shoulders. "Don't worry, the time will come soon enough. You'll make a fine warrior."

The boy perked up. "Thanks, Pa. Maybe—"

Pallaton stuck his head out from inside the teepee. "Igasho, Jeb, come."

Floyd picked up Buck's reins and handed them to Mika. "I'd be obliged if you'd take Buck and Browny to water and give them a good rubdown."

Several of the younger men, under supervision of the women, had already removed the elk from Browny's back, had it hanging, and the women were deftly skinning it. They would clean and tan the hide for Wirasuap to take back with him. Once the hide was off, the animal would be carefully butchered. Everything would be used.

"Sure, Pa. I'd be glad to."

"Thanks." Floyd, with Jeb at his side, headed for the chief's teepee. Bending to pass through the opening made by pulling the flap back, he followed his friend through the entrance.

As he straightened and looked around, his mind traveled to the first time he had been in Pallaton's teepee. It was after his encounter with the grizzly. That bear had been a big surprise. He had been setting a new trapline when the massive brute burst from a thicket. The bear was on him before he had time to get his rifle up. He managed to kill the grizzly, but not before the bear's huge claws slashed through his left forearm and ripped through his scalp. He was fortunate that Pallaton and several of his braves had been watching. They brought him back to their camp, where Nina and Leotie nursed him as he battled the infection in his arm. He rubbed his forearm unconsciously, feeling the deep scar.

Clearing his mind of thoughts of the past, he sat where Pallaton indicated, and Jeb dropped alongside.

Wirasuap was on the opposite side of the small fire. To his right sat Pallaton. On his left was Kajika, son of Chief Pallaton. Lesser chiefs and several of the braves completed the circle. The meeting began by Pallaton lifting the ceremonial pipe, lighting it, taking a puff, and passing it to Wirasuap. The shaman took a deep draw and passed it to the next man. All eyes were on Floyd, or Igasho as most of the Shoshone knew him, named for his far travels. All Shoshone of the tribe were well aware Floyd did not smoke, and of all the things he could do well, smoking the pipe was not one of them. It would send him into an embarrassing coughing spell.

Jeb took the pipe, inhaled deeply, and then let the smoke slowly flow from his mouth. Finished, he handed it to Floyd, who took it with the caution of a man handling a rattlesnake.

3

The Shoshone told many stories of Floyd Logan's bravery, but he continued to lose his battle with any kind of tobacco smoke. If he tried inhaling it, he would break out in uncontrollable coughing. He looked across the fire to Pallaton. The chief's dark eyes gazed intently back at his friend, his face solemn.

I swear he's laughing inside, Floyd thought. *He's waiting for me to take a puff and start coughing, but today, Pallaton, chief of the Shoshone, will be different.* He moved the pipe to his lips, watching the curl of smoke drift upward. Cautiously, he placed the mouthpiece to his lips and began to inhale. Instantly, he could feel the tickle of the smoke traveling down his throat and into his lungs. *This time, . . . maybe . . .* A short cough, much like the bark of a deer, burst past his lips.

He yanked the pipe away as the paroxysm of coughing took over his body. It lasted only moments, but when it was over, he heard several grunts and mms and noticed money changing hands. He even saw Jeb receiving a coin from Bidzil. Floyd turned and gave him a dirty look. Jeb grinned and shrugged. He noticed Pallaton handed Kajika something. Defeated again, but head held high, he passed the pipe to the next man, glad to be rid of it.

After it had made the round, Pallaton respectfully laid it aside and spoke. "Wirasuap has made a long journey. Though he is tired and needs rest, his words are important for us to hear."

Wirasuap, his face thin and drawn, began, "It is good to see my brothers. Too many moons have passed since we were together." He lowered his eyes to the fire, closed them, and waved a wrinkled hand slowly from side to side. The men waited, watching the shaman. He would speak in his own time.

After minutes passed, he opened his eyes and looked around the circle, holding each man's gaze for a moment before moving to the next. When he came to Pallaton, he patted him on the knee and began, "I have had a dream. It came to me while my eyes traveled along the river for which the white man has named us. I watched the flow of pure water move quickly past, leaping over rocks and rolling around itself to churn white at the top. In my dream, I saw the buffalo grazing across the plains, happy and content, scattered yet together as one.

"But as they fed, they came to a point of land that rose, slowly at first, then faster and higher with craggy cliffs no buffalo could cross. Reaching this point, the two buffalos separated, one going to the right of the point, the other to the left." Wirasuap stretched his arms before him, palms together, slowly separating the two palms and moving his hands farther apart. "Others followed the leaders until the buffalo had split into two groups and drifted far apart, the mountains now obscuring their distant companions."

He stopped and allowed his gaze to take in each of the listeners before continuing, "Soon, winter and the wolves came. The gray shadows kept coming until there were more wolves than buffalo, because they were no longer as one. The wolves attacked each group, and slowly the number of buffalo dwindled until there were only drying bones glistening on the plains."

He stopped his story and looked at the fire, as if seeing the dream play out in the flames. Floyd watched his friends, his eyes stopping on Pallaton. He could see the worry in the man's eyes and could feel the foreboding driving deep into the souls of the men in the teepee. These were his friends. Their concern was his. His head turned back to the shaman as Wirasuap resumed speaking.

"You," he said, turning to the chief, "have led your people far from their home along the river. We are separated, and our numbers are small, like the buffalo. You did it to find a place rich in game and sheltered from the winter winds of the north. You did good for your people, but now it is time to return. We *must* join together again."

He looked across at Floyd. "Igasho, will the white man's number increase?"

Floyd looked around the circle of worried faces, his gaze coming to rest on Wirasuap's. "Yes, Shaman. They will increase."

"Will it be good for the Shoshone?"

Floyd felt himself on the spot, but he couldn't lie. "It will not be good for the Shoshone."

Wirasuap's arm shot out, his finger pointed at Floyd. "Listen to Igasho. He is one of us. He and Jeb Campbell have taken our women to wife. They have fought the Blackfoot with us. Today, Igasho saved my life. Had he not been there, I would be dead, and you would not be hearing my dream. The Great Spirit guided him to me. Thanks to Igasho, you will be saved if you follow my direction."

Pallaton turned to Wirasuap and said, "What is it you would have us do, Shaman?"

Wirasuap nodded. "It is good you ask, Great Chief Pallaton. You lead your people well. One of the reasons is that you listen to the Great Spirit. I have come to tell you he has given me this dream, and he has given me the answer to saving the buffalo in my dream. My people."

With his palm down, he extended his arm and slowly swung

it from left to right, encompassing the men in the circle and the village. "The buffalo can be stronger by retracing their steps that they might join together again. They will toss the wolves with the points of their horns and grind them into the ground with their forefeet. In this way, they will sustain their lives and their way of life much longer. Like the buffalo, the time is here for you, Pallaton, to bring your people back to the river of our homeland and join again with those who have remained."

Pallaton nodded. "It is good. I, too, have been feeling the need to lead my people back to our brothers. The Great Spirit has placed that feeling deep in my breast." Floyd watched as the chief lifted his right hand, made a fist, and clapped it once, hard against his chest. The others let out a single yell of agreement.

Wirasuap raised his arms and head toward the sky, held the position for a moment, and then lowered them. "You are a good leader, Pallaton. You have been good for your people."

Floyd's head turned slightly as Kajika spoke. "Shaman, you say that if we return and join with our brothers, we will be like the buffalo and last much longer."

The shaman nodded.

"And you said that the buffalo together would be strong and able to kill the wolves?"

The shaman nodded again.

Kajika looked across to Floyd and Jeb. "Does that mean we will kill the white man?"

The shaman didn't hesitate. "It means we will be stronger if we must fight."

Kajika's eyes found Floyd. "Floyd, Jeb, do you think we will have to fight the white man?"

Jeb spoke up. "I hope not, my friend, because if you do, you will lose."

A murmur raced around the circle, and frowns covered several faces.

Jeb held up a hand. "Wait, you are my friends. Do not misunderstand me. The Shoshone are noble warriors. And you may win many battles, but you cannot win a war with the whites. I will give you two reasons the Indian nations cannot win against the whites."

He leaned forward and pointed at Kajika. "My friend, you are a great warrior, strong and young, but if you are killed, who will replace you?"

Floyd watched Pallaton's face. The chief listened intently.

Kajika pointed to Bidzil, sitting next to Jeb. "The great warrior Bidzil."

"And if Bidzil is killed."

Kajika pointed to another brave.

"And if he is killed?"

Pallaton spoke. "What are you saying, Jeb?"

"Great Chief, the Shoshone are many, but as their braves are killed, they cannot be replaced quickly. The People will dwindle, becoming fewer and fewer. Spirit warriors cannot fight. They cannot hunt the buffalo or provide for those of their people who remain. Winters will be harsh and without food. Many more of the Shoshone will die until . . ."

A doleful silence descended on the council. Finally, Kajika spoke. "But the same will happen to the white man. Perhaps that will stop them, and the Shoshone will grow again."

Floyd glanced at Jeb, and his friend nodded. Floyd said, "The white man is hungry, not for buffalo or venison, but for land. They have heard, far across the great water, about all the open land, and they will rush to have a piece of their own. It is a great yearning for my people. Across the water, in what is called Europe, most men do not even own their own teepee, but must rent from their neighbor."

Floyd could see the dismay on the faces of his friends on the council. "They will not stop coming. If you fight, when one falls, there will be ten more to take their place."

Floyd felt the sadness of his words, for the Shoshone had

become his family. He loved the wild freedom they enjoyed. Life was hard, but good. At night, stars were bright, not wiped out by the light of ten thousand lanterns, or the smoke of that many fires. The smell of the forest or plains was always there, not hidden by the stench of thousands of people's garbage. And the sound. The sound of the forest could be easily heard, not blocked by incessant wagons rolling or machines clanking. It might even be said that it was harder on him and Jeb and the rest of the mountain men who remained in the mountains, for they knew the results of what was inevitably coming.

Pallaton broke the silence. "Jeb, you said you would give us two reasons."

"I did," Jeb said. "Here is the second. Have you wondered where the rifles and pistols come from, the powder and the lead? It is all made in large buildings in the east. In these buildings, day after day, men work to produce the powder, the rifles, all of it. They make many rifles in one day, and they improve them. You have seen the new Colt revolving rifle and the Paterson pistol that Floyd brought back from his trip to the east. Those guns will shoot many shots before reloading. They are made in what we call factories. These people who make the guns will provide the army and the settlers with as many of them as they need." He paused here and, while looking around the council circle, asked, "Where are your factories? Who will make your guns?"

Wirasuap stood for the first time. "I hear our friends, Floyd and Jeb, speak of the coming advance of the white man. It causes my old heart to soar with the eagle, knowing I will not live to see this plague upon our land. All men die, but we must live and die like men. My dream shows the first step. You must return with me to our land."

He lifted his arms to the sky again, palms up. "And if, as the buffalo did in my dream, it comes to a fight to preserve us, though we die to the last man, woman, and child, we will die together!"

Wirasuap lowered his arms. "But we are not there yet, and I

hope our great chief will not be forced to make that decision. For now, the thing we must do is move back to our river." The old man staggered with fatigue. Both Kajika and Pallaton leaped to their feet. Each took an arm of the shaman. He smiled and nodded his head. "I am old and have come a far distance. I must rest."

"Yes," Pallaton said. "The meeting is over. We will begin preparations, and our shaman will rest."

Nina led the old Shoshone over to a bed that had been prepared for him and helped him lie down.

It's hard to believe he made it alone all the way from the Snake River. He is one tough old codger, Floyd thought, moving toward the teepee entrance.

After stepping outside, he turned to Pallaton, who had followed them out. "How long do you think before you break camp and head north?"

"It will be at least seven suns, maybe longer. We need to kill and dry as much buffalo as possible. A far travel awaits us."

Jeb watched Floyd. "What's got yore mind workin', boy?"

Floyd looked east, toward the Greenhorn mountains. "A week would give us time to make it over to Bent's Fort and purchase supplies. With our mules and extra horses, we can bring back more grub. It oughta help for the trek."

"I reckon."

Pallaton held Floyd's gaze. "It is good what you do. We could use powder and lead."

"Powder and lead, it is."

Kajika had joined them. "I will ride with you and bring two extra horses. Spread the load, and the travel will be faster. You may also need an extra gun with the Apache near."

"Good," Floyd said. "We leave at daybreak." Floyd and Jeb headed toward their teepees and their wives.

Walking back to his home, Floyd eyed the camp. It was more like a village. Almost two hundred teepees dotted the southern end of the valley. Smoke drifted from each, for the day, waning as it was, brought with it cooler temperatures at these higher elevations. Much of the snow on the mountains that closed the valley to the north and west had melted, but it would still be a cold trek back to the Snake River country if they took the mountain route.

They had made a good life here. Buffalo were plentiful on the plains. Leotie and Mika were happy. They saw few white men, except along the Santa Fe trail, which turned south well east of them. With most of the beaver market disappearing, the majority of mountain men had either headed back east or moved on west. Nowadays, they had little company besides the Utes, and they kept to themselves.

Yep, he thought, *I hate leaving this valley. I oughta go on down to Santa Fe, look up the fella who owns it, and maybe work out a deal with him. We could make a home here.* He shook the thought from his mind and stepped into his teepee. More important things required his immediate attention, and they didn't involve a trip to Santa Fe.

The smell of elk liver and wild onions cooking bombarded his nostrils. Immediately, his mouth began to water. "You make enough for all three of us?"

Leotie smiled up at him, her white teeth shining. "I am always glad to share with my family, even though they make fun of me and *my* elk liver."

Floyd grinned and winked at Mika. "I'm mighty glad you're so generous. Aren't you, boy?"

Mika, his eyes fastened on the skillet, missed the wink, but said, "Yes, I am very glad. I will be even more glad when it is ready."

Leotie smiled at her son, then turned a serious face toward Floyd. "We will go soon?"

"You spoke to Nina?"

She shook her head, holding his gaze. "No. I just know it is time."

His head tilted quizzically. "Sometimes you amaze me, wife."

Mika looked back and forth between the two of them. "Going where?"

"I just came from the meeting with the shaman. He says it's time for us to be moving back to the Snake River country. Without talking to anyone, it seems your ma already knew."

Mika, his face serious, said, "Yes, the spirits are strong within her. She knows much."

Floyd watched a look pass between Leotie and her son. *I wonder how much of that was passed on to you, boy.*

Mika's face lost the momentary serious demeanor, and his eyes widened with excitement. "When do we leave, Pa?"

Floyd lowered himself into a sitting position next to Leotie, drew the Paterson revolver, and placed it within reach at his side. "Pallaton plans on having everyone ready to leave in seven days. Jeb and I are heading over to Bent's Fort for a few additional supplies. We'll take off in the morning. Kajika is going with us, and I thought, if your ma could spare you, you could come along."

The boy looked like he might explode with excitement, but strived to remain calm as he turned to see his mother's response.

She continued to work with the food, almost as if she had heard none of Floyd's last words. She dished the liver and onions onto the metal plates that Floyd had bought them. Giving Floyd the largest, her almost-warrior son the next, she took the smallest. Floyd smiled inwardly at her action. She was always taking care of others before herself. A prime reason she was so important to the tribe, as was Nina. The two of them were also the tribe's doctors.

He leaned over and, with a fork, exchanged his larger piece with hers.

Her head jerked up, full lips pursed, and brow knitted.

"Now, Leotie," Floyd said, "you're the one who wanted elk

liver. I reckon you should have the largest piece. You've been talking about this stuff for days."

For a moment, the frown remained, but slowly it changed to a wide smile as the wrinkles disappeared. "You are too good to me, my husband."

His smile turned to a grin. "Sometimes, only sometimes."

She nodded her head. "Ahh, yes, I see." Her face became serious as she turned to her son. "Mika, your pa and Jeb will be leaving for the fort tomorrow, but I must start packing for our long trek back to the Snake River. It will be much work, and I could use help. I will leave it for you to decide. Which task should you undertake, going with your pa, or helping me?"

The anticipation and excitement fell from Mika as quickly as it appeared. A cool breeze wafted through the opening where the teepee flap had been folded back. Floyd felt the coolness across his neck and thought of the times his mother had used this same logic on him. He knew what a responsible man his son was growing into, which meant he had no chance. She had given him a choice between responsibility and fun. Mika would stay.

After a few moments of thought, Mika turned to Floyd. "Pa, I cannot go. Ma needs my help."

Floyd nodded, understanding the decision, but disappointed. His son needed to get out and meet other men and boys of his age outside of the tribe. White boys, who might be friendly or who might not. He needed to be prepared for the world. But just as Mika would make the responsible decision and help his mother, Floyd also chose not to discuss this with his wife in front of the boy. There would be other trips, other opportunities.

4

Floyd Logan pulled the red roan to a stop and looked over Bent's Fort, the multitude of teepees near the entrance, and the Arkansas River in the distance. His three companions followed suit. The mule and horses immediately began munching grass.

He hitched himself around in the saddle and looked over their back trail. As far as he could see were the brown, curly-haired brutes all the tribes depended on—buffalo. They had been amid them since making the turn west out of their valley at the southern base of the Greenhorn mountains. As far to the north and west as his vision could reach, the sea of brown extended, flowing, twisting, undulating. Returning his gaze forward, he pushed his slouch hat to the back of his head and said to Mika, "You ready to see Bent's Fort?"

The young Shoshone, eyes shining, tore his gaze from the buffalo and looked toward his new adventure, the fort. "I am ready."

"Then let's go," Floyd said, kicked Rusty in the ribs, and let out a shout. The big horse charged down the hill toward the fort and the teepees. Jeb, Kajika, and Mika followed, all whooping.

Before reaching the first teepees, Floyd slowed Rusty to a walk, and the others joined him. He glanced at Mika, whose laughing face had become stoic against the backdrop of the teepees. His son rode as tall in the saddle as his youthful body would allow.

Gratitude filled the mountain man's heart as he watched the boy, and he said a quick thank you to Leotie. She had left their bed early to prepare for their departure. It was she who had awakened Mika and informed him it was his responsibility to go with his father and learn of the white men and the other tribes who would be at the fort. More like a child than his years would dictate, he'd thrown his arms around her in a tight hug.

Jeb nodded toward an Indian standing by a teepee they would pass. Floyd had seen him only once or twice since they had first met eight years earlier. He subconsciously rubbed the scar on his left bicep where the Comanche arrow had impaled his arm. Riding up to the Comanche, he swung down and extended his hand, gripping the Indian by the forearm.

"Chief Black Hand, brave leader of the Comanche Nation, it is good to see you."

The older man's powerful hand gripped Floyd's forearm. "And you, Pawnee Killer. You have grown much since first we met. I hear many stories about you. You and the great bear. You and the Blackfoot. Your path is wide but difficult for any man to follow." Humor briefly slipped across his face. "You rub your arm. It bothers you?"

Floyd smiled. "Occasionally, in cold weather, it reminds me of my good fortune."

Black Hand nodded. "And ours. It is good the Comanche arrow struck only your arm."

The others had stepped from their horses.

"I think you know all but my son, Mika."

The Comanche examined the thirteen-year-old and extended his hand. The two shook. "He is good size, Pawnee Killer."

"Yes. His blood father, you may have heard of him, Ahiga, was killed fighting the Blackfoot. His wife took me into her teepee, and I am happy to call Mika my son."

Black Hand gripped the boy's shoulders. "The Great Spirit blesses you to have had two powerful fathers. Do not let them down." He turned to Floyd. "Tell me, what brings you to the fort of the Bents?"

Floyd looked to the northwest and pointed to the mountains. "The great Shoshone medicine man Wirasuap traveled many days from the Snake River to our little valley. He brought Chief Pallaton a message. It is time to move back north, to the Snake. We are here for supplies before we leave."

The old chief nodded. "I know of Wirasuap. The Shoshone are family. He is family. You will leave your valley with the Shoshone? It is a good place, though too cold for my old bones."

"I will leave. Now that I have a family, I must go with them. But before I go, I must tell you. The shaman was attacked by Apaches west of our camp. He was not hurt, but I felt you should know. The Apache is near."

Black Hand smiled. "It is good you tell me. I have not taken an Apache scalp in many moons. Perhaps there will be an opportunity." He shook hands with Floyd and nodded to the others. "Safe trip, and good hunting." Without another word, he turned and disappeared inside his tent.

"Interesting," Jeb said. "That old chief has other enemies right here." He looked around at the Pawnee teepees and the Blackfoot. "The Bents have sure figgered out how to keep peace around their forts."

"Yep," Floyd said, swinging back into the saddle. "I'm surprised to see the Blackfoot down here. Makes my back itch."

"Come to trade," Kajika said as they rode slowly through the encampment, dogs barking and little kids dashing in front of their horses.

"You're right there," Jeb replied, "but I sure wouldn't want to meet any of 'em a ways from this here camp. Reckon they'd be intent on rippin' off my scalp, and a mighty fine scalp it is, too, if I do say so myself."

Floyd eyed Jeb's head appraisingly. "Doesn't look near as thick as it did back when we met."

This brought a snort from Jeb. Kajika nodded and gave a grunt.

"You cain't be agreein' with Floyd," Jeb said to his Shoshone friend. "My hair's way thicker than his. It'd make a much better trophy. Why, sometimes I'm tempted to scalp myself, it looks so good."

Riding through the gate, Floyd reexamined the adobe walls of the fort. Almost a yard thick, they would withstand a major attack. A walkway erected six feet below the top of the wall allowed defenders to stand and fire safely over the parapet.

Floyd recognized the two men striding down the stairway access, two good friends, Shorty and Morg. It had been quite a while since he had last seen them. He raised a hand in salute.

Jeb leaned over and softly said, "I'll betcha a five-dollar gold piece they're arguing when they get here."

Floyd shook his head.

As the two men drew nearer, Shorty's gravelly voice could be heard. "That weren't no Black Hand what stopped them boys. I'm telling you for sure. You've been havin' problems with your seein' parts for quite a while. Next time we go to Saint Louie, you need to get those peepers checked. Probably need a pair of spectacles."

Walking up to the group, Shorty spoke before Morg could open his mouth. "Floyd, who was that you wuz talkin' to out there? Morg swears it was Black Hand, and I know different. There's Blackfoot camped out there. That Comanche wouldn't be seen around a bunch of Blackfoot unless he wuz chasin' 'em to lift their scalp."

"Howdy, Shorty, howdy, Morg," Floyd said. He looked at

Morg. "You'll be glad to know the Comanche chief I was talkin' to was none other than the infamous Black Hand."

Shorty yanked his hat from his head and threw it to the ground. "Dagnabbit, Floyd. I *know* that weren't Black Hand. Why you go tellin' me somethin' like that?"

Morg grinned at Floyd while shaking his hand, his slow drawl flowing smoothly. "Good to see you, Floyd. I'm sure glad you come in to convince Shorty that was Black Hand. Otherwise, I would've had to take him out there and prove it to him."

Kit Carson and Jim Beckwourth were standing along the wall, peering over the top. They both turned and waved. Kit called, "Both Jim and I tried to convince Shorty it was Black Hand, but he wasn't having any part of it."

Shorty picked up his hat and smashed it back on his head. "Well, that ain't so bad. Here it is May, and that's the first mistake I made."

Morg let out a whoop while everyone around started laughing.

Shorty shook his head. "Morg, I just don't know why I put up with you. I shoulda left a long time ago." He looked around. "Anybody hungry?"

Morg stopped laughing long enough to say, "I'm shore thirsty."

"We're definitely ready to put on the feedbag," Floyd said. "Give us time to get our horses taken care of, and we'll join you at the cantina."

"You too," Jeb called up to Kit and Jim.

They waved as the group rode on to the stable in back of the fort. Once inside, Mika jumped from his horse, grabbed a pitchfork, and started throwing hay into the feed trough.

Floyd swung from Rusty's back and removed the tack. He picked up a handful of hay and began wiping the horse down. Once finished, he turned Rusty loose into the pen. The big roan immediately rolled, dust flying everywhere.

"We about ready?" Jeb asked.

Floyd checked Kajika and Mika. They both nodded. All the animals had been stripped of gear, rubbed down, and were loose in the pen with food and water. He grabbed the Colt revolving rifle and his saddlebags. "I'd say we are." Turning to the young fella working in the stable, he said, "Our kits'll be alright here?"

The man looked up. "You know they will be, Mr. Logan. Ain't no one would dare steal nothing from a Bent stable."

"Course I do, just asking," Floyd said. "Come on, boys. Let's go put on the feed bag."

They walked through the fort, looking at the different people. There were Mexicans, Indians from several tribes, and white men, even a few French. Everyone seemed to get along, at least for now, except for the occasional drunk, or maybe Morg and Shorty.

They twisted and turned through the people, following the row of adobe buildings backing against the fort's wall. Each of the buildings, all owned by the Bent brothers, held vendors, all with something to trade or sell. From the blacksmith's shop, smoke and steam rose as the burly blacksmith heated and hammered out new tires for wagon wheels. Next door stood a dry goods store, crowded with people eager to part with their hard-earned money or trade furs. Adjoining, the next store beckoned with an old musket hanging beneath a sign proclaiming *Guns Fixd*.

Floyd watched Mika's head turn quickly from one fresh sight to another. The boy's face was filled with wonder. Reaching the cantina, Floyd pushed the door open. The interior was divided roughly in half. The front portion was occupied with circular tables and chairs. Each table would seat at least eight men or women, more if they squeezed together. At these tables, food was being served. The area behind the eatery, but with no visible separation, was the space reserved for drinking and gambling. Into this area, no decent woman ventured.

Floyd was interested in food, though he knew Morg would

prefer to keep walking to the back of the cantina. The tall man was always thirsty.

It took several moments for his eyes to adjust to the darker interior. He spotted men at one table as they pushed their chairs back and stood. He turned to his son. "Mika, run over there and grab that table. We'll be right behind you."

As Mika took off, Floyd turned to Jeb and Kajika. "I figured Morg and Shorty would be here, but they must have been dela—"

His head whipped back at a gruff yell. "Git away from this here table, kid. This un's ourn." A heavy man with a thick beard and broken teeth had Mika by the forearm and was about to throw him across the room. Floyd, his Colt rifle in his right hand and the gear in his left, took three quick, long steps, putting himself in range.

He used the rifle barrel like an axe, raising it high and driving it down into the crook of the man's right elbow. The big fellow had turned his head toward the hulk entering his field of vision in time to see the rifle barrel descending. He tried to twist away, but his move only gave Floyd a more open target. The barrel crashed into the unprotected elbow, causing the fingers gripping Mika's right arm to jerk open.

Simultaneously, the man let out a curse of pain and went for his knife with his left hand. Floyd saw the man's movement. He knew, with his hands full and Mika between the two of them, there was no way he could prevent that knife from finding a home in his body.

He caught another movement lower. It was Mika. Quick as a striking snake, the boy yanked his knife from his belt and drove it into the man's left forearm.

The big man screamed, dropping his knife and jerking his arm back and up, ripping Mika's blade from his grip. The knife had driven to the hilt, and the razor-sharp blade had sliced through clothing, tough skin, and flesh to extend out the opposite side of the arm, dripping blood.

The five companions of the impaled man started for their guns as Morg, Shorty, Kit Carson, and Jim Beckwourth stepped into the cantina. The perpetrator and his friends found themselves staring into eight rifle and pistol barrels. They quickly changed their minds and lowered their weapons, deciding to look to their companion's needs.

William Bent, the owner of the fort and the saloon, pushed his way to the table. "I saw it all." He looked down at the big man, who had dropped into the chair and was attempting to hold his skewered left arm with a right that wasn't as yet following any commands. "Mister, you picked the wrong people to tangle with. If you don't know them"—he nodded at Floyd—"he is Floyd Logan, the boy you grabbed is Mika, his son, the man next to him is Kajika, the son of a Shoshone chief, and I wouldn't sleep too soundly because his name means walks without sound, and the man next to him is Jeb Campbell. Then there's Shorty and Morg, and Kit and Jim. So it looks to me you unleashed yourself some awfully bad poison by grabbing that boy."

Bent took a breath. "Also, the boy was at that table before you, so on top of everything else, you had no right to claim it. Normally, I don't step into disputes, but I thought I'd step in here to protect you. Now why don't you take yourself on over to the doctor's office and get that scratch looked at?" Here Bent looked at the man's companions. "I'd suggest you gentlemen accompany him."

"Wait just a second," Floyd said. The man was starting to get up from the table. Floyd grabbed the man's arm above the knife with his right hand. His left closed around the hilt, and he yanked it from the arm. Blood chased the knife blade.

The man yelped and grimaced in pain. Floyd locked his cold blue eyes on the bleeding man. "Reckon you oughta follow Mr. Bent's direction and get on over to the doctor. Be glad this happened here. If you'd done this anywhere else, I'd a killed you. Now git."

Floyd wiped the bloody knife on the man's shirt and handed it back to Mika. He could feel the rage that had flashed when he saw the man's hands on his son beginning to subside. *I shouldn't have said that,* he thought. *But I know it's true. There's a side of me that scares even me.* "I'm much obliged, Mr. Bent, and I'm really sorry about making a ruckus, but I'll not allow any man to lay a hand on my son."

Bent laughed. "I guess not." He placed his hand on Mika's shoulder. "Seems the two of you were cut from the same stock. The boy here didn't much like the idea of someone pulling a knife on you."

A man at the adjoining table spoke up. "I seen it all. The boy beat that feller to the table. Anyways, I'm right with you, Floyd. Lay a hand on my kin and expect to meet yore maker."

Floyd nodded his thanks.

Bent held his hands up and spoke loud enough for everyone throughout the cantina to hear. "Alright, folks. The entertainment's over." He nodded to Floyd and strode back to the bar.

The group seated themselves around the table. Mika sat next to Floyd on the left, with Jeb on the other side of the boy. Kajika sat to Floyd's right. Everyone else grabbed a chair and found a spot.

They had no sooner seated themselves before a buxom young woman made her way to the table. With a full and confident voice, she spoke over the din of men drinking and eating. "My name is Kim." She smiled at Jeb. "We've got elk stew or buffalo steaks. For the fine young man with the quick knife, I bet I can find some buffalo tongue. Who wants what?"

It was divided between stew and steaks, but Floyd knew Mika definitely wanted the tongue. While the others were ordering, Floyd placed his hand on his son's shoulder. "Mika, are you all right?"

The boy turned wide, serious brown eyes on Floyd. "Yes, Pa. I didn't think. I saw him drawing his knife on you with your hands full. Before I knew it, my knife had found his arm."

"Thank you, son. You kept me from getting stuck. You made the move of a man."

Kajika, who had been listening, said, "Yes. You have drawn blood and counted coup. When we return to the village, we will celebrate your action to save Flo-yd. Songs will be sung about you."

With Kajika's words, Mika's eyes grew wide, and he sat a little higher in his chair.

The food arrived quickly and was devoured nearly as fast as it had arrived. Kim seemed to end up next to Jeb each time she returned to the table. He just grinned, but didn't encourage her. Floyd nodded to himself. There was a time when Jeb would have latched on to the girl, but he was different now. He was devoted to Aiyana and his new son.

Kit Carson finished his piece of apple pie and looked at Floyd. "I hear you'll be traveling back to the Snake River."

Floyd looked at Jeb.

His friend said, "Yep, Pallaton plans to leave in less than seven days. We'll be loading up with supplies and headin' back."

Jim Beckwourth swallowed a sizeable chunk of pie. "You're traveling toward cold country." With a knowing smile, he continued, looking at Floyd, "And I understand the Blackfoot don't have the welcome mat out for you."

"That's a fact. I'll have to keep a lookout, but I do that anyway." He grinned at Beckwourth. "Maybe you can put in a good word for me."

Jim Beckwourth flashed a grin back at Floyd. "Maybe."

Floyd's countenance turned serious. "A piece of information you may not have, Apaches are moving north. Wirasuap was attacked by three, only a half-day's ride from the village."

Carson and Beckwourth looked at each other, but Shorty,

who had been unusually quiet, spoke up. "Early. I told you, Morg. Them Apaches would be moving early this year. Yep, winter was early last season and pushed 'em back south, away from the buffler. Now they're moving up early this year."

Morg refused to rise to the bait and kept eating his pie while glancing at the bar in the back of the cantina.

"What happened?" Morg asked of Floyd.

"Wirasuap has three new Apache scalps."

Morg looked at him suspiciously. "He kill all three? That's mighty good for an old shaman."

Floyd shrugged. "I might've helped."

Morg took a long swig from his tankard, then wiped foam from his mustache and beard, smacking his lips. "I reckon."

Kajika spoke. "Igasho, Flo-yd, killed two of them, but Wira-suap shot an arrow through the neck of an Apache. The man fell dead at his feet."

"Yep," Shorty said, "your shaman may be getting up there in years, but it ain't faded out any of his gumption. That's a long trek from the Snake down here. I'm thinkin' he was pretty worn, but he still stuck an arrow through that Apache's neck. That's potent medicine, mighty potent."

Morg nodded, emptied his tankard, and held it in the air until he was sure Kim saw it. "We been thinkin' about headin' back to the Snake River country ourselves."

Shorty's head popped up from his pie. He stared at his partner for a moment, took another bite of pie, and said, "Yessir, that's a fact. It's time we wuz gettin' back up there. Ain't seen that country for a while."

Floyd began to respond when the door of the cantina flew open, and a man burst in, shouting, "Wagon train comin' in from Independence."

5

M any of the cantina patrons leaped to their feet and rushed to the door. The wagon train would bring news from back east and, hopefully, newspapers from the metropolitan areas.

"We'll be going," Kit Carson said as he and Beckwourth stood. "I'd like to get my hands on one of those papers before they're gone."

"Good to see you fellers," Beckwourth said, turning for the door. "Watch yore hair. Especially you, Floyd. If I know them Blackfoot, and I do, they'll be fit to be tied once they hear you're back up north. I don't know if my word'll make much difference to 'em."

Everyone waved, and the two men disappeared through the door, following the rest of the crowd.

Shorty shook his head. "We should be goin' on out there, Morg. All them papers'll be gone afore we can get nary a one."

Kim had brought Morg another beer, and he had the rim against his mouth. Finally lowering it, he said, "You just keep your seat, and you'll know ever' last thing what's in them papers from right here in this cantina. A few minutes ain't gonna change a thing."

Kajika finished his dessert. "Pie good." He had seen Morg raise his tankard, so he held up his dish. Sure enough, Kim saw him and was over in a flash.

"Want some more pie?"

"It is good. I would like another piece."

She smiled at the Shoshone warrior, wheeled around, and headed back to the kitchen.

Floyd watched Mika's longing eyes track Kajika's dish back to the kitchen. "You want another piece, son?"

Mika turned to look at Floyd. "Would that be too much, Pa?"

"Reckon not. Let's both have another piece to celebrate you keeping me from getting stuck like a pig."

Mika gave a single, emphatic nod. "Good. I like that."

By the time they had finished their second piece of apple pie, folks were straggling back into the cantina. Floyd was watching the door when his good friend and mentor entered the cantina, along with Kit Carson.

"Look who I found," Kit said.

Floyd had already risen and moved swiftly toward his friend. When Hugh stuck out his hand, Floyd just kept going and wrapped the man in his big arms, hugging him tight. They hugged for a few moments, then each stepped back.

"You are looking fit, son. It is good to see you. The last time these old eyes laid on you, it looked like you were headed for prison. I'm sure glad that didn't happen."

"It didn't happen because of you, Hugh."

"I am thankful I arrived in time." Moving toward Mika and Kajika, he nodded to Shorty and Morg. "Good to see you two. I'm glad to see you haven't yet killed each other."

Shorty grinned. "Shucks, Hugh, you know I wouldn't hurt this tall drink of water. If'n I did, who would I argue with?"

Morg nodded back to Hugh. "Nice to see you, too, Hugh. It's

come close a couple of times, but I just consider where it's comin' from."

Shorty's head pulled back. He glared at Morg. "Why, mister, one of these nights when you're snoring so loud it's shaking them stars, I'm liable to stuff a horse apple down yore gullet."

Hugh stepped by the two friends. Mika and Kajika stood. He clapped a hand on Mika's shoulder. "Your ma is feeding you well. You are close to being a full-grown man."

"He saved my life today," Floyd said.

Hugh's eyes widened and eyebrows lifted. He shook the boy's hand. "Later, you'll have to tell me all about it." He then extended his hand to Kajika and said, "It is always a pleasure to greet the brave Kajika."

Kajika took the hand and inclined his head. "And it is always a pleasure for me when I can see Hugh Brennan, good friend of the Shoshone."

"Thank you. Now everyone, sit. I have news."

They made a place for Hugh and seated themselves.

Kim came over with a thick buffalo steak, alongside which rested a large baked potato. Shorty saw the potato and said to Kim, "We didn't get a potato."

She smiled sweetly at the man. "You're not Hugh Brennan."

"Humph!" Shorty said.

Hugh thanked Kim and began eating and talking. He talked about the presidential election and inauguration. "I think all of you are aware William Henry Harrison is now president of the United States. Just maybe we will have someone who can leave us alone and turn this economy around." Several heads around the table nodded. "There is much more we can talk about, but the other news can wait. This outweighs everything else."

Hugh turned to Floyd. "Salty has been hurt."

Floyd felt a deep stab of concern. Salty had been the first employee of Hugh Brennan Floyd had met. The old man's disposition went along with his age, and at first he'd irritated Floyd to no end. But his dislike changed into a close friendship, and Salty's lessons on the west and the handling of men had been invaluable.

Brow wrinkled with worry, Floyd asked, "How was he hurt, and is it bad?"

Hugh turned his chair to face Floyd. "You will not like this, but you can't go blaming yourself. Sometimes bad things happen no matter what you do."

"Come on, Hugh. You don't have to soften me up. Give it to me straight. Is he going to live?"

"I saw him again just before we left Independence. He's looking better. The doc says he's too ornery to die."

Those who knew Salty chuckled in relief.

Hugh continued, "He'll be laid up for a spell. He's had some internal bleeding. There for a while, according to the doc, it looked like Salty was a goner."

Floyd's mind raced. *What happened? What caused the internal bleeding? Did a mule or horse kick him, or maybe a wagon fell on him? He was getting old, but he still insisted on working at the Brennan barn.* "Hugh, how did it happen?"

Hugh nodded. "A knife wound. The doc said it came close to his liver. He didn't think his liver was cut, though. He said if the knife had hit his liver, he would've bled to death for sure."

Floyd could feel the anger rising. *A knife wound? Salty's an old man. Could it be a longtime grudge?* "Who did it?"

Hugh placed his rough hand on Floyd's shoulder. "It was the Akers bunch."

Floyd felt like the knife driven into Salty was stabbing his heart. *I knew it. I should have stayed. This is all my fault.* He could see the concern on Hugh's face as he felt the man's big hand squeeze his shoulder.

"This isn't your fault, boy. You had to get back to your family and make sure they were all right. Don't go blaming yourself."

"Salty's going to be fine?"

"Yes. Like I said, it'll take some time, but he'll recover. Salty is one tough old man. He told me to tell you it wasn't your fault. He also said he winged Roscoe."

"How'd it happen, Hugh?"

"Salty had a run-in with them in the Trailhead Saloon. Seems they were looking for you. According to Doc Bessel, Salty tried to goad them into a fight. They almost bit, but Clarence's ten-gauge persuaded those hillbillies that would be a terrible decision. They backed off and left the saloon, but they didn't leave town.

"Seems they waylaid him when he left the Trailhead. They were trying to get information on you. Roscoe Akers wants you for killing his two boys."

A grim-faced Floyd said, "I reckon that can be arranged." The words came out cold and heavy.

"Now look, Floyd," Hugh said, "you just got back from the east. You—"

Floyd stared into Hugh's eyes. "You said Salty winged Roscoe."

Hugh sighed in resignation. "Yes, it was the weapon you gave him. In fact, he thinks he wounded at least one more. That's what got everybody to him so quickly. Doc Bessel said it sounded like a war going on in the alley next to the Trailhead. He got off four shots. Said those Akers scattered like a covey of quail. Last anyone saw of them was their backsides as they raced out of town. But Salty did see something else." He paused for a moment. "Henry Page was with them."

Kajika had been silent until now. "Is this the Henry Page we did not hang?"

"That's the one," Shorty said, his face twisted as if he had just taken a dose of castor oil.

Floyd shook his head. "We did what we thought was right. Leotie said he didn't hurt her. She told us it was all Van McMillan's doing." His big head turned toward Shorty, flashing the scar on his left cheek. It had almost disappeared in his sun and wind weathered skin, but was now a scarlet line running from his cheekbone to his chin. "He'll hang this time. It's been a long time coming."

"Look, Floyd," Hugh said, "you have your family to think about. Kit told me about the tribe moving back to the Snake. You need to be with them."

"You're right. I have my family to think about. If this Akers bunch finds them, they'll try to kill them. It's my job to stop that from happening, and I aim to do it."

"Well, you ain't doin' it alone," Jeb said.

Floyd shook his head. "You need to be with Aiyana and the baby. They need you. This is going to be a hard, fast trip."

Kajika spoke. "It is time for the tribe to support you. We will take braves and find this Akers and those who are with him. They will die, and it will be over. We will then return to the tribe."

Floyd shook his head. "Kajika, think about what you are saying. The tribe will be moving. Braves will be needed to defend against the Apache, the Ute, Blackfoot, and possibly the Sioux. Without warriors to help defend against enemies, the tribe will be vulnerable. You and they must stay."

Kajika was silent. Slowly, he nodded. "I do not like it, but you are right, my friend. The tribe must come first."

"Thanks for the thought, but what you say now is true. The tribe must come first."

Morg spoke up. "We're with you."

"Danged right we are," Shorty said. "We'll show that Akers bunch what it means to stick a knife in a friend of ours. Plus, I'd also like to see that Henry Page get his comeuppance."

Floyd turned back to Hugh. "Did you hear if Bobby Sutton is all right?"

"He is. Owen Fisher said the boy and his aunt made it past the Akers bunch. They should be relaxing back home in Nashville, none the wiser."

Floyd let out a sigh of relief. "Good, and when we take care of old man Akers and his boys, they'll never have to worry."

"So, you're going after them?"

"Hugh, there's nothing else I can do. I can't wait for them to ambush us somewhere along the trail. They may not be from these mountains, but they are canny, dangerous folks. Akers and his whelps have lived in the hills their whole life. Tracking is bred into them. They're not city folks. I've got to find them. Then we'll see how it goes when I find those fellers."

"Not just fellers."

Everyone around the table looked at Hugh.

Floyd asked, "What do you mean?"

"Roscoe has a daughter. According to Owen Fisher, she is quite lovely physically, but he said she's as bloodthirsty as the rest of her family."

"That might create a problem, but we'll deal with it when the time comes. In your trip from Independence, did you hear anything along the way about Akers or his bunch?"

"I did. We camped at Pawnee Rock. Some traders coming down from Fort John joined up for the evening."

Forehead wrinkled, Floyd said, "I'm not familiar with Fort John. Is it newly built?"

"Sure you are," Shorty piped in. "That there is the old American Fur Company fort they called Fort William. It got fancied up, all nice and adobe like, on the bluff above the Laramie. The old Fort William was run-down and fallin' apart."

"Thanks, Shorty." He turned back to Hugh. "So what'd they say? Did they come in with you?"

Hugh shook his head, and Morg held up his tankard for a refill. "No, they took the Cimarron cutoff. But they told me about some men looking for you. Said a Henry Page was with them. He also said they had a really pretty girl with them."

Floyd considered what his friend Hugh had just told him. *Why would Page take them north? Doesn't he know I'm down here? Surely he heard the bar talk from teamsters and trappers. Was he just not listening? Does he think I'm still on the Elk River? That has to be it.*

He looked at Kajika. "Page thinks we're still on the Elk River. I bet that's where he's headed."

"Good," the chief said, "you can cut them off. Kill them all."

Shorty grinned. "I like yore thinkin', Chief."

Morg said, "At least we have an idea of what they're doing."

Floyd shook his head. "Don't think so. They were only five or six days from Elk River when the traders talked to them. By now they've been there and know we're nowhere around. So what'll they do next?"

Jeb spoke up. "No tellin'. Page'll know about the Shoshone on the Snake River. He's liable to head in that direction."

Floyd nodded. "True, but he could run into someone who knows us. They'll tell him we're down here. In the time they've had to travel, they could almost be here, or halfway to the Snake. I'm thinking we need to cover both situations."

He looked at Jeb. "My friend, as much as I would like to have you with us, with this information, I think it extremely important you be with your wife and baby. That will strengthen the People and protect our families. Shorty and Morg can go with me, and we'll head for the Snake."

The corners of Jeb's mouth pulled down, and his brow wrinkled. "I ain't likin' it, but it's about the best thing we can do. If they should come for us, we'll be prepared."

"Good," Floyd said. "Let's line up some extra horses, get the supplies, and plan to be on our way at daylight."

As DAWN BROKE, they waved goodbye to Hugh Brennan and his Santa Fe–bound wagon train. With their backs warmed by the rising sun, they rode silently toward the distant mountains. When the sun stood at its zenith, they stopped, built a small fire, and ate their last meal together for a while.

Father and son sat next to each other, eating bacon and

sopping cold biscuits in their bacon-grease gravy. Around a mouthful of biscuit, Floyd said, "Mighty good, Shorty."

"If you boys like that there bacon, you'll love this." He walked to a pack, opened it, and gingerly lifted two pies from inside.

Mika's face brightened. "How did you do that, Mr. Shorty?"

Shorty shot a wide grin toward Mika. "Well, son, I just packed 'em mighty careful like so you could have some pie today."

"That's a fine treat, Shorty," Floyd said, his friend cutting each pie in thirds.

"Reckon each one of ya gets a third. If you're the first, be right careful not to latch on to what ain't yores."

Floyd watched Mika carefully separate his part, making it disappear quickly. When the boy finished, he handed it to Floyd, who passed it on to Kajika. "You go ahead. I'll eat last."

The Shoshone took the pie and ate his portion as carefully as the boy. When he was done, he passed the remaining third back to Floyd, who made quick work of it.

Morg finished his at about the same time. "Shorty, you may not be the best cook in the world, but you make the best apple pie I've ever tasted."

Shorty eyed his partner. "I noticed you weren't too slow lappin' up that there bacon. In fact, I can't rightly remember you ever turning down something I fixed."

"Boys," Floyd said, "before you get started off on another squabble, let's get this fire out and these animals loaded. We need to be parting ways. All of us have a lot of traveling ahead."

The men went to work loading horses and mules, cleaning the campsite, and putting out the fire.

When they were finished, Floyd walked with Mika to the boy's horse. "I'm sorely beholden to you for what you did in the cantina, son. You saved my life. I'm proud of you. You tell your ma what has happened and why I'm headed out ahead of the tribe. Tell her I'll miss her and hope to see her before you reach the

Snake." He grasped the boy's shoulder and squeezed. "Take good care of yourself. I'll miss you."

"Me too, Pa. *You* be safe." They stood silently, looking at each other. Then Mika turned and jumped into the saddle.

Floyd moved to Kajika. "I wish you were going with us, but you'll be needed in the move. Tell Pallaton what has happened, what we're doing, and to watch out for renegade white men. He'll understand." The two men shook hands, and Floyd walked over to Jeb, who had already mounted.

"Don't say it," Jeb said. "I know, I need to take care of Aiyana and the baby, and I'll be helpin' Mika take care of his ma. I'll tell you though, I'm gettin' almighty tired of missing out on yore fights."

"Hopefully," Floyd responded, "you'll miss out on this one if we've made the right decision. If not, you'll be in the middle of it. Plus, I'll be kickin' myself for this fool move."

Jeb nodded and stuck out a scarred, calloused hand. "Reckon it's probably the right one. But if you hear different along the way, come running." Bumping his horse in the flanks, he said, "See you."

Floyd watched his son and two friends ride off, leading their pack horses. Mika turned once and waved, then they disappeared over a low rise. Picking up the reins, Floyd patted Buck's neck and swung into the saddle. "Boys," he said, "what say we go find Roscoe Akers and his bunch?"

Both Shorty and Morg gave curt nods, turning their horses alongside Buck.

Shorty said, "Page too. It's time we took care of some unfinished business."

6

Henry Page, thankful the fire was between him and the old man, said, "I'm tellin' you, Mr. Akers, this is where he was when I was out here. He was livin' right here with a tribe of Shoshone. I rode back to Independence with a bunch of mountain men, and they told me he lived here. They said that those Injuns saved his life. In fact, he rescued that Shoshone woman from my partner and then killed him—hanged him like a sack of oats."

Roscoe Akers tracked Page with pale gray eyes reflecting the color of flint in the firelight. His hand massaged his left side where Salty had fired the Paterson's .36-caliber lead ball into him. Fortunately for him, it had gone through without damaging any organs. He was stiff and sore, souring his always nasty disposition and making it even worse. His voice hammered at the guide. "Page, I hired you 'cause you said you could find Floyd Logan." He held his arms out wide, turning his upper body to show the darkened mountains. "Do you see him anywhere around here?"

Akers glared into the shadows, looking to each side. "How long's it been since you talked to those *mountain men*, Page?"

"Well, sir, it has been a while, a few years."

"How many?"

Page looked at his cup of coffee no longer steaming in the chill mountain air. "Reckon maybe six or seven."

Akers stood, cursed, and threw his empty cup across the fire at Page. The cup missed the man's head and sailed into the darkness. "Six or seven years! How do I get involved with so many stupid people? Do you think he or them Injuns might have moved in six or seven years?"

Page remained quiet, looking to the others for help. Cold, blank eyes stared back at him. *How do I get mixed up with this kind? Roscoe Akers may even be worse than Van McMillan, and he almost got me hanged by Logan.*

Akers pulled his pistol from behind his belt and aimed it at Page. "Feller, you been asked a question. When I ask a question, I expect an answer."

I'm a dead man, Page thought. *If I'm gonna live, I've got to come up with something.* "Sorry, Mr. Akers. I was just trying to figure out where they might've gone. The Shoshone aren't movin' people. They stay in one place. They might move temporarily to stay up with the buffalo, but mostly they find a place and put down roots. That's what I expected. I'm as surprised as you are."

Akers kept the gun leveled for a moment, then lowered it and shoved it behind his belt. "Alright, considering that might be true, you have any idea where they could've taken off to?"

Page knew he had to come up with an answer. He had led these people to Elk Creek, hoping Logan would be here. He knew it was a long shot. But it was his best chance of finding Floyd Logan. There were some old campfire rings, but that was the only sign that anyone had ever been here. It was obvious they had been gone for years. *What can I say? This crazy old man and his equally crazy kids are liable to gut me like a hog if I say the wrong thing.* "I don't know."

The old man's hand went to his waist, but this time he pulled the long-bladed knife he whetted every night.

"Wait. I said I don't *know*. None of us do, but I have an idea. There's a large group of Shoshone who live on the Snake River to the northwest. It's near the trail to Oregon country. There's a good chance Logan's group decided to join back up with them." He nodded his head for emphasis. "Yep. I bet that's what they did. Those Shoshone like nothing better than to be with their own people. In fact, that's what they call themselves, the People."

Akers returned to his seat and pulled his whetstone from his pocket. It was wrapped in an oily, stained piece of deer hide. He removed it, folded the hide, shoving it back into a pocket, and began stroking the blade on the stone. "Mary Grace, git me another cup of coffee."

"You threw your cup in the woods, Pa."

Speaking slowly, as if he were talking to a young child, Roscoe said, "Then go into the woods and find it. When you find it, fill it with coffee, and bring it to me."

"Pa, it's dark. I can't see out there. There's timber rattlers all around, and, anyway, how can I find yore danged cup in the dark?"

The old man raised his head from his task and stared across the fire at his daughter. "Girl, I ain't a-gonna tell you again."

She stood, reached into the edge of the fire, and pulled out a lighted brand. Carefully, she made her way into the darkness. Page could hear her mutter, "Mean, ole—"

Almost in the same tone, Roscoe said, "I've still got good hearing, girl. If you prize yore backside, you won't finish what you're saying."

Page watched the girl. She was mighty pretty. The shadows outlined her body, accentuating her bottom and chest. It excited him, much like the Shoshone girl Van had bought from the Blackfoot. Van had been so stupid. He'd beaten the girl and raped her. Page had been smarter. He'd waited until the girl was unconscious from Van's beatings and then took her. She was never the wiser, and Van never knew. Page had only done it when Van wasn't around. It had been so funny. The girl had actually defended him to Logan and the others. *I am so smart,* Page thought. *I can think circles around these backwoods hicks.* He felt better.

Page tore his eyes from the girl's body and looked around. No one had noticed him watching her. There would be a time for this girl, too, he thought. *She's dirty and hill-country trash, but she's pretty. Clean her up and keep her mouth shut, and she'd be fine.* He felt better. He was smarter than any of this bunch. They were even dumber than that Floyd Logan. Why, he'd have her and be long gone before they ever knew anything was wrong. He'd done it before. He'd do it again. One more glance around the fire, but this time Gent Akers was staring right at him, grinning. The man held his gaze, almost as if he knew what he was thinking, then winked.

I've got to be careful around Gent, Page thought. *He may be smarter than the others.*

Roscoe Akers looked up from his knife. "How long you reckon it'd take us to reach them Shoshone Injuns? I'm gettin' all-fired anxious to skin me a Floyd Logan."

At Roscoe's mention of skinning, Cooter Akers looked up. His eyes gleamed with excitement. "Can I do it, Pa? That'd be mighty fun. I'd love to do it. I like to hear 'em scream."

Roscoe ignored his son. "How long?"

Page did some fast figuring. It would be at least a three-week trip, if he could even find the camp. *I'm not a mountain man,* he thought. *Most of this country I've never seen before, but I have heard the trappers talking.* "Mr. Akers, there's some mighty rough country betwixt here and there. Much of it's like this, mostly up and down. Some of it's almighty flat and dry."

"Page, I didn't ask you to tell me about it, I asked how long."

"That's right," Cooter joined in. "Pa wuz askin' how far?"

Though tempted, Page didn't respond to Cooter. He knew the younger fella had an awful temper. He had seen it demonstrated on a trader they'd met shortly after leaving Fort John. One second, the boy had been sitting by the fire, laughing with the trader. The next, the man was dead. Cooter had shoved his big knife—it seemed they all had one, even the girl—through the trader's brisket. Page had watched the man's stunned gaze fix on Cooter as the boy pulled the knife from the man's chest. The trader had given a couple of coughs and fallen dead.

Page had jumped to move the man's head from near the fire. Cooter, still holding the knife, a faraway look in his eyes, had asked him, "Whatcha doin'?"

Thinking back, he realized then was the first time he had doubted his trip west.

"Didn't want the stink of burnin' hair around."

Cooter, silent, had stared vacantly at him and slowly wiped the blood from his knife blade onto the man's jacket.

Gent had spoken up. "Leave him be, Cooter. I don't like that smell either, especially when I'm eatin'."

Cooter had slowly turned his head toward Gent. He'd appeared to be considering what his brother had said. Moments later, his eyes had seemed to light up. "Oh, yeah, Henry. Reckon I know what you mean," and he'd slid the still bloody knife back into his belt scabbard.

Page nodded at Cooter and responded to Roscoe. "Reckon we'll be lookin' at close to a month, give or take a few days."

Roscoe held his frown. "Long time. What if'n he ain't there?"

"We should meet other traders or trappers along the way. They may be able to give us more information. Once I get you headed in the right direction, I'll ride ahead and see if I can come across Logan's sign."

"Humph," Roscoe said, "sure as I turn you loose, you'll skedaddle off on yore own. We'll not see hide nor hair of you from that time on."

Page shook his head emphatically. "No, sir. That's not gonna happen. I want to see Floyd Logan stretching a rope. There's no way I'd leave that opportunity."

The old man shot Page an icy grin. "Now ain't that big of you. You want to be there. Wouldn't that just be peachy." His face turned grim. "No, you stay with us."

Page shrugged. "Alright, it's up to you. But if you're afraid I'll run, you can send one of your boys with me."

He could see Roscoe considering it, and elected to stay quiet.

It was Gent who spoke up. "Shoot, Pa. He ain't gonna run. But if you want to send someone with him, send someone what won't be needed. You could be needin' any of us boys. Why don't you send Mary Grace with him? You know if he tried anything, she'd shoot him quicker than Cooter would. She'll keep him in line, and with just the two of 'em, not having any mules, they could travel a lot faster than us."

Page held his breath. *Is it possible he might send her out alone with me? I couldn't choose a better guard.* He let his head turn and eyes focus on Mary Grace. *Yeah, a little dirty, but mighty pretty.*

"That's a fine idea there, Gent. She don't do much around camp. Anybody can fix a meal or two." His head whipped around to his daughter. "Girl, in the morning, you go with Page. If he tries anything, shoot him."

With a high, nasal voice, she whined, "Pa, I ain't got no use for Page. I've caught him staring at my upper parts."

"Girl, I told ya, if'n he tries anything, you can shoot him."

She turned her face toward Page, the corners of her beautiful dark eyes crinkled with humor, as if she'd just heard the funniest joke, and her full mouth broke into a grin. She giggled. "I'd be likin' that, Pa. I surely would."

"Girl, listen to me. I said *if'n he tries anything.* We still need him 'cause he knows this country better'n we do. You go and kill him for no reason, we could be in trouble. So don't you kill him unless you have to. You understand me?"

Mary Grace's lower lip shot out in a pout, and she said nothing.

Roscoe stopped paused and yelled at his daughter, "You do what I tell you, girl! Now do you understand me?"

She looked at him under hooded eyes. "Yeah, Pa."

Page tried to hide the chill that shivered through his spine. *I swear,* he thought, *all these Akers are crazy as loons. I've got to get away from here.* He cleared his throat. "Best be saving all that shooting for Blackfoot. They range this far south, and they love to scalp white men."

Cooter glanced nervously into the dark timber, his gaze settling on Roscoe. "We ain't afraid of no Injuns, are we, Pa?"

Gent grinned at his brother. "We ain't, Cooter. How 'bout you?"

Cooter's hand dropped to the hilt of his knife. "I ain't neither, Gent, and don't you go saying I am. You be careful, or I'll spill yore guts all over these here pine needles."

Roscoe slapped Cooter on the back of his head and glared at Gent. "Leave it be, Gent. Cooter, you ain't gonna be spillin' anybody's guts unless I say so. You shouldn't have kilt that trader. You get ahold of your temper, and I mean right now."

Cooter pulled his head in like a turtle and slowly turned a malevolent gaze on his pa.

"Don't you look at me like that, boy. I was using a knife long before you sucked air. Now settle down."

Cooter looked down, took his hand from his knife, and glanced over at Gent. Gent was grinning at his brother.

Page observed the family interaction and thought, *Why did I let my hate for Logan overrule my good sense? I was nice and comfortable in Independence.* He shook his head. *Look at me now, in the middle of Indian country with a bunch of madmen. I hope watching Floyd Logan hang turns out to be worth all this.*

He unrolled his sleeping gear, sat, and pulled off his boots. "Best get to sleep, Mary Grace. We'll start early."

"Mind your own business, Henry Page. You ain't my boss. I'll be goin' to sleep when I'm ready."

Though Page faced away from her, he could feel the venom. Without another word, he lay down, pulled his blankets under his chin, and closed his eyes, hoping he'd still be alive in the morning.

He awoke to a flash of pain as a boot toe slammed into his thigh.

"Get up, Page," Roscoe Akers said. "It'll be daylight afore long. You need to be on yore way."

He rubbed his thigh and threw the blankets off. The mountain chill was upon them. Grabbing his boots, he pulled them on as far as they would slide, stood, and stomped them on the rest of the way, then stretched into his coat. *Heck of a way to start the day,* he thought, *but at least I'm alive.*

With a sinking feeling in the pit of his stomach, he saw Cooter saddling his horse. Mary Jane was seeing to the coffee and the last of the grits. She'd cooked up a bit of bacon to go with it. The bacon smelled good. He felt hunger pangs jab. "What's Cooter doing? Is he going to be scouting around this morning?"

Roscoe Akers coughed hard and spit a wad of phlegm into the fire, where it momentarily sizzled and popped. He cleared his throat and said, "Changed my mind. She ain't much of a cook, but she's better than any of us men. Mary Grace is stayin' with us. Cooter's goin' in her stead."

"You look a little disappointed, Page," Gent said. His wide, taunting grin accompanied his observation.

Roscoe looked up. "Nothin' to be disappointed about. Cooter can spot an Injun ten mile away, and there ain't no better fighter around." He exposed jagged, rotten teeth in a grin that could chill blood. "Course, you don't want to rile him. That boy does have a mean temper."

Page yanked his gloves from a pocket and slipped them on. He grabbed his cup from his saddlebags and gripped the hot coffeepot handle, pouring himself a cup of the wicked-looking brew. This was a motley crew, and the old man had assigned the worst of the lot to ride with him. He took his first sip, feeling the hot coffee burn as it made its way to his stomach. Coffee would help. It had always worked much like a drug for him. Everything looked better after his first cup. "We'll need supplies."

Roscoe pointed to an almost filled tow sack. "That one's yores. Cooter already has his loaded." The old man looked over at his wild son. The boy was standing by his horse, ready to go. "Get a move on, Page. The boy's already loaded up and waitin' on you. You're the one who said you needed to leave early."

"Yeah," Cooter said, "do like Pa said. And hurry up. I'm ready to go."

I'm going to enjoy killing that boy, Page thought. He cleared his throat. "As soon as I get some vittles in my belly, we'll be on our way."

Roscoe turned to Mary Grace. "Dish him up a plate." Then to Page he said, "Git loaded up. You can eat in the saddle."

Page stood and walked to his horse. Once he had finished saddling and tying the bag of supplies behind his saddle, he turned back to Roscoe.

Mary Grace was standing there holding his plate.

"Wait until he's in the saddle, girl. Page, mount up."

Page turned, swung into the saddle, and Mary Grace handed him the plate. With her back to everyone else, she winked and moved back to the fire. He puzzled over the wink. What did it mean? Was she gloating because Cooter was going with him, or did she like him? *I bet she likes me,* he thought. *Women always take a shine to me. She has probably seen the error of her ways and wants to let me know.*

Roscoe's harsh voice broke into his thoughts. "I want you two back here in three weeks or less. We're gonna hang around and do a little scouting ourselves."

"Three weeks is cutting it a little short, Mr. Akers."

The old man eyed Page, then turned to his son. "Cooter, did you hear me?"

"Sure did, Pa. Three weeks it is." He leaned over towards Page, grinned, and slapped the end of his reins across the rear of Page's horse.

The bay gelding leaped forward, Page barely keeping his seat while he threw the plate of food to the ground. Incautiously, he momentarily glared at the laughing man. Regaining his composure, he slapped the spurs to the bay, and they galloped from camp.

7

Turning in his saddle, Floyd watched the fractured clouds pouring down the peak of El Capitan, plummeting much like a waterfall, and disappearing as they plunged into the warmer air below. He scratched the four-day stubble, feeling the southwest wind's heat against his cheek. The same wind brought the faint smell of pine, even this far onto the plains. He stood in the saddle and stretched, his back sounding several audible pops.

Shorty glanced at his friend and shook his head. "Old."

Floyd, having passed his twenty-seventh birthday in February, said nothing. He knew Shorty was just trying to bait him and chuckled to himself. Physically, he had never felt better. Since being home with Leotie, he had eaten well, run and wrestled with the braves, and practiced the moves Lontac had taught him so many years ago.

While his eyes searched the foothills ahead, his mind drifted back to his training with Lontac. He had been but a boy of sixteen when, upon arriving in Santa Fe, Hugh Brennan had persuaded Lontac to train him. In the rustic room of the small man's house, he'd learned the moves, thrusts, and parries used by those trained in the Filipino art of defense and attack. Lontac's teachings had saved his life on several occasions. He shook his head at the rapid passing of the last eleven years. So much had happened.

Eleven years of doing what he had so wanted to do as a boy, of trapping, hunting, exploring, and living his own life in these mountains. A deep breath of satisfaction expanded his wide chest. The smell of the ponderosa pines mixed with that of the tall green switchgrass and Indian grass that brushed Buck's belly. The soft fragrance of the purple star-shaped flowers of the milkweed added to the sweet blend. Yep. He was glad to be here, but he for sure owed his life to Lontac. *I wonder how he's doing. He was old when he taught me. Could he still be alive? I'd sure like to see him.*

They were just coming out of the dry creek bed, which twisted through the shallow valley. Tall cottonwood, their silvery leaves flashing, towered over the twisted dark green scrub oak, both growing along the sometimes flowing creek. *A man has to stay alert out here*, Floyd thought. *You never know where or when someone might wait to lift your scalp or your money pouch.*

Wrinkles across his forehead deepened, and his eyelids pulled tight as he concentrated, examining the distant rocks, grass, and brush. There were cuts and ridges, dry creeks and narrow valleys slashing through these foothills. Buffalo were near. It was buffalo-hunting time for the Indians. Some of those hunters were friendly, some weren't. Even the friendly ones might get notional.

Morg looked toward the mountains. "If I had my druthers, I'd be in them trees yonder. I ain't much taken with ridin' out here across this open land."

Shorty, not having gotten a rise out of Floyd, shook his head. "Morg, how many times have I told ya we can move faster out here? You ain't skeered of a little Injun or two, are you?"

Morg's big shaggy head turned slowly toward his partner and fastened him with dark, deep-set eyes. "A man in this country who ain't skeered of Injuns might as well scalp hisself, 'cause it's comin'."

The crack of a rifle blasted his statement home. Floyd kicked Buck in the flanks and, leading Rusty and Browny, raced out of the creek bottom across the undulating plains and through the tall grass. Once Buck was settled into a run, Floyd looked back. Pawnees. At least seven or eight and not far. Where did those blasted Indians come from?

Morg and Shorty were both pounding after him, leaning low over their horses' necks. He wasn't worried about the Pawnees hitting anyone from the backs of their running horses. He was worried about being pushed into a trap up ahead. Morg was right. He'd sure like to be in those mountains to the west. He glanced in that direction, and spotted a stream of at least five Pawnees paralleling them and closing. Automatically, he looked to the east. Five more out there pushing in toward them. Even as he looked, he saw one of the Indians' horses yanked down from the front like he'd been roped.

"You see that?" Shorty called.

"Yeah," Floyd shouted back. "Stepped in a hole."

Floyd glanced back again and could see Shorty peering ahead.

Shorty saw him look. "That could happen to us out here in this tall grass. We cain't see nothin' till we're on top of it."

Morg yelled, "Big buffalo wallow to our right!"

"Head for it," Floyd shouted. He turned Buck and could make out the depression ahead.

The Pawnees to the east must've seen the wallow at the same time. They started yelling, and their shooting picked up. Floyd could see they were trying to get to the wallow before them. The race was on. Turning either right or left gave the pursuers behind them the angle, allowing them to draw closer. Floyd made sure his revolving .52-caliber Colt ring rifle was loose in the scabbard. He checked both of his .36-caliber Paterson revolvers were easy to hand as they beat through the high grass toward the wallow.

They were almost to the wallow.

Shorty went down. No more than twenty feet from safety.

The Pawnees to the east were almost on top of them. Floyd yanked Buck to a sliding stop, his horse's haunches almost dragging on the ground. He leaped from the horse and raced to Shorty, who had rolled clear of his mount as they were going down. The animal had jumped up and trotted toward the wallow.

A rifle fired from behind him. Morg. He must have made it to the wallow. Floyd raced to his downed friend.

Shorty was trying, unsuccessfully, to get to his feet while holding his two single-shot pistols. Floyd reached Shorty just as the leading brave brought up a wicked lance to drive through his friend's chest. Floyd's rifle shot slammed into the charging Indian's breastbone.

The point of the lance dropped, driving into the earth. The Pawnee had the lance trapped in his right armpit, and when it stabbed into the ground, the dying man was propelled over the rear of the horse, slamming him into the ground.

Floyd swung the revolving rifle to the next brave. With no time to aim, he one-handed the weapon and fired it like a pistol. With the other hand, he had grabbed Shorty's collar and was dragging him toward the wallow. The .52-caliber ball drove through the lower jaw of the Pawnee and exited through the back of his head. The brave rode past, swaying, dead in the saddle.

Floyd pulled Shorty over the edge of the wallow, dropped him, and with his .36-caliber pistol, fired at the nearest target.

They were all around them. He fired again. He felt a burning sensation in his neck, but couldn't stop to check it.

A brave built like Shorty rushed Floyd, his tomahawk raised. It flashed down, and Floyd blocked it with his rifle barrel, knocking it to the side while shooting the man in the ear with his handgun. From the corner of his eye, he could see Shorty in a death struggle with an Indian half again as big as him. Floyd spun while raising the Colt rifle high above his head and brought it down on the back of the man's head with all the strength his adrenaline-filled body could muster. He could hear and feel the heavy barrel crunch through the skull and into the brain. The barrel wedged in the dead man's skull.

He yanked. The rifle wouldn't come out. He couldn't leave the weapon for fear a Pawnee might get it. One more desperate yank freed the rifle.

Floyd could see a form breaking into his peripheral vision from his left. He let his body continue to swing from jerking the rifle out of the dead man's head, the rotation of the ten-and-a-half-pound rifle building up speed. It slammed into his assailant's shoulder, knocking the brave sideways. The blow allowed Floyd time to again pull the ring, rotating the next loaded chamber into the firing position, move his finger from the rotation ring to the trigger, and fire into the man's belly. The Pawnee staggered back with surprise and pain, then with grim determination, leaped at Floyd, a shiny steel eight-inch blade stabbing toward the mountain man's throat.

With no time to think, he dropped both weapons, grabbed the man's wrist in his left hand, twisting it as if he were intent on ripping the arm from its socket. He made a fist of his right hand and drove it like a sledgehammer into the Pawnee's overstressed elbow. The crack of the breaking elbow was lost in the grunts and yells of desperate men locked in death struggles. When his elbow snapped, the Pawnee's hand opened, dropping the sharp blade. Catching the falling knife in his right hand, Floyd slashed back, the blade slicing deep across the Indian's neck. Spurts of blood followed the glinting steel.

Floyd, his face covered with blood and contorted in a grimace of rage and determination, examined the killing ground for other attackers. He released the dying man and snatched up his revolver and rifle.

Morg too was red with blood, his tomahawk in one hand and knife in the other. Three Indians lay dead or dying around him. Shorty sat, holding his pistol by the barrel and his knife in the other hand, a hefty Pawnee dead beside him.

"Looks like they're gone—for now," Shorty said.

Floyd nodded. "How bad you boys hurt?"

Morg wiped his 'hawk and knife on a dead Indian's leggings. "Reckon I ain't nicked. Appears only you and Shorty got scratched up a bit."

Shorty gazed up at Floyd. "How much of that is Injun blood?"

"Most of it. Morg, why don't you keep a lookout and check the horses? I'll take a look at Shorty."

Morg began reloading weapons while he scanned the surrounding plains and moved toward the two remaining animals.

Floyd knelt down with Shorty. "How you doing, pardner?"

"Fine. Nary a scratch but this here leg."

A bloody Pawnee arrow rose like a flag from the front of his left thigh. On the opposite side, it was embedded down to the fletching. "Came close to hitting my horse. I woulda hated that." He looked up and winked at Floyd. "Pretty lucky, huh?"

"Yeah, Shorty, you've always been lucky. Now let's get this arrow out of your leg." He grasped the shaft in both hands, one big hand resting against his friend's leg. "Ready?"

"Break away."

Floyd snapped the shaft and looked at the bloody arrowhead, recalling when the Comanche arrow had driven through his upper arm. It had hurt like the blazes. He knew what Shorty was feeling. He handed it to Shorty. "Gotta pull the shaft back through."

"Well, get with it." Shorty glared at the bloody arrow in his hand and rolled over, exposing the back of his thigh.

Floyd wrapped a big hand around the fletching, gripped the shaft tight, and yanked. Shorty never uttered a sound. The only sign of pain was the sweat rolling down his forehead. Floyd gave the remaining portion of the arrow to Shorty.

The injured man held the two pieces together where the break meshed. "Now, ain't that a pretty sight? Who wouldn't like a lovely little stick like that shoved through their leg?" Disgusted, he tossed it away.

Morg called, "Shorty, they got all of yore horses. Left us with one of mine and one of Floyd's."

Standing, Floyd said, "I guess the good thing is that they didn't get them all. We've got to get those stolen animals back and soon. I'm thinking they'll be eating Browny tonight."

Shorty shook his head. "Yeah, them danged Injuns do like mule." He started to get up.

"Wait," Floyd said. "We've got to get that leg doctored up, or it's liable to sour on you. We don't want that to happen. Morg, you don't happen to have any Who-Hit-John left, do you?"

Morg grinned. "Yessir, I surely do. I had some in our packed gear, but the Injuns got it. Reckon they'll have a fine time with it, but I also kinda spread it around amongst the animals, just in case." He turned away and moments later returned with a bottle of whiskey.

Floyd took the bottle. "Shorty, if you don't want me to mess up those fine trousers any worse than they are, you best get 'em down." He nodded toward Buck. "I've got an old, light blue, homespun shirt in my saddlebags, Morg. Would you mind getting it for me?"

"Now wait," Shorty said. "Ain't no need of you messin' up one of yore shirts for me. I'll be fine."

Floyd shook his head. "It's an old shirt. I never figured on wearing it, anyway. I keep it around for just such a happening, so stop arguing."

When Morg brought the shirt, Floyd ripped several long bandages from the back of the shirt. While he was tearing the shirt, Shorty pulled down his pants.

"I've got to say," Morg said, "that's about the ugliest excuse for a leg I think I've ever seen."

Shorty looked up at his partner. "Ain't you supposed to be lookin' out for Injuns? If you don't keep a lookout, they'll be pullin' yore pants down and roastin' those bony legs of yours. At least these here have some meat on 'em."

Floyd poured liquor over a portion of the torn shirt he had folded over to make a pad. Then he cleaned both the entrance and the exit wounds. He glanced up at Shorty, whose jaw muscles stood out like cords and his forehead poured sweat.

"Don't look at me. Get on with it. That there leg's just hankerin' for a drink."

Floyd nodded and, giving the bottle to Morg, said, "When I get this wound open wide, pour it in."

Morg gave a quick nod.

Floyd placed a big hand on each side of the wound and spread it wide. He knew full well the pain his friend was suffering from this action, but it had to be done. When the wound gaped open to his satisfaction, he nodded to Morg. The bottle tilted, and the brown liquor poured into the raw flesh. Though Shorty never uttered a sound, the muscles around the wound spasmed. Excited nerve endings caused the flesh to quiver and sent frantic signals of pain to the brain.

"Roll over," Floyd said. He had to get to the entrance wound. After first cleaning it with the dampened pad, he and Morg repeated the process. Once doused with the liquor, Floyd wrapped the wounded leg in the homespun bandages. "All right, we're done. You should be as good as new in no time."

Morg, who had been standing over Floyd, said, "You need to take care of that bullet wound on your neck."

"What?" Floyd looked up at his friend, thick dark brows raised in question.

"Give me that pad, and I'll clean it up and give you a dose of Shorty's medicine."

Floyd reached to the left side of his neck, where it joined his shoulder. Sure enough, he could feel the open channel where the bullet had coursed across his flesh. "It doesn't feel that bad."

Shorty grabbed Floyd's arm. "We ain't got time to argue. Let him do it, and we'll be on our way."

Floyd tore another piece of shirt, made a pad, and handed it to Morg, then loosened his shirt and pulled it away from his neck. He could hear the mountain man pouring the liquor onto the pad.

"Here it comes," Morg said.

When the liquor-soaked rag hit his neck, Floyd remained stationary, though his brain screamed at him to jerk away. It felt like a red-hot coal had been crushed into his open flesh and now was moving across every living nerve in the wound. Finally, it stopped.

Then Morg said, "I'm pourin'."

The rag was nothing compared to this liquid fire that reached down into every pain receptacle in the wound channel. He sat still, no expression on his face, only a few beads of sweat popped out across his forehead.

"Done." Morg held up the half-empty bottle as he carried it back to his saddlebags. "Don't know if you two are worth all this."

Shorty struggled to his feet and pulled his trousers up. "Thanks, Floyd. I owe you." Then he looked at Morg. "You enjoyed that, didn't you?"

"Reckon I did. Does me good to hear that mouth of yours shut for a change."

Shorty's chin shot out, and his eyes narrowed. He gingerly took a step toward Morg, winced, and stopped. "Listen, you backwoods old geezer. If I didn't have this here arrow wound, I'd stomp you all over this wallow."

Morg winked at Floyd. "I guess we're gonna be hearing about the fierce Indian fighter and how many times he's been shot with them arrows."

Shorty glared at his friend, then broke into a big grin. "I reckon you are, so you just better git ready."

"If you two can take a break from arguing, we might oughta try to figure out what we're going to do. Those Pawnees have taken most of our supplies, and I'd like to get the horses back before Browny gets eaten."

Shorty spoke up again. "I cain't imagine them leaving all these dead braves. I'm thinkin' maybe they haven't gone far. Maybe they're planning on hittin' us again."

Floyd nodded. "Could be, but we hurt them pretty bad." He looked around at the number of dead braves. "They lost almost half of their force, and we have no idea how many might be wounded. I'm guessing their desire to tangle with us again may have gone down a bit. I could be wrong, but they looked more like a hunting party than a war party. There's going to be some unhappy wives when they get back home. I think they'll hole up somewhere, eat mule, drink Morg's liquor, and lick their wounds. If we can get to them early, we might save the animals.

"If we can't, we'll have to head back to Bent's Fort. That'll cost us another two weeks. I'm for getting after them. We've evened up the odds a little, and we should have the benefit of surprise."

"Sounds good to me," Shorty said, "but how's this gonna happen? We ain't got but two horses."

Floyd had moved over to Buck, checking him closely for injuries. Finding none, he rose and said, "I'll trail them, and you two follow on Morg's horse."

Morg and Shorty nodded as Floyd swung into the saddle. He laid the revolving rifle across his legs, adjusted his pistols, and walked Buck up the edge of the wallow. The prairie looked open and empty, which meant nothing. There were so many canyons and washes, creeks and cuts, a thousand Pawnees could hide out there across the waving, waist-high grass.

Reaching the top, he pulled Buck up. "You see me coming back like my tail's on fire, you know I found more than I could handle, so get ready. Otherwise, when I find them, I'll wait as long as I can. It's possible I may have to open the ball without you."

"That'd be a danged fool move," Shorty said, swatting Morg's helping hand away as he swung into the saddle.

Morg mounted behind Shorty, his feet dragging in the high grass. "Luck, Floyd. We'll be along as quick as we can."

Floyd turned the buckskin toward the mountains, angling a little south of the Pawnees' trail. The last thing he was going to do was ride straight down on them. For sure, they would have look-outs watching their back trail. He did like that they were headed for the mountains. He couldn't get off these plains fast enough.

8

Once the Indians' direction was well established, Floyd turned Buck farther south of the trail and put him into a trot. He had no reason to think the Pawnee braves would change course. Though they had taken terrible losses, they would have no thought of being trailed by the three men.

No, Floyd thought, *they're heading to the mountains. Once they stop, they'll go through our supplies first and find Morg's stash. Hopefully, Morg brought enough to make them forget their hunger. That'll give me more time to get there. I'd hate to see anything happen to Browny. That's one fine mule.*

He raced the sun to the mountains. As he drew nearer to the slopes, so did the sun to the peaks. The tall grass had given way to scrub oaks and mahogany bushes. There was still a carpet of short grass with thick patches of sedge. Piñon and juniper scattered along the rocky red buttes. Floyd slowed Buck to a walk, taking care to prevent stumbling into the Pawnees' camp. He halted the horse often to examine rocky outcroppings and bluffs.

Time slipped by. Nearly three hours had passed since leaving

Morg and Shorty. He felt sure the Pawnee braves would have stopped by now. A steep bluff ahead would make a good lookout.

Floyd pulled Buck to a stop behind a piñon tree, slipped from the saddle, and eased to the edge of the piñon's green needles. He removed his slouch hat and extended his neck until he could examine the bluff. It was wide and steep. Made up of layers of rock that reminded him of the way Ma used to stack layers on a cake. The rock layers ran horizontally and varied from a deep red to a soft yellow, their edges rounded over time from the wind and sand. Juniper and oak jutted from deep crevasses.

After closely examining the bluff for anything that might be out of place, a moccasined foot, a smooth brown arm—for no rock, brush, or branch had the texture of a human's skin—or maybe a shining eye, he eased from behind the piñon and quickly made his way to the base of the rock hill. He climbed slowly, quietly.

A chipmunk, blending nicely with the rock it was squatting on, sat still as Floyd climbed. Floyd's head came level with the tiny squirrel. The little animal's alert brown eyes watched him, its tiny nose working rapidly, attempting to decipher the unusual bouquet rising from the man who stared at it with huge blue eyes.

Floyd had always liked these cute little squirrels. He had first become acquainted with them at Jeb's trapping camp. There had been one that would sit on the woodpile next to the cabin. He had gotten so used to Floyd, he would eat piñon nuts from the palm of the mountain man's hand while sitting on his big, calloused thumb. How could you not like the inquisitive little face, with the brown stripes running from nose to ears, the tiny soft red-furred body and the black feet? Those had been good days of learning from Jeb.

He winked at the chipmunk, and when his eyelashes moved, the tiny squirrel scurried to a nearby shallow outcropping, under which it stopped, spun around, and stared again at Floyd. *Come on,* Floyd thought. *Get your mind on your business. If you're not care-ful, that could be the last chipmunk you'll ever watch.* He continued his climb toward a low-hanging juniper along the ridge. Reaching the top, he eased under the hanging limbs of the tree, removed his hat, and raised his head above the rim.

Surprised, he thought, *How could I be so lucky?* There below him, no more than two hundred yards away, were the Pawnee braves. They had stripped the packs off Browny and Morg's and Shorty's packhorses. The supplies were scattered across the ground. He let out a silent sigh of relief. Browny stood there unharmed, cropping grass. He did like that mule.

The Indians had found Morg's stash. He started counting. One, two, three, four, five—astonished, he thought, *How many bottles did Morg bring?*—six. *There are six bottles going around.* He counted the braves, nine. Nine Indians and six bottles. He watched as one man jerked a bottle away from another, who had it tilted up as if he was intent on downing the entire contents.

Floyd scoured the surrounding area. He could see no sign of anyone other than those gathered around the bottles of liquor. He looked back to the east along his trail. From this vantage point, Morg and Shorty would be visible on their approach, but nothing moved.

A narrow draw meandered its way from the east to the south edge of the Pawnees' camp. It looked deep enough to hide him until he was on top of his quarry. Slightly past their camp, he could see an elk trail coming up out of the draw. A small, twisted juniper struggled for life at the edge of the wash next to the trail. The juniper would be his marker. Once out of the draw, he was sure they would spot him immediately. But he would be on top of them before they could do anything. It was only thirty yards from the draw to the camp.

With Morg and Shorty nowhere in sight, he would have to carry out the attack on the Pawnees himself. He made his way back down the ridge. The chipmunk had come back out onto the rock where Floyd had seen him. The mountain man looked at the little animal as he passed. In a soft voice, he whispered, "Best be careful, little fellow. You sit on that rock too often or too long, and you'll be a meal for a hawk."

The chipmunk's only response was the sniffing wiggle of his tiny nose.

Floyd continued down to the bottom and quickly moved to Buck. He checked the loads in his handguns, slipping them behind his waistband. They were uncomfortable there, but they wouldn't be there long, and the holsters might drag. He slipped the holsters from his belt and dropped them into his saddlebags, returning the belt, with his knife and tomahawk, to his waist.

He checked his Colt ring rifle and also his Ryland. He had a plan. The ring was certainly better than a single-shot muzzle-loader, but it wasn't that great in a close-up fight. He'd ride in, shoot the ring once, the Ryland once, and go to his pistols, which would give him twelve shots. After that, he'd have to fall back on his tomahawk and knife. *Hopefully, fourteen shots will be enough,* he thought.

Though the wind was pouring down the mountains onto the prairie and should mask any noise, Floyd slowly led Buck back the way they had come. He couldn't take a chance on the Indians hearing him.

When he was a comfortable distance, he turned north and gradually worked his way to the wash he had marked. Finding a trail down into the bottom, he led Buck into the wash and mounted. His hands brushed the butts of the pistols. He touched his knife hilt and tomahawk. Everything was in place. It was time.

He bumped Buck lightly in the flanks, and the big horse began walking slowly up the draw. Floyd could feel the tension in his shoulders. The bullet crease along his neck burned from the sweat running into it. A fight was coming, and he felt good. These men had tried to kill him and his friends. They had stolen their horses. To a white man, there was hardly anything worse. He had lived with the Shoshone long enough to know the red man felt differently, but Rusty and Browny were like family, and he sure didn't want them eaten.

A robber jay flew over. He watched the bird, hoping it would stay quiet. It glided by, uttering no sound. A porcupine sunning in the dusty bottom of the draw shuffled reluctantly up the brushy side and disappeared over the edge. *Don't rattle those danged quills,* Floyd thought, for he was nearing the trail leading up and out of the draw. The disturbed porcupine silently shoved his head back through the grass at the edge of the draw to watch the horse and rider quietly pass.

Floyd halted Buck at the base of the trail. The Pawnee camp was less than thirty yards from him. He could hear the Indians arguing. They were slurring their speech. Floyd took a deep breath. He hoped Morg and Shorty were close enough to lend a hand, but he wasn't betting on it. He kicked Buck in the flanks, and the big horse leaped halfway up the elk trail. Floyd's head and shoulders jerked above the rim of the draw. Heads turned at the noise. As Buck was taking his second leap up the trail, Floyd assessed the camp while the ring rifle came to his shoulder.

Browny was pulling back on his reins. The other end was held by an Indian, who had the reins in one hand and a knife in the other. "No mule meat today, mister," Floyd yelled. He settled the sights on the man's chest and pulled the trigger. The two-hundred-and-thirty-grain ball caught the man in the center of his chest, destroying the right side of his heart. The Indian dropped, and the reins fell free.

Floyd didn't see the man fall, but there was no doubt in his mind where the ball hit. He dropped the rifle into the scabbard and pulled the Ryland. A brave was charging him as Buck charged the camp. He gripped the Ryland like a pistol, earing the hammer back as it came out of the scabbard and shoving it toward the oncoming brave. The muzzle was no more than ten feet from the man when it fired, the ball striking him in the nose and blowing out the back of his head.

The camp had turned into bedlam, but none of the Pawnees were running away. They were all running toward Floyd, surrounding him. On his left, an Indian was pulling his bow to full draw as he brought it up. Floyd snapped a shot with his Colt Paterson and missed. The man let the arrow fly. His mind registered the flight of the arrow straight for his head even as he fired his second shot with the Paterson, striking the man low in the belly. He felt the arrow hit the edge of the brim of his hat, and then the burning as it coursed across his scalp, taking his hat with it.

He yanked out the remaining Paterson and shot the fierce-looking Pawnee grabbing for his right leg. His horse screamed and reared high, front legs flailing. Floyd shot into another Pawnee. He saw Buck's front hooves smash into an Indian's head, driving him to the ground.

At that moment, he heard a familiar whoop and the twin blasts of rifles firing. Two of the remaining Indians dropped. He felt the weight of a Pawnee as he leaped astride Buck. Floyd twisted in the saddle as a hand grabbed his hair, and shot his attacker in the throat. The bullet ripped through the Pawnee's spine, and the knife he had been clutching beat him to the ground.

Floyd pulled Buck to a stop, swept the camp to ensure there were no remaining threats from the Pawnee. Once his sweep confirmed they were all down, he leaped from his horse and began examining the animal. Buck had screamed, so he had to have been hurt. He found a deep cut on the horse's right foreleg, but fortunately, nothing else. His attacker must have been the man Buck stomped. The bleeding from the wound was down to a seep. He patted the animal on the shoulder. "Looks like you're going to make it, boy. You're a real fighter."

"Cain't you ever wait? I swear you've got the patience of a

hungry buffler calf," Shorty's shrill voice sounded as the two rode up on Morg's horse. "If we'd pushed Morg's nag any harder, we woulda been walkin'."

Floyd pointed to the dead Indian nearest the draw. "If I'd waited any longer, Browny'd be roasting over a fire. That Injun was about to cut my mule's throat when I came out of the draw. He was the first one I shot."

Floyd left Buck and started checking the Indians. "Make sure they're dead. There's been a few mountain men killed by Indians they thought were dead."

Shorty joined in. Morg was examining his bottles and muttering. Each one he'd pick up, shake, then drop it and head for the next one.

He started shaking his head. "These fellers drained all them fine bottles. What does a man have to do to keep hisself a drink in this here country? It's a blasted shame. At least you fellers didn't use up my spare bottle. There's a couple of swigs left in it."

Floyd had gone back to Buck and was examining the wound. "I need to talk to you about that, Morg."

Unlike Shorty, the tall mountain man seldom complained, but at Floyd's statement, he looked up, an empty bottle still held in one big hand. "What are you tryin' to say, Floyd?"

"It looks like I'll be needing another shot out of your bottle for Buck. This cut needs to be cleaned."

In a rare burst of emotion, Morg threw the bottle against a boulder, glass flying in all directions. "I'm gonna end up out here with nary a drink for months, and it's all because some danged Pawnees wanted a few scalps."

Shorty limped over to Floyd and stood examining Buck's wound. "He does get testy when a body starts messin' with his liquor. He'll be like that for a while, but he'll get over it."

Floyd had watched his friend hobble over. "How's that leg feeling, Shorty?"

Shorty was gazing at Buck's wound. At Floyd's question,

Shorty's head snapped around toward him. "How you think it's feelin'? Let me stab one of these here Pawnee arrows through your leg, then you can explain to me how it's feelin'."

"Calm down," Floyd said. "I just noticed your limp is more pronounced. Why don't you drop your trousers and let me take a look? You might need a little more of Morg's elixir on it."

Shorty started to say something, thought better of it, and lowered his pants. The exit wound had already turned bright red around the bandage.

"Turn around."

Shorty, muttering, did as he was told.

Floyd pulled the edge of the bandage back and examined the entrance wound. It was looking fine, but he didn't like the redness on the front of the leg. He stood and removed his canteen from the saddle, started to kneel back down, and changed his mind. A large, rounded boulder, most of it buried in the reddish-yellow dirt, extended about two feet above the ground. He motioned Shorty toward the boulder. "Why don't you go sit on that rock so I can take a good look at this."

Shorty frowned. "Floyd, we need to load these animals and git. There's no telling who might come to investigate all this shootin'."

Floyd nodded. "You're right, but I want to take a look at your leg first. This exit wound on the front isn't looking too good."

Morg returned from his horse, carrying his last bottle. A wide grin spread across his face. "Well, Shorty, ain't you cute. I swear . . ." His voice faded when he saw the worried look on Floyd's face. "What's wrong?"

"Look at this," Floyd said. He had exposed the inflamed wound. He touched the edge of it.

Shorty winced. "It's a little tender. I ain't stupid, boys. I know that ain't good."

Floyd shook his head. "I should've put a piece of prickly pear pad on there. I was in too big a hurry to get our horses and gear back."

Morg jumped up. He handed Floyd the bottle. "I seen a patch a short way back. Won't take me long."

Floyd, kneeling, watched Morg take off, and looked up at Shorty. "I've got to clean this up again, Shorty. It's gonna be a lot worse than before."

Shorty nodded and looked over the ground. He pointed at a small stick. "Hand me that, pardner. I ain't hankerin' on breakin' any teeth."

Floyd picked up the stick and gave it to his friend. He watched Shorty position the stick in his mouth, bite down, and nod. Floyd poured a small amount of the liquor onto his hands to wash them off. He took a piece of bandage and soaked it with Morg's dwindling supply. After wrapping the bandage around his right index finger, he gave Shorty a curt nod and pushed the bandaged finger deep into the wound, turning and sawing it up and down.

Shorty's body stiffened, quivering with the pain. Floyd could hear his friend's teeth grinding into the stick, but he kept working. *I've got to get this cleaned out,* he thought. *I made a mistake the first time. Now's the time to correct it.*

Finally, he slid his finger from the wound. Blood gushed. Floyd caught it with the old bandage, preventing it from running down Shorty's leg into his boots and pants. "It's over, Shorty." He looked up at his friend. The man's face was as white as one of Ma's sheets after it had been scrubbed with lye soap.

The smaller man removed the stick from his mouth, deep tooth marks cut into it, and shot Floyd a stiff grin. In his gravelly voice, he said, "Shoot, I was hoping you'd do that for a while longer. It was right bracing."

Morg slid his horse to a stop. Spit on the point of his big knife was a prickly pear pad. Careful not to drop it, he jogged up to Floyd, staring first at Shorty's bloody leg and then his friend's pale face.

"Thanks, Morg," Floyd said. "How about laying it on the rock and getting a shirt for me, in my saddlebags."

While Morg went after the shirt, Floyd carefully scraped all the thorns and fine stickers from the pear pad, skinned one side, and cut it into two pieces.

Morg returned with the shirt, extending his long arm to hand it to Floyd, who shook his head.

"Tear as long a bandage as you can get from the shirt back."

Shorty looked at the shirt, his leg, and Floyd.

He started to speak, but Floyd beat him. "You can buy me another one when we get to a town. I never liked that one, anyway." After Morg had torn the bandage from the shirt, Floyd nodded at the wounds where he had placed the pads. "Alright, Morg, why don't you wrap that bandage so it'll hold these pads in place."

The tall mountain man bent. Slowly and deliberately, he wrapped the bandage around Shorty's leg, trapping the prickly pear pads in place. He tied it tight around the wounds and straightened.

Floyd admired their work, nodded in satisfaction, stood, and turned to Morg. "You two need to head back to Bent's Fort. They've got a doctor there."

9

Istaka fumed as he drove his lathered horse northward. He knew the danger of riding through the tall grass at such speed. He had seen others die or suffer injuries when their horse stepped into a gopher hole or pitched into a wash. Only this morning, Kuruk had shown the risk of chasing the trappers. Kuruk's horse had found a hole. Its front hoof had dropped into the gopher's lair, breaking the horse's leg, throwing and killing Kuruk when the warrior's head struck a boulder.

But there was no time to think of Kuruk. Istaka had to get back to the tribe. He would not stay with the fools as they drank the firewater of the white man. He would have nothing to do with the white man's ways. When they had ridden away from the attack with the horses, Istaka had tried to persuade them to turn around and finish the trappers. The short one was on the ground, injured. Another, the man he hated and longed to feel his knife sink deep into his chest, was bleeding from the neck. It had been his rifle shot, so close. Another attack would see the end of them. But no. His companions and the leader were satisfied with the horses and supplies they had stolen. They would ride to the mountains, camp, and check their booty.

He derided them, cursed them as women, but they would not listen. He considered going back on his own, but his logical mind convinced him it would be foolish.

After a long ride, they made it into the land of the big bluffs and piñon. It was there that they decided to stop and look through their treasures. It was there that they found the firewater. He knew there would be no persuading them then. He cursed them again, reminding them of their dead brothers crying for revenge, but they only drank and laughed at him. Patience gone, he swung onto his tired mount and headed north.

Hate burned deep in the heart of Istaka. Today he had seen the white man who killed his father so many summers ago. Racing across the plains, his mind drifted back to that day.

He had been only a boy brought along on his first raid with his father to take scalps. Samoset, just a year older, but much bigger, had also been there. Father had placed Samoset in charge and told Istaka to do what the older boy told him. It had been only one wagon, two women, one sick man, and a trapper. He was young. Only four summers older than Istaka.

Samoset and Istaka were to stay in the trees until the fighting was over, then come forward and feel the power of counting coup. His father had planned the ambush. Arrows first to disable the trapper and the woman, but what had seemed so simple suddenly turned into a massacre—theirs.

The young trapper saw them before the first arrow was released. He fired, killing the bowman. Istaka wanted to charge with his father, but Samoset held him back, telling him he must listen to his father's words.

The trapper and the woman were deadly with their rifles, killing three of the warriors before his father was upon the boy. The young trapper, using his pistol, blocked his father's tomahawk. He knocked it from his father's hand and hit him in the nose with a fist. Blood sprayed from the blow. Istaka was shocked.

He had never seen a man fight with his fists. He tried to jump up again.

Samoset's ironlike grip held his bicep. "Stay," he said. "Look at those rifles." He glanced momentarily at the woman. She had reloaded both rifles, and now the sick man stood in the tent's doorway, holding a pistol.

Istaka remained still in the tight grip of Samoset. It was his father's wish. He watched his father first draw his knife, then wipe the blood from his nose, smear it over his chest, and grin at the young trapper. Istaka nodded. His father would kill the boy.

His father leaped forward, made a slash, and drew blood, then used a feint he had taught Istaka. The boy fell for it. He was so young and stupid. The boy stepped in, showing the eagerness Istaka's father had warned him against, and chopped at his father's wrist, which was no longer there.

Of course, he missed, opening up his chest and throat. Istaka's heart leaped with joy, but the boy was surprisingly quick. Instead of finding the boy's throat, Istaka's father's knife slashed deep into and along the young jaw. For an instant, Istaka could see the white flash of bone, then blood gushed from the wound. Though it had not been the killing strike Istaka had hoped for, the bleeding would weaken the boy and slow his reaction. It would only be moments before his father was victorious.

He saw the boy's foot scrape against the log, saw him stumble. Istaka was elated. But his hope plummeted in despair when he saw it was a trick. That bleeding, feeble boy had fooled his noble father. His father overextended, his knifepoint stabbing for a chest it would never find. The boy stepped in and drove his long knife deep into his father's side. That moment, his father's death and the trapper's slashed face were printed indelibly into his mind.

Samoset held him and whispered, "If you want to live to avenge your father, stay quiet and slip to the horses with me."

The last thing Istaka saw was his father slumped across the log, and the woman rushing to the aid of the boy trapper.

A wash appeared ahead, jerking him back to the present. He turned the horse to parallel the shallow stream and slowed the animal to a walk. Istaka lifted his rifle, swung a leg over the horse's neck, and slid to the ground. The animal was breathing in short, raspy breaths. He would have a dead horse and be walking the remaining distance to the Pawnee camp if he didn't let the animal rest.

The horse pulled the reins, trying to turn toward the water, but Istaka jerked him back and continued walking along the stream. He would not let him drink until his breathing slowed. His mind slipped back to the attack on the white men only a short time back.

Finding the trail of the white trappers had been good luck. They had been elated. Theirs was a large hunting party after the buffalo, but the three trappers and their many horses were a huge bonus, and the trappers had at least one mule. Mule. He had tasted mule only once, but it was delicious. They had joked about thanking the white men before they took their scalps.

All such thoughts had disappeared when the big trapper rose from inside the buffalo wallow and Istaka saw his face. The face was older, more mature, but it was the same face with the scar on the left cheek running from cheekbone to chin. In haste, he had thrown his rifle to his shoulder and fired. The bullet only grazed the man. He saw his brothers going down, he began to reload, and their leader yelled, "Grab the horses and mule."

Moving swiftly, while the white men fought for their lives, he grabbed the reins of the animals, rode out of the wallow, and turned north toward their main camp. His leader yelled over the din of the battle. The man was pointing west, toward the mountains. Istaka had no idea why they were going in that direction. Istaka shook his head and pointed north. He heard pounding hoofbeats behind him. He looked back and saw they were all leaving, coming with him.

He pointed his rifle toward the battle. "We must kill the white men."

"No," the leader shouted. "There will be another time. Take the horses to the mountains."

Istaka allowed his horse to drink and wiped the lather from its body with handfuls of grass. Before the animal had its fill, he pulled it away from the water and continued walking. He did this three times, allowing the horse to pull at the grass between drinks. Satisfied the animal was in good enough shape to continue, he swung back into the saddle and pointed the horse north.

Another two hours of riding and he would be there. It had been a hard day, but the day wasn't over. Once there, he would get a fresh horse and lead a large group of men. They would head back tonight and catch the now-grown trapper. Istaka would have the pleasure of skinning the trapper, strip of skin by strip of skin, until nothing remained except exposed flesh. Then he would turn him over to the women. They would know how to make him scream long into the night and the next day. The trapper's price for killing Istaka's father would be high.

He rode on.

. . .

Floyd's forehead was wrinkled with worry lines as he watched Morg and Shorty ride southwest out of camp. Neither of the two was happy with having to abandon him, but Floyd knew Shorty was especially angry at himself. His friend took the blame for getting shot with the arrow and for it turning sour. He had argued furiously against, first, his going back, and second, the necessity of Morg accompanying him. But Floyd knew if Shorty's wound grew worse, he would die without help. He only hoped the two of them would make it back to Bent's Fort in time.

He had switched the saddle to Rusty, allowing Buck to trail along. Hopefully, the horse's wound would heal quickly. Browny was again loaded and stood waiting for Floyd to lead them onward. He checked Browny's packs one last time to ensure everything was secure and the load was evenly distributed. He scratched the mule between the ears. The long-eared animal's lips blew contentedly. A few pats for Buck, and Floyd swung into Rusty's saddle.

He took one last look at the disappearing mountain men and turned west toward the distant tall pines of the mountains. There was way too much activity on the plains. The last thing he wanted was to run into the Pawnees again, or the Sioux, or heaven forbid, the Blackfoot. He bumped Rusty in the flanks, and the two horses, rider, and one mule moved toward the darkening mountains.

Floyd pushed for two more hours toward the mountains. Finally, he spotted the vermillion cliffs he had been aiming for. Shortly after seeing the red rocks, he could make out the tall cottonwoods that announced the presence of Mount Vernon Creek, which flowed a short distance below the red cliffs.

The farther Floyd rode into the vast Rocky Mountains, the better he felt. This was the wrong time of year to be riding through buffalo country, and he was glad to be climbing out of it. Plains tribes and mountain tribes would travel great distances to hunt the massive buffalo that covered the plains. He needed to travel fast to find the Akers bunch, but it wouldn't help anyone if his hair ended up on some Indian's lance. Floyd and his friends had traveled a great distance on the plains, making good time, and had been fortunate until running into the Pawnees. Now he would have to go it alone. Floyd chuckled and whispered to Buck, "That's what I came west for, wasn't it, Buck? To be in the mountains alone."

He continued riding toward the huge red upthrust that made up the cliffs. They rose high above the fifty- or sixty-foot-tall cottonwood trees that lined the creek. The cliffs, boulders, and wooded creek would provide plenty of cover for Floyd, but tonight, he would still forgo a fire. He'd miss a cup of coffee, hot beans, and the warmth, but he'd slept well many a night after a supper of water and jerky. He'd have both tonight with a bonus. At Bent's Fort, he'd picked up a sack of lemon-drop hard candy. After the jerky, he'd suck on one of those until he went to sleep.

Floyd's face grew somber while thoughts of his friends making their way back to the fort drifted through his mind. *I hope Shorty's alright. That arrow left a nasty wound.* Reaching the edge of the timber that followed along the creek, he paralleled the thick brush bordering the big cottonwoods. If he remembered correctly, not far ahead, there should be a small park along the water, shielded by the brush. After a few minutes, his search was successful. Barely visible behind the shorter wild plum and maple trees, he could just make out an area large enough for him and his animals.

He pushed through the thick edge into what amounted to a natural corral with an abundance of bluebunch wheatgrass. The grass was nutritious, and with the thick brush on the border of the creek, he wouldn't have to worry about his stock wandering away, though he would still stake them on a long rope. Floyd always staked his animals in the mountains. He didn't want hobbles on them if they had to fight off a mountain lion, wolves, or even a bear. Nearby, the icy water of the clear creek gurgled as it jumped and twisted over rocks and roots. Snow-fed, the little stream originated high in the mountains, near their tops.

Floyd dismounted and soon had the tack stripped from Buck and Browny. He tossed long lead ropes over the three animals and led them to the creek to drink. With the day ending, the air was cooling, and the wind currents were flowing down the mountains, making the cottonwoods' silver leaves dance and the limbs moan. The mountain man listened to the sound he knew so well. Unconsciously, a smile spread across the big man's scarred face. He had always loved the sound of the wind in the trees. It was his own mountain symphony.

When the horses finished drinking, he rubbed each one down with dried grass, gave each a bit of corn he had picked up at the fort, and staked them for the night. The sun had disappeared behind the mountains, rapidly chilling the air and draping darkness across mountains and plains alike. Floyd arranged his bedding with his saddle as a backrest, laying his weapons where they would be readily at hand. Dropping onto his ground cloth, he pulled several strips of jerky from his saddlebags and let his mind wander to Leotie and Mika.

I wonder where they are now, he thought. *Are they near?* He shook his head. *No, they may not have even left yet, but knowing Pallaton, he would have them moving. He knows the importance of their getting to the Shoshone River before hard winter sets in.* He pictured Leotie, his wife of almost ten years. *Has it been that long? Time has gone by so quickly, but she is even more beautiful than the first time I saw her, and Mika. Little Mika is growing into a man. Fortunately, he is not the hot-tempered kid I was.*

His mind slipped back to Leotie. It was so clear he could almost smell the tanned hide of the teepee and the faint odor of smoke drifting through the air as it made its way to the smoke hole in the top of the teepee. His fingers could feel the softness of Leotie's bare shoulder and the warmth of her against him. She had turned a good life into a life of wonder, happiness, and love.

His face grew grim as he thought of the Akers bunch. *I'm from that part of the country. I know how tight those mountain people hold onto their grudges. I should have waited and put an end to their thirst for killing.* He shook his thick mane of hair in aggravation at himself. *The past is. It can't be changed. Now is what counts. I must find the Akers and Henry Page and ensure they will never threaten my family again.*

Floyd's eyelids grew heavy. He stretched out, pulling the blanket up around his neck, and relaxed as a picture of Leotie smiling up at him calmed his mind. Moments later, he greeted the night with a soft snore.

ISTAKA RECEIVED an icy glare from the Pawnee chief after raising his voice in argument for returning and killing the white men. The chief, Long Hunter, had put him off, in anticipation of the return of the rest of the hunting party with the horses and supplies. Time passed, and the men did not arrive. There was concern among the wives and children, and as the shadows lengthened, it became apparent the Pawnee braves would not be returning. Wives broke out in wails, and children began to cry.

Earlier, Istaka's wife, Little Dove, tried to calm his anguish over the escape of the white man. "The chief knows best, Istaka. Our people need the buffalo. If we don't get enough, the starving time will bring death, and already many of the hunters have not returned. We can't lose more. What will happen to our tribe?"

Istaka knew she spoke truth, but his thirst for revenge ravaged his reason. "I must go."

Istaka had left his teepee, gone back to the chief, and was rebuffed again. He couldn't stand it. He felt as if he would burst if he didn't get on a horse and pursue the white man. "Listen to me, Long Hunter. This man has killed my father. The others have not arrived, so he has killed them. He keeps killing. I have learned the Comanche dogs have given him the name Pawnee Killer." Istaka was normally a calm, reserved man, but when it came to Floyd, his passion for killing overrode everything. "All the tribes laugh at us when they use that name. Pawnee Killer. He cannot be allowed to live. He cannot even be given a noble death. The mountain man must be skinned and dragged through the dirt, his screams erasing his courage. We must mount up and search for him. He is near right now. We can find him and bring him back. We must!"

His last statement had been emphasized by drawing his knife and thrusting it toward the sky. Several young men, having returned from a successful hunt, stood around, listening. They also drew their knives and, like Istaka, thrust them skyward, yelling and jumping.

The chief shook his head. "We cannot follow one person's need to kill, no matter how justified it is. Look around you, Istaka. See the faces of the women and children? Do you wish to kill them, too?" He spoke not only to Istaka but also to the other men eager to ride the warpath. "As sure as you mount your horses and ride after Pawnee Killer, you will kill these wives and children. Do you not care for them?"

Istaka followed Chief Long Hunter's instructions and looked around the camp. He saw the women and children watching the argument, but he really didn't see them. All he saw was Floyd making the final thrust of his knife into his father, and he wanted to kill the white man. "We can go after him and be back in four days with our prize. We will lose only four days. Give me three men, and the rest can stay and hunt."

The chief, incredulous at the remark, stared at Istaka. "Only three men for four days? How many men have we already lost? Even now we may not take enough buffalo to satisfy our winter's needs, and you would take away more? Wait until the hunt is over, and then you may freely go."

Istaka had to restrain himself. In a cold but calm voice, he said, "But he is close now. At the end of the hunt, we will have no idea where he may be. It will be a search of futility. We must leave now."

Chief Long Hunter raised his left hand to the darkening sky. "You would leave now, even as the sun has gone to rest? How could you travel or track anything? To leave now would be the act of a crazed man."

Istaka gave a curt nod and then another. "Yes, yes. You are right. We could not leave now." As he spoke, he thought, *But we could have if you had not put off your decision until darkness.* He took advantage of the chief's comment. "Are you saying that if we wait until morning, we can leave then?"

The chief had drawn himself to his full height. "You are making a decision that will, I promise you, condemn your and many other families to death. But I see you are set on the killing of this Pawnee Killer. Therefore, I will not keep you from doing something that stirs your blood so strongly. Sleep on this decision, and if you are still determined to condemn your people and satisfy your thirst for blood, I will not stop you. I can only hope you will come to your senses before morning."

Istaka gave a curt nod and turned away from the chief. Almost immediately, he was surrounded by young men eager to join him.

10

F loyd opened his eyes to see the stars twinkling beyond the tops of the cottonwoods. He glanced at his animals and was gratified to see the horses asleep and Browny munching on the wheatgrass. He lay still, listening to the sounds of early morning. The prominent sound—the gurgling creek— joined an insomniac dove cooing high in a cottonwood, and the light wind rustling the tall tree's leaves. Floyd smelled the fresh scent of the grass and the creek, mixed in with the sharp but faint smell of the pines only a short distance up the mountains. He wiggled his toes and threw his blanket off, immediately feeling the chill of the morning, which brought the desire for coffee, but there was no way he'd trade the taste of coffee for the loss of his hair.

At Floyd's movement, Browny turned his head and laid a steady gaze on him. Buck and Rusty, their sleep interrupted, lifted their heads, glanced at him, and began pulling large mouthfuls of grass. Floyd traded the soft feel of his moccasins for his stiffer boots and stood. It felt good to be alive. Shoving the moccasins into his saddlebags, he tied the flaps and rolled his bedding.

Once finished, he scanned the prairie, still dark, but with a tiny strip of light running along the horizon. Dawn was on the way.

He wanted to be well behind the massive upthrust of red rocks before the rising sun lit the slope. He quickly watered the horses and Browny and then allowed them to crop wheatgrass while he fastened the packsaddle on Browny and saddled Buck. Floyd hurried to beat the light. Swinging into the saddle while there was barely enough light for him to work his way through the boulder field, he guided Buck to the edge of the brush and scanned for friend or enemy. Nothing was in sight. He bumped Buck and, with Rusty and Browny on short leads, began their climb past the red boulders and up into the tall mountains and thick pines.

Floyd held to the southern slope of the short east-west ridge lines that coursed down to the vermillion rocks. It kept him and his horses in shadow as dawn filled the morning. The longer he could remain hidden before reaching the tall pines, where he could disappear, the better he would like it. He thought, *I know there are more Pawnees than just the ones who attacked us. If they decide to send a war party after me, I at least want them to have to work to find me.* He ultimately arrived at a high north-south ridge-line he could not get around or remain in shadow to cross, but cross it he must. He was at a notch that provided a crossing, but it was open, only low mahogany brush providing concealment. Fortunately, it was a narrow notch, and their exposure would be short.

Still in the shadow, Floyd paused the animals and pulled his brass Thos. Harris & Son telescope from his saddlebags. After removing the lens covers, he extended the optics, checked to make sure the sun wouldn't reflect off the lens, and lifted the precision instrument to his eye. Surveying his back trail, he could make out a faint dust plume on the edge of the plains. It appeared stationary, which meant the dust plume, and therefore the riders were moving in his direction. He watched for a minute or two longer, but they were too far away for him to make out the individuals. Floyd closed the telescope, replaced the lens covers, and returned it to his saddlebags. *It was too much to hope for,* he thought. *I guess they have more men than they know what to do with, or someone really wants my hair.*

He bumped Buck. "Come on, boy. Let's get this done. I've got an idea that, if they're aching to take my hair, just might work." He had a choice. He could slowly walk the horses across the exposed portion of the ridge or race them across. Either way, they would be moving, and Floyd knew movement drew the human eye. It was possible to disappear in the open as long as a person was still. The Apache had perfected the maneuver. Floyd's question was, would speed make any difference, and he felt sure it would, so he ambled the horses and mule across the open ground. He was only exposed for two minutes at the most, but he knew if eyes were searching for him, his exposure would be time enough.

Once through the saddle, Floyd picked up speed for a while, then slowed again to a walk. The slope had steepened, and he couldn't take the chance of wearing out his animals, for today, like many days to come, was going to be hard on all concerned. He had to stay away from the Indians. Pawnees were the threat for now, but he was moving into country sometimes roamed by the Blackfoot, and they had cautioned him about returning to their land. He understood the gravity of the warning, but he had to stop the Akers gang before they reached Leotie, Mika, and his people, the Shoshone. The tribe could be moving north, even as he climbed, and he had to protect them. He just hoped he remained clear of the Blackfoot.

Floyd climbed toward the majestic peaks. Once past those, he'd drop into a valley and then have others to cross, but this was a special valley, and it just might work to help slow his pursuers. He'd hunted and trapped in this country and knew it well. He was moving toward where Leotie had nursed him back to good health after the bear attack, and he pictured Mika as a little boy.

He had been traveling for a couple of hours now and was deep in the tall pine and aspen forests. His eyes searched every thick-trunked ponderosa pine. Some were so big, several men could hide behind them. Shiny blue spruce occupied the outer edges of the stand of ponderosa, combined with juniper. He eased to the edge of the trees to check his back trail.

Floyd had left a false trail before doubling back and climbing this long plateau. The edge, where he was now, dropped off into a near-vertical wall for three hundred feet. If the Indians fell for his feint, they would ride into a box canyon. Their only chance to catch him would mean doubling back, and with the time they'd lose, he'd be long gone. He really didn't expect them to fall for the false trail unless they were in a hurry or really thirsty for his blood, and after losing so many Pawnee braves yesterday, he expected them to be as mad as a swarm of hornets. It was time to take a look.

He stopped at the trees' edge. Between the trees and the cliff lay about forty yards of massive round boulders and huge jagged rocks. Once sure he was alone on the plateau, he walked the horses into the boulder field, picking his way carefully through the rocks.

Still thirty feet from the edge, Floyd removed his telescope from his saddlebags and hung it around his neck with its leather strap. Dismounting, he pulled his Ryland rifle from its scabbard, ground-hitched his animals, and walked carefully toward the vertical edge. Having already picked out a pair of boulders to hide behind, Floyd eased up to them, laid his rifle carefully on the rocks, removed his hat, and slipped the side of his head into the crack formed by the two boulders. Moving just far enough to clear his eye, he had a limited view of the valley, but it was enough. Surprised, he saw the Indians below him in the box canyon. Floyd brought the spyglass up, extended it, and shook his head. Their horses looked as if they would drop at any moment. They were covered in lather and gasping for breath.

He recognized one man, young but older than the other three. He had been at the ambush where Shorty had taken the arrow in the leg. This was the Indian who had shot him. An inch to the left, and he'd have bled out in the buffalo wallow. Floyd examined him closer. The man's face nagged at him. It was a familiar face, but one Floyd was sure he had never seen before, other than yesterday's attack.

He continued to watch as they rode through his field of vision. Four men. When they rode out of his vision, he leaned back against the rock and mulled over his questions. *Where have I seen that Pawnee before, and why is he so determined to catch me?* He chewed on the thought, but couldn't come up with an answer. Whatever the reason the Pawnee brave might have, Floyd need no longer worry about them. They were riding plains horses, not mountain horses. Without time to grow used to the high mountain air, a man could kill his horse in one hard run, and, unfortunately, those horses would be dead in another hour if they didn't get rest and water.

Floyd considered throwing a shot at them as a warning, but the last thing he wanted to do was advertise his position. There was no telling who else might be near enough to hear his shot echo through the mountains. He moved to the other side of the boulder, raised the spyglass, and continued watching the braves.

It looked like two of his companions were arguing with the leader. Watching the hand motions, Floyd could tell they were arguing about the horses. The leader finally said something, pulled his horse to a stop, and stepped to the ground. Floyd could tell the man was angry, but the Pawnee pulled a handful of grass and began wiping down his gasping horse. The two who had been arguing followed suit.

He considered stepping out and letting them see him, so they would know he'd had them under his sights and could have killed them. However, as young as they were, they might start firing at him, which would be just as loud as if he opened up on them. His best bet was to slip away and leave them be. They were far up the box canyon. Their horses were exhausted, and those fellas would be lucky if they made it back to their camp.

He returned to his animals, grabbed their reins, and hastened toward the concealment of the trees. Stepping past the line of spruce and juniper and into the tall ponderosa forest, he gave a silent sigh of relief. Not far ahead was a spring he had never known to run dry. His animals needed water, and so did he, but he'd wait, along with them, until reaching the spring. Floyd's goal at the moment was to get as far away from this spot as he could. He mounted and continued walking his animals toward the next line of towering peaks.

ISTAKA WANTED TO KILL SOMEONE, preferably the mountain man, Pawnee Killer, but right now, either of his three companions who had forced him to stop would do. While he wiped down his horse, he considered their common-sense suggestions and, at last, admitted to himself they were right. His horse looked as if it might die at any moment. *Why didn't I notice?* he thought. *Without horses, we are dead. I am dead, and then who will avenge my father?*

Slowly, the horses began to breathe easier, but they needed water. The closest water was behind them, and he detested the idea of turning around. He poured a little water into his hand from his water bag and held it for his horse. The exhausted animal drank it dry and licked Istaka's hand. Two of his companions, who had dismounted, followed his example.

Even as he was thinking about returning to the water, Chayton spoke up. "We should go back to the water now. Our horses will die if we do not." He cast an accusing stare at Istaka. "You pushed them too far. They are plains horses. Remember what we were told about how the mountain gods can kill our horses."

Istaka could feel his temper rising again. Chayton was small only in stature. The man had no fear and would fight or speak his piece any time he felt it necessary. Istaka took a deep breath, glared at the remaining mounted rider, and ordered, "Everyone dismount."

Ojai gave him an insolent look. "I do not walk."

Chayton responded, "You will walk now or later when your horse is dead. It is your choice. If it is later, we will leave you."

Istaka nodded. "Chayton speaks the truth. We pushed them too hard. Now we must walk them to the water and allow them to rest."

Keme, the quiet one, gave a single nod. "Istaka speaks the truth. If we do not allow them to walk slowly to the water, we will be in these mountains without horses. We have seen the Cheyenne, Shoshone, Comanche, and Utes. The only reason we were not attacked was that we were on the plains, hunting the buffalo. We are no longer on the plains. We will need our horses if we should run into any other tribes."

Ojai swung down. "You are all women." He jerked his horse around and stepped out ahead of his companions. They shared a glance and followed.

Returning along the canyon floor, they led their horses at a easy walk. The animals' gasping had stopped, and their breathing had almost returned to normal. It had been an hour, and Istaka tried to put the widening gap between Pawnee Killer and them from his mind. The past hour had given him time to think, leading to the realization that their only chance of survival was to return to the tribal encampment after the horses were allowed water. Though the animals had stopped breathing hard, their heads hung low. *We will be lucky,* he thought, *if we haven't permanently injured these horses, and horses are valuable. The trip back to our camp must be slow, or these animals will never recover.*

Ahead, he could see the tops of the cottonwoods sticking above a distant ridge. They plodded forward until reaching the ridge, cautiously approached the top, and scanned the creek. Seeing it was clear of intruders, they led the horses down the slope and to the much-needed water. Reaching the creek, and well hidden under the trees, Istaka spoke softly. "They have rested long enough to allow them to drink, but not too much. We don't want one to die on us now."

Ojai snorted. "You think we do not know? We are not children. We are skilled warriors. Do not insult us with your directions."

Istaka seethed. He had brought Ojai only because he was the chief's son. The man was arrogant and difficult to control. Since the warrior was aware of what needed to be done, Istaka elected to say nothing in response. With water, the animals were looking better, now alternately drinking and pulling at the grass next to the creek.

Suddenly the sound of rolling stones and horses' hooves reached them from down the creek. Water splashed as the horses crossed from their side of the creek to the opposite bank. The four men acted in unison, one hand tightening the reins and the other going to their mount's nose, hoping to prevent them from whinnying. Their horses remained silent, and Istaka signaled not to mount yet, but to be ready to leap on and ride like the wind if they were spotted. He thought, *Tired as these horses are, we will be easy prey for whoever is downstream.*

The riders didn't stay downstream long. They rode single file just outside the treeline. Through a tiny space in the brush, he glimpsed the intruders as they passed, heading southwest into the mountains. *Utes,* he thought. *If they see us, we are dead men.* He counted ten. The last two men were riding side by side and talking. He heard one give a short laugh, and they rode out of sight. Soon all sounds of them were gone.

Ojai glared at Istaka and jabbed a finger at the departing

Utes. The finger then pointed at his horse. Istaka shook his head and mouthed the silent word, No! The brave sneered and turned to his horse. Istaka could not stop the Indian. Chayton was between him and Ojai. Istaka saw that Keme, almost as big as himself, was watching, and he motioned for him to stop Ojai if he tried to mount, which the brave did, almost at the same moment.

Keme, a large man, stepped forward and grabbed Ojai's arm, pulling him from his horse. Off balance, Ojai fell back and would have fallen to the ground if Keme hadn't hung onto his arm until he regained his footing. When both men were steady, Keme released his arm, and Ojai's right hand flashed to his knife.

Istaka had moved quietly around Chayton and his horse. Drawing his own knife as he hurried, he shoved the point against Ojai's neck, sinking the tip far enough to draw a steady stream of blood. "I will kill you like a dog, Ojai, if you continue drawing your knife."

Ojai's hand had frozen on the hilt of his blade, jerking his fingers wide but showing no pain. "I will not kill Keme, but upon our return, I will kill you."

Istaka waited, allowing Ojai to contemplate the noise and possible result of trying to attack Keme. When he deemed Ojai cooler, he removed the knife tip from the arrogant brave's neck. "Be quiet, pick up your knife, and lead your horse from here. This time we must slip away. The Utes are too many."

Ojai turned to glare at Istaka, one side of his mouth drawn up in a sneer. He kept his voice low, though the words dripped with anger. "Too many for you, Istaka? You are a coward."

Istaka turned his back on his adversary, moved to his horse, and, making sure he remained in the grass and away from any rocks, which could roll or click against the animal's hooves, led the way down the creek and toward the plains.

Well clear of the Utes, they mounted and slowly walked their horses toward camp. It would be late into the night before their arrival, and they would be met with shaking heads and ridicule from the chief. Istaka played their return over in his mind.

In their anxious pursuit of this demon mountain man, they had taken a decoy trail into the box canyon, which was made clear after they turned back. *Why didn't I see where he back-tracked?* Istaka thought, berating himself. On their return, they had seen where the mountain man had backtracked and turned up a steep but navigable trail that disappeared along the canyon wall. They didn't have the time, nor did their horses have the strength to follow it, but he knew the steep trail would have led to the top of the canyon. Istaka shook his head in disgust.

We were tricked by the mountain man, just as he tricked my father so many years ago. A six-year-old boy would have seen it was a false trail, but not me. I could see nothing but his skin separating under my knife blade. I was blind. On top of my stupidity, we are returning without Pawnee Killer, and, because of him, our horses may be ruined forever, good only for a mediocre meal at best. Worst of all, I will have to fight Ojai to the death. The old chief was right. This chase has been cursed from the start.

They rode steadily but slowly toward the camp, but suddenly the evil buzz of rattlesnakes filled the quiet of the evening. Ojai's horse jumped sideways. The men were tired, and aside from Istaka, who was wide awake and berating himself, the others were nodding in their saddles.

When Ojai's horse leaped sideways, it caught the half-asleep Pawnee brave completely by surprise, and before he could lock himself on the animal's back with his strong thighs, he was unseated and airborne. The curse had not ended.

Ojai landed on his back on a small rocky shelf at the edge of the dry ravine they had been following. During the day, they might have seen the multitude of diamondback rattlesnakes sunning on the ledge, but in the dusk, they blended with the rocks and sparse grass. The reptiles had been in the process of slipping below the surface into their subterranean labyrinth for the night, but had stopped at the approach of the horses.

Ojai was a powerful brave, and in any other situation, his speedy reaction might have saved him, but landing on his back on the solid rock shelf knocked the wind from the athletic brave, and he was an instant too slow.

The strike of the first rattler hit the brave in the palm of his right hand, sinking its fangs deep into the fleshy part below his thumb. Before he could react to the single bite, fangs pierced every part of his unprotected body from large and small rattlers.

With the strike of the first, he had begun to rise, but was driven back by snake after snake slamming into him. His head jerked from side to side, fangs embedded in his cheeks and throat. Snakes whipped with the snap of his head, tails rattling, jaws clamped.

Istaka and his two other companions sat their mounts, watching in horror. It happened so quickly there was nothing anyone could do. One moment, Ojai was among them. The next instant, his horse jumped, and he was dead, covered in writhing, buzzing killers.

Once Ojai stopped moving, the snakes gradually released the Pawnee brave and slithered into crevasses and unseen holes to slide down into the protection of their den. Within moments, the snakes were gone, and Ojai lay, a grotesque caricature of himself, hands pulled into claws, eyes wide and empty, lips drawn back in a silent scream.

It was the smallest of the remaining three braves, Chayton, who spoke. His voice was soft and almost reverent. "What do we do, Istaka?"

Istaka shook his head. "There is nothing we can do. Ojai lies in a den of vipers. Darkness is upon us. His body is covered with the poison of the snakes. If we go near the den, we could join him. If we touch his body, the poison may find its way into our bodies. There is nothing we can do. Ojai has met a horrible death

I would not even wish on Pawnee Killer, but there is nothing we can do now. He has fallen like a warrior. Fighting to his very last breath. He will lie here as a warning to others. The snake gods have been appeased, and I, for one, will not offer myself to them. We will continue."

Keme spoke softly into the night. "Our chief will not be happy."

Istaka shook his head. "No, he will not." He turned his horse away from the den and made a wide circle. Though Ojai's horse had jumped, it stood only a few feet from the braves. Istaka guided his horse close, leaned from his saddle, and grasped the reins. "Come, we will continue to camp."

The three men slowly turned their horses to the east. Moving at a walk into the darkness, Istaka thought, *At least there is one bright spot in this cursed trip. I will not have to fight Ojai.*

11

F loyd Logan traveled a long trail of high mountains and deep valleys. At last, he rode across the Elk River to the campsite where he had first met Leotie so many years before. Floyd hoped whoever was leading Roscoe Akers and his group might have camped there.

He was right, for he found tracks of several riders with shod horses, relatively fresh signs of fire, plus the detritus from their camp. They had taken neither the time to bury their refuse, nor to dig holes or slit trenches. The place was a mess. He tried to follow their tracks, but soon it became impossible. The mountain showers had washed out their trail. He would find Akers, but first, he must locate the Shoshones Pallaton was leading his tribe to join.

Floyd guided his animals down the Elk River until reaching the Yampa. From there, he turned west. After several days, he turned northwest and crossed the Little Snake. It was his goal to cut the Green north of the massive gorge that had saved his life so many years before.

After many more days of travel, he was riding beneath tall lodgepole pines. Scattered Engelmann spruces added their perfect shape and dark green beauty to the high country. The pines thrust a hundred feet into the clear morning sky, and the faint whisper of Rusty's, Buck's, and Browny's hooves through the thick bed of pine needles was muffled by the rustling of limbs in the steady wind.

Finally, his journey finished, he halted his animals inside the treeline and examined row upon row of Shoshone teepees set in the tall grass bordering the Green River Lakes. Trout constantly rose to the surface, inhaling the latest hatch, while young children fished with hand-lines. Smoke emerged from the tops of the teepees, to be torn away, disappearing in the wind's grasp. After many days of travel, he felt relief and happiness at having successfully completed this portion of his long journey, but disappointed he hadn't found the Akers bunch. He patted Rusty's neck. "We'll find them yet, boy, and when we do, we'll remove their threat from this land, once and for all."

He took in the picturesque view of the scattered teepees, conscious he was seeing a picture that could be gone in only a few short years. He thought, *This is what I dreamed of. I wish Ma were here to see it.*

Framed by pristine blue-green water and tall pines scattered among Shoshone teepees, Squaretop Mountain jutted forth to the sky. The monolith appeared close enough for Floyd to reach out and touch. He removed the telescope to examine the village more closely. Floyd searched the peaceful scene for danger while his mind drifted back to a time when he had been farther north, across the Missouri, almost to Canada. He smiled to himself. *A hard throw of my tomahawk would have landed it in Canada.*

Ten years ago, Leotie and Mika had been grabbed by Blackfoot braves who were stealing horses from the Shoshones. The same Shoshones who had saved his life after his encounter with the grizzly. The kidnapping had been bad luck for all.

Mika was little and had awakened needing to relieve himself. Leotie, Mika's little hand in hers, took him away from the teepees toward where the horses were pastured. It was during their excursion that the Blackfoot attacked the horse guards, killing them and, along with the horses, taking the mother and son.

When Chief Pallaton found out, he immediately led a grueling foot chase over the mountains, which, though barely recovered from the grizzly mauling, Floyd joined, resulting in the death of the Blackfoot braves and the rescue of the desperately needed horses. However, the Blackfoot had divided their force, and the two Shoshone captives had been sent with the other band.

Floyd led the chase to recover Leotie and Mika, joined by a much younger Kajika, Morg, and Shorty. Their chase took them to the rendezvous, where they found Leotie had been sold to trappers. The Blackfoot had kept Mika to adopt into their tribe and raise him as their own. After rescuing Leotie, a long chase followed in their search for Mika.

Floyd continued examining the mountain slopes surrounding the village. Satisfied at last, he stowed the glass and urged Rusty forward. Leading Buck and Browny, he stepped from the treeline, breaking into the tall grass-covered valley. Within moments, all eyes were on him, and three mounted Shoshone braves raced from the village toward him.

"Rusty, I'm sure glad that's a Shoshone village instead of Blackfoot, otherwise we'd be in a heap of trouble right now." He looked at his mule, Browny. "Especially you. You'd be on the menu quicker than you can blink."

The distance quickly closed sufficiently for Floyd to recognize two of the braves. They were big men, all at least six feet tall, with wide shoulders, war clubs grasped in scarred hands. The brave Floyd knew to be the leader, Tocho, stood, switched his war club to his left hand, raised his right, palm forward, and gave a piercing call, "Igasho!"

Floyd duplicated the man's actions, standing in his stirrups, raising his empty right arm high, palm forward, and called, "Tocho!"

Reaching him, the three men pulled their horses to a stop, and Tocho thrust his arm forward. Floyd clasped his forearm. The brave was several years older than Floyd and exhibited an assortment of visible scars. His face carried a wide smile, and he began speaking rapidly in Shoshone. "Igasho, it is good to see you." His dark eyes roved over first Floyd and then his animals. "But it looks as if your travels have been long and hard."

"Yes, but I bring you good news." He turned to the man on the opposite side of Rusty and grasped his shoulder in a tight grip. Still speaking Shoshone, he said, "Atohi, it brings a smile to my face to see you are doing well. His eyes turned to the young brave riding behind and to the left of Tocho. And who is this strapping warrior?"

The young man's chest swelled. Tocho spoke, his pride obvious. "He is my son. You remember Mato?"

Floyd feigned astonishment. "No, this cannot be Mato. It is not possible. He was so little when last I saw him. Look at those shoulders. I would hate to meet him in battle. He would make my heart quake."

The two older men laughed while the boy beamed. His father slapped the young man on his thick arm. "There are times he makes his mother's heart quake in fear." Tocho laughed, turning his horse. "Come, Igasho, there are many in the village who will be glad to see you, and will be eager to hear your story."

HENRY PAGE, tired from their long but rapid trip to the Shoshone village, glanced to his left at his companion, Cooter Akers. The violent young man's eyes were locked on the camp they were approaching. *I should have killed him when I had the chance,* Page thought, *and I had so many opportunities.* He looked away and shook his head, then glanced quickly at Cooter, concerned he might have observed the headshake, but Cooter's attention was fixed on the camp. With the headshake, Page was thinking, *But if I had killed him, the old man would have blamed me and followed me just like he's doing Logan. How did I get myself into such a mess? Even worse, if Logan finds out what I did to his wife, he'll string me up or turn me over to the Shoshones.* The thought made him shudder.

Cooter's harsh voice yanked him from his thoughts. "What you lookin' so sour about? We're gonna be drinkin' Mary Grace's coffee mighty soon. That's worth smiling about."

Page looked back at the killer to see beady eyes fixed on him. "Cooter, I'm just sorry we didn't find Floyd Logan at the Indian camp." His words were the opposite to the relief he had felt to learn Logan wasn't there and hadn't been there.

Cooter barked out a harsh laugh. "Yeah, I just bet you are. Pa's gonna be some kind of mad. Shoot, Page, he might even cut you." With the last statement, he laughed again.

They had drawn close enough for the laughter to draw the attention of those in camp, and Page watched Mary Grace and Roscoe Akers walk around behind the lean-to. Akers had a cup of coffee in his hand. He turned to his daughter, pointed at Page and Cooter, and said something to Mary Grace. She turned and stomped out of sight. Akers remained in place, joined by three strangers, two of them with rifles resting in the crooks of their arms. The group watched them close the distance to the camp.

When the men stepped into view, Cooter let out a whoop, ripped his hat from his head, and waved it high. Grinning, he turned to Page. "Them fellers standing with Pa are all three cousins. They got a different last name, but it don't matter. Pa's sister, my aunt, raised 'em like true Akers. All three of them are danged near as mean as Pa. Why, I've got in fights with every one of them boys, and though I ain't been beat, there for a bit, I thought I was gonna have to cut every single one of 'em. They's fighters from who flung the chunk. That Floyd Logan won't stand a chance now." He kicked his horse and galloped toward the waiting men.

To maintain an appearance of eagerness, Page bumped his animal in the flanks and pushed him up to a gallop, just a few feet behind Cooter. Reaching the men, Cooter yanked his horse to a stop and leaped from his saddle. He charged the closest man and wrapped him in a bear hug. It was returned with equal gusto. The reunion was repeated with each of the newcomers.

Swinging down, Page waited to be introduced, but no introductions were forthcoming, so he stepped forward and extended his hand to the first woolly-looking newcomer. "Hi, my name's Henry Page."

The man grinned, took Page's hand, and tightened down on it, but when Page met him with superior strength, the man's grin disappeared. He released the hand. "Jethro."

Cooter had stepped back, and pointed to the taller man in the middle. "That's Gomer, and the tall one is Elmer."

Gent walked around the lean-to, wearing a big smile. "Well, Mr. Page, it looks like you survived your trip with Cooter. You find out anything about that Floyd Logan? I'm ready to haul my freight back to civilization. This place is starting to get downright cold at night."

Pa Akers spoke up. "Gent, quit complainin' and make yoreself useful. Take care of their horses."

Gent's smile disappeared. "But Pa, I want to hear about what's going on with Logan."

The old man's eyes narrowed. "Boy, I said take care of those horses. They'll be close enough that you can hear just about everything what's going on." Akers turned for the campfire. "Come on, boys, let's hear what's been happening with Floyd Logan."

The men trooped around the lean-to and settled on logs that had been dragged near the fire, and Pa Akers locked cold eyes on Page. "Where's Logan?"

Page cleared his throat. This was the moment he had hoped would never come. He had no idea how the old man would react, but he knew it wouldn't be good. "Well, Mr. Akers, to sum it up, we think he is near Bent's Fort."

The old man's face darkened, and if the opportunity had existed, Henry Page would have risen and rapidly left to anywhere other than here. But his only chance was to convince Akers he was valuable to them, or he'd feel the steel of Cooter's blade. He had no doubt about his value. "Mr. Akers, we found out that several months back, a tribal medicine man left the northern village to contact the Shoshone tribe Logan is living with. His message to the chief was to return here with the tribe."

Akers's face lost its scowl. "Have they heard anything from him?"

Page shook his head. "No, they've heard nothing since the man left in the spring, but if he made it, they should be getting ready to move or already on their way."

The old man spat and pulled out his knife. He started trimming his long fingernails. His voice was almost a growl. "And he could be dead and scalped somewhere. We're heading to Bent's Fort. You know how to get there?"

Page had never been south of the rendezvous. He knew nothing more than what he had heard and had never considered himself a mountain man. He much preferred the comfort of the cities to the extremes and discomfort of the mountains, but had, unfortunately, believed the tripe about getting rich on beaver furs. If Logan hadn't come along and killed all of his friends, he would have left in the spring. The mountains were too dangerous and unpredictable. If the cold didn't get you, then the Indians or a grizzly would. It was just a matter of time. "Yes, sir. Been there many a time. We'll head east until we hit the plains and then turn south. Should be there in a month or so."

Mary Grace had brought Page and her father a cup of coffee. In giving Page his cup, she bent over, thick black hair cascading over her shoulders, her face near his. It was difficult for him not to notice that the top three buttons of her shirt had been unbuttoned. When he glanced at the cleavage, she smiled and winked at him.

She did that on purpose, he thought. *That's the second time she's winked at me. I'm sure she likes me. Just you wait, girl. Your time is coming.* For only a moment, he watched the sway of her hips as she walked away, but when he turned his eyes back to the old man, those cold gray eyes were locked on his, and the bushy eyebrows raised.

Page lowered his eyes to his coffee, cleared his throat, then concentrated on taking a sip of the hot brew. It flowed into his mouth, delicious. That girl could make a mean cup of coffee.

"You think you could tear yourself away from enjoying Mary Grace's coffee and tell me more about your trip?"

The gray eyes were still on him.

He cleared his throat again. "You might get Cooter's perspective."

Pa Akers's head slowly turned to his son, who sat between Gomer and Jethro. "How do you think the trip went, boy?"

Cooter's brow wrinkled, and his eyes narrowed in a threatening glare at Page, but when he turned to his Pa, on the other side of Jethro, he was grinning. "Mighty good, Pa. Other than dealing with the Shoshones, we never saw nary another Injun. They just weren't out." He nodded his head toward Page. "He said they was all trying to fill their storehouses with buffalo. This is a busy time of year for them. That's what he said."

"Is that right, Mr. Page?"

Page swallowed. "Yes, sir. That's exactly right. Even the Shoshone village was missing many of its warriors and their families. They're all out harvesting buffalo and getting the meat ready for the winter. They call it the starving time. Quite often, it happens even if they kill plenty of buffalo. The end of winter is a very hard time out here. In these mountains, it is almost impossible to find game, and you have to travel on snowshoes. At least in most places."

The old man sat nodding and staring at Page. Finally, he spoke. "When do you think we should leave?"

Page groaned inwardly. *Why did I get involved with these animals?* he thought. *The last thing I want to do is sit in a saddle for another month, but I sure don't want to spend the winter in these mountains. If we can find Logan and kill him, I can get out of here.* "Mr. Akers, I'm thinking we should pull out in the morning or the day after tomorrow at the latest. Those Indians are probably on their way back, and Logan with them. We catch them on the move, that would give you your best chance at Logan."

"In the morning, then. You say a month?"

"About that, barring any problems."

The sun was sinking toward the rugged mountaintops. Pa Akers ran his loveless gaze over his brood. "Tomorrow it is. You boys get everything we won't be needing in the morning packed and ready to load. I want to be out of here nice and early. There's no sense wasting time."

Jethro was up first. "Come on, Cooter, give us a hand. We'll have this place ready to go."

Cooter nodded as the others stood. "Get up, Page. It's time you did some work."

Page slapped his hands on his knees and began to rise.

"Hold up," Pa Akers said. "Page, you stay. I want to talk to you."

Cooter's lips pursed as he glared at Page, then he turned to Mary Grace. "Alright, girl, it's time you pitched in."

"Nope," Pa said, "she stays, too. She needs a rest. She's been working hard. Come over here, girl, and sit down next to Page, so I can talk to you."

Cooter glared at his sister, but she stuck her tongue out at her brother and dropped on the log next to Page, who felt his heart quicken.

12

Floyd had been gone from the Shoshone village for four days when he saw them. He was working his way through a thicket of aspen when, between the white trunks, he caught movement downslope. He froze, halting the animals and attempting to make out how many and of what tribe. Immediately after stopping, he recognized the markings on the horses, Blackfoot. *That's the last thing I need,* he thought.

Floyd Logan, old at twenty-seven years, calculated his chances as he counted. He had been in the mountains for going on eleven years. They had been good years.

Hugh had taught him the business of buying and selling pelts. Jeb had given him the survival skills that had brought him successfully through the turbulent months and years. Lontac, the little Filipino, had shown him he had the power to control his temper and to fight more with his wit than his brawn. But Leotie had brought him love. *Sweet Leotie,* Floyd thought, *I will miss you the most.*

He loved his Leotie and his years in these mountains. They had been hard, sometimes on the very edge of survival, but they had also been exhilarating. The mountains, the dreams of his youth, had been the most beautiful classroom he could have asked for, and Leotie had blessed his life more than he could ever have hoped. Floyd was not a fatalist, but when the number of Blackfoot braves reached fifteen, he accepted reality. Now was the time to put all thoughts of Leotie and everyone else out of his mind. He must focus on the task at hand, survival.

He was in a thick growth of aspen. The white and gray trees, a pattern of confusion thrusting their golden leaves to the sky, might provide enough concealment to hide him from the passing braves. But with fifteen sets of eyes, always searching, always hunting, like fifteen eagles, he had little confidence in his concealment. It was only a matter of one set of those dark eyes spotting an out-of-place smooth fragment of buckskin hide, white skin, or rifle glint, and he would be in the fight of his life. They would have a difficult time getting to him through the slim trees, the trunks growing so close together, but he too was limited. It would be impossible for him to turn the horses, and there would be no racing through the trees. No, possibly his ultimate battle would be here among the beautiful aspen in his beloved mountains.

Interestingly enough, death did not bother him. Oh, he didn't want to die, nor would his death come easily for the Blackfoot, but it wasn't himself he was sad about. It was his mule, Browny. The braves would most likely kill and butcher the devoted mule that had been with him since he left Hugh Brennan in Santa Fe ten years ago. *I'm sorry, Browny,* Floyd thought. *You've been a fine companion, but they'll slit your throat. At least death will come quickly for you.* He began checking his weapons.

Two of his revolvers hung in his saddle holsters, and one on each hip. He knew there would be no talking with these braves. He could see the war paint, and Tocho had told him the Blackfoot had killed a party of soldiers along the Missouri. Slowly, he slid his Colt ring eight-shot rifle from the scabbard and pulled the ring in front of the trigger to index the cylinder and cock the hidden hammer. Now, while the braves, cutting diagonally across the slope below the thicket of aspen, moved ever closer, he waited for the inevitable.

The fifteen warriors looked magnificent. This was a sight with the high mountain backdrop any artist would die to paint. Floyd chuckled to himself. *That's the truth. Any artist seeing this would never live to get paint on canvas before Blackfoot arrows filled his body.*

The braves were riding single file, keeping their trail as concealed as possible. Considering the angle they were cutting, at the closest point, it would put them within fifty yards of his position. He took a deep breath and felt his pulse slow. Battle was near, and he could feel his nerves calming. He reached his right hand to his side, behind his holster, and flipped the loop from his fighting knife. He was ready.

Floyd felt no fear, only the anticipation of a fight, one that would probably be his last. He took a deep breath, tasting the sharp smell of pine sap from the majestic lodgepole pines thrusting forever up to heaven. Glancing up, he was surrounded by flickering gold leaves of aspen welcoming winter. Not far away, a porcupine shuffled through the pine needles, and the scratching of a pair of racing squirrels in the nearby trees was barely audible.

He waited.

A cool breeze caressed the long scar on his cheek while Floyd absorbed his beloved mountain forest. A magpie sailed over his head from left to right. He could see the lead brave's head turn to follow the movement of the black and white bird. The Blackfoot brave tracked the magpie until it was directly above Floyd, and his head stopped moving. His eyes met Floyd's. Holding the stare, the brave snapped something to those behind him and, in one smooth movement, bent and strung his bow. The remaining fourteen heads turned toward Floyd. He could see them searching, and then, almost as one, heads stopped. Arms and hands were following their leader's actions, reaching for weapons.

Floyd kicked himself for watching the Blackfoot so intently. He knew better, but the fat was in the fire now. He waited motionless, the butt of his ring rifle resting on his right thigh.

The leader, carrying one arrow in hand with his bow, whipped its notch into the string while turning the Appaloosa he was riding. Several of the others carried rifles, while the rest were armed as their leader. Much like cavalry on parade, the fifteen men turned their horses toward Floyd in unison, fired, and raced toward the aspen stand. Bullets slammed into and ricocheted off trees, to whine their useless wail as they sailed into the distance. None struck Floyd. Those with rifles dropped them to hang on leather straps fastened to the saddles, and reached for their tomahawks or war clubs.

Floyd would not worry about those reaching for clubs or tomahawks until they were within striking distance. His worry now was the bowmen. They could fire faster than he could shoot the ring rifle. He heard a whoosh and felt a sudden burning in his left ear, but his aim never varied. When the Blackfoot wheeled, he had thrown the rifle to his shoulder, centering his front sight on the leader's chest. Now, he squeezed the trigger, saw the instant bloom of blood on the man's wide chest, and pulled the ring, positioning another round and cocking the rifle. He fired again at a brave pulling his bow to full draw, and was gratified to see the man tumble from the saddle, the arrow wobbling into the air only to drop a few feet distant from the dead brave. Two down and thirteen to go.

Again he pulled the ring, but it stopped halfway to its locking position and would move no farther, jammed. He dropped the rifle into its scabbard and yanked a .36-caliber Colt Paterson from its saddle holster.

Blackfoot braves were in the thicket of aspen, and one had found a direct route through to Floyd. He was swinging his war club high to smash Floyd senseless. Floyd leaned away from the man and shot him in the armpit. He yanked the hammer back and shot him again. This time, blood sprayed from his neck. The club dropped to the ground, but Floyd had no time to follow its fall. He leveled the Paterson on another brave, this one carrying a tomahawk, and marveled at the man's youth. He thought of Mika as he pulled the trigger, striking the young man in the chest.

An arrow sliced his neck, but he had no time to worry about the fresh wound. Blackfoot braves were almost on top of him. He fired, knocking another from his mount, and drew his remaining saddle Paterson while dropping the empty one into the waiting holster at the same time. With his right hand, he whipped his fighting knife from the scabbard.

Another arrow clipped his ribs, fired from only ten feet away, but the brave had had to lean around two aspens and a companion in front of him to get the shot. Floyd drove his knife deep into the chest of the companion who was on top of him, and while the man slumped against him, he fired his revolver over the man's shoulder. The first shot missed the brave who had just released the arrow, but the second caught him in the shoulder.

Floyd's mind raced, knowing he was about to die, but calculating which man should be his next target. He realized he was almost surrounded.

Two braves wove through the trees, each approaching from opposite sides. Floyd had to make a choice. One of the two would reach him. He didn't have time to shoot both. He shot the bigger man, who slumped in his saddle, and Floyd turned, leaping out of his saddle at the other, the bloodied blade of his knife poised. At the moment he was airborne, the brave jerked to the side. A spray of blood shot from his chest. Even in the cacophony of battle, he could hear the boom of a Hawken.

He couldn't stop himself. His leap carried him onto the dead brave, and the two of them slammed into the ground with Floyd on top. He jumped to his feet, only to feel something hammer into his left shoulder. His arm went numb. In falling, he turned to see a brave of about his age standing above him. The man's face was a grotesque mask of hate and anticipation of the death of this mountain man, for his next blow would certainly crush Floyd's skull. But it wouldn't, for a Hawken fired again, and the brave fell lifeless into Floyd's arms. He threw him off his body and leaped to his feet, his knife swinging for the next attacker.

But they were gone. He counted nine Blackfoot racing down the grassy slope, two with their arms wrapped around their companions. Floyd tried to move his left arm, and all he could do was wiggle his fingers. He drew his remaining unfired Paterson and surveyed the carnage. His chest rose in gasps as he sucked in the mountain air. He remembered the Hawken shots and looked around.

From the edge of the aspen, a familiar voice called, "If you ain't the ugliest sight I ever did see. I was just tellin' Morg, here, I was gettin' almighty tired of chasin' yore scrawny body, and now look at it, bloody as a butchered hog."

Floyd shook his head. "Shorty, is that you?"

"'Course it's me, boy. Who else would take the time to save yore ornery hide? Now would you get yoreself out of them aspens? We ain't fools. You won't catch us ridin' through a thicket like that."

Morg spoke up. "You alright, Floyd? You need some help?"

Floyd shook his head while he looked around for the Paterson he had dropped. Finding it, he shoved it behind his gunbelt and turned for the horses and mule. "No, I'm fine. Let me get the horses." He remembered Buck's shudder during the fight and fast-walked back to the buckskin. His horse had blood running down its thick neck. He checked the other side, bleeding as well. Floyd gave Rusty and Browny a quick check. Miraculously, with all the bullets and arrows flying, Buck was the only casualty. Browny had two arrows sticking in the packs, but neither had even scratched the mule.

Relieved, he picked up his reins and lead ropes and led the animals from the field of battle. Blood was everywhere, but there were only two bodies. It was the last two shot with the Hawkens. Though they were being fired upon by unseen assailants, the remaining Blackfoot had taken the time to grab all the wounded and most of the bodies of their dead friends.

Floyd stepped out of the aspen thicket. He could make out Shorty and Morg in the shadows of the pines. Shorty waved him over. "Get over here, boy. No sense standing around jawin' with you out in the open. We ain't hankerin' to get our hair lifted. Especially after the hornet's nest you stirred up."

Morg stepped up to Floyd, his big hand extended. "It's good to see you, pard. Are you sure you're alright? I don't think there's an inch of your body that ain't covered in blood. Man, that was a fight to behold. Them Blackfoot will be telling stories about this for years to come."

"I think most of it is Blackfoot blood. They sliced me a little with their arrows." He raised an eyebrow at Shorty. "It's a good thing I was in those aspens. It was hard enough for me to get a shot at them, but they had a really tough time trying to weave those arrows through to me, and not a rifle shot reached me."

"Humph, so you say. How was yore chance of turning around and getting out of there with those animals?"

Floyd nodded. "You've got a point. When they stepped out of those pines, I knew I was a dead man. If you boys hadn't come along when you did, I'd be shaking hands with Saint Peter right now. I'm mighty glad you showed up." He nodded toward his friends' rifles. "Those Hawkens saved my life. They surely did."

Morg nodded his head toward their back trail. "There's a canyon back a ways with a fine stream and beaver pond. Let's get back there so we can get you cleaned up and see if any of those arrows did any bad damage." He saw the blood on Buck's neck. "You need to change horses?"

Floyd shook his head. "Not now. It was an arrow that went all the way through. Fortunately, it's high, so if we can keep it from getting infected, he'll be fine." With his last words, he clucked at

Buck, and the horse led off in the direction they had just traveled. "Speaking of infection, Shorty, how's your leg?"

Shorty slapped his thigh. "Right as rain. About halfway back to Bent's Fort, we ran into an army patrol. They had a sawbones with them. He looked at it and said it looked fine. He said you did a mighty good job of getting all the trash out of it. Anyway, he put some stuff on it, bandaged it, and said I could do whatever I wanted, as long as I dodged those Pawnees, and that's what we been doing."

"I'm mighty glad to hear it, Shorty. You are one lucky fella. You could've died or at least lost that leg."

"Reckon I know that. If I woulda lost that leg, I might as well have died. But thanks to you, I'm still here keeping Morg in line. He even managed to talk the Doc outta a couple of bottles of you-know-what." He winked at Floyd.

Morg frowned at his friend. "You cain't keep yore mouth shut for no amount of money." After holding the glare for almost a minute, he turned back to Floyd. "It's only for med-i-ci-nal purposes. You ain't got no reason to be worrying about me."

Floyd nodded, but said nothing. His side was hurting, and, surprisingly, his ear was hurting almost as bad as his side. His neck stung a bit, but it wasn't bad, though he could feel blood still running down his left shoulder and back, but that could be from the ear. He chuckled to himself and shook his head. Shorty caught the movement.

"What's on your mind?"

This time, Floyd laughed aloud. "So I get sliced with an arrow on my left ear and the left side of my neck. The bear got me on the left side of my scalp and left forearm. The Comanche arrow caught me in my left bicep." He ran a finger down the knife scar he'd received from the Pawnee. "Plus this."

Shorty joined in with a chuckle. "Boy, yore left side is mighty unlucky. You ain't got much left on that side that ain't been shot, poked, or sliced." He roared this time. "Get it, much left. Heh, heh, heh. I could be one of them jesters."

Floyd glanced at Morg, who was grinning at him.

They rode in silence for another two miles. Floyd took advantage of the time to reload his Patersons. *I'll save the ring rifle for later,* he thought, *when I have time to figure out what went wrong.* Following a trail that led into a deep canyon with a wide stream, they made their way to the bottom. It was level, with a nice stand of grass around the pond, thanks to a family of beavers. Their pond was clear and inviting.

The men led the horses to the edge of the water to drink. Removing the saddles right now was not a good idea, in case the Blackfoot were on their trail. All the animals drank greedily. Floyd opened his saddlebags and pulled out a sealed container. Inside were some medicines, twine for sewing wounds, needles, and clean rags. He removed several rags, dipped one in water, and began cleaning Buck's wounds.

Both the entry and the exit wound looked clean. Floyd worked on the buckskin's wounds until he was satisfied they were clean. Buck tried to step away, but he held him still and patted the horse on its shoulder. "Good boy. Just a bit more time here, and you'll be good as new." When he finished with Buck, he moved to the other two, rubbing the neck of each. "You fellas did real good back there. I'm proud of you. If you'd started kicking up a fuss, I woulda been in real trouble."

He then stripped his clothes off to doctor his wounds. He was lucky. All were superficial except maybe the ear. The arrow had sliced his ear as if it had been clipped with shears. The back had a distinct notch cut out of it.

Morg cleaned the wounds as Shorty watched and commented.

"Floyd, I'm tellin' you, that arrow must've been spinning right smart, 'cause it made a perfect notch cutout. It looks like an ear notch those Texas cowhands use to mark their stock. Yes, sir, that's mighty even. You'll have a notched ear for the rest of yore born days."

"You have anything else to comment on?"

"Well, actually, I do, boy. That cut on your neck won't hardly be visible at all. There ain't nobody who'll be seeing that. It's down below your collar. Reckon that's how your shirt got messed up. It'll take a mite of sewing."

Morg rolled his eyes at Floyd as he worked on his wounds.

"Thanks, Shorty," Floyd said. "That's mighty calming to know."

Shorty nodded again. "It is, ain't it, mighty calming."

Morg leaned back. "Looks like we're done here, Floyd. I'd say you're none the worse for wear."

"Thanks. You boys watch this stuff. I'm gonna take a quick swim to get this blood off." With his last statement, he stripped the rest of his clothes off and dove into the pond.

As his head went underwater, there was a hail from the rim above them. "Hello the camp. Mind if I come down?"

Shorty grabbed his Hawken. Morg picked up his and called to the stranger, "Come on."

13

The man was with no riding stock, not even a broken-down mule. He carried no rifle. All he had with him was a .54-caliber flintlock pistol and his possibles bag, and it looked pretty light. There couldn't be much powder and ball in it. He also lacked any kind of stores.

Floyd washed off the remaining blood quickly, threw his clothes into the pond, and weighted them with a large rock. After putting on the clean clothes he had laid out by the water's edge, he pulled on his boots, swung his gunbelt around his hips, and picked up his Ryland. He could depend on this rifle even if it was only a single shot.

The stranger looked pretty weak as he scrambled down the trail. His clothing was worn, and it hung on him as if it were three sizes too big.

"Name's Gideon Billings. I ain't lying when I say I figure the good Lord sent you fellas, 'cause I knew it was only a matter of time, and it wouldn't be long in coming, before I would meet him face-to-face."

Floyd frowned. "Your name's familiar, mister, but I can't place from where."

"Back before the beaver prices went south, I was a fur buyer. Most of the time, I worked south. There was so much competition at rendezvous I never came up this far. Did most of my trading with Hugh Brennan in Santa Fe."

Floyd's frown changed into a wide smile. "Yes, sir. I remember you. In fact, you bought me lunch one day right after I started working for Hugh."

Gideon leaned forward, staring at Floyd. His eyelids pulled together until his eyes were almost completely hidden except for tiny slits. Then he smiled. "Why, I swear. You are that young fella who worked for Hugh, Floyd Logan! You've made yourself quite a name in this country." He thrust his hand toward Floyd. "It's good to see you. Course, seeing is a manner of speaking. They took and smashed my glasses. I can't hardly see my hand in front of my face without them."

Floyd shook the extended hand while Morg walked to his saddlebags and pulled out several strips of elk jerky. The tall man stepped back and held out the jerky. "You look a mite hungry there, Gideon."

Taking the strips, the man said, "Mister, you have no idea. I have had no food except for wild onions and a few berries for longer than I'd like to think. I got away with my pistol, but I can't see well enough to take anything down with it." He thrust a strip of jerky between his teeth, tore off a piece, and went to chewing.

The man had piqued Floyd's interest. It wasn't the norm to find a man in the mountains alone, starving, and almost blind. "Tell me, Gideon, who took your glasses?"

Between chews, he told his tale. "I came up from Bent's Fort in search of a good area to establish a trading post in this north country. I'm on good terms with most of the tribes, though the Blackfoot are a bit standoffish."

"Humph," Shorty said, "you can say that for sure."

Gideon squinted at Floyd. "The gunfire I heard was you defending yourself against the Blackfoot?"

Floyd nodded. "Yes, sir. That was us."

"It sounded like quite a battle."

Shorty couldn't stay quiet. "Quite a battle? You should've seen it. When we come up on Floyd, he had set to with about fifty Blackfoot, and they was dead set on lifting his fine hair."

Floyd shook his head. "Shorty tends to exaggerate. There were only fifteen, but that was more than enough. If it hadn't been for my pardners showing up, I'd be buzzard food right now, but Gideon, that's another story. You were saying about your plan for a trading post."

Gideon looked from Shorty to Floyd. "Yes, well, I was on my way north. I've been all over the south country, that is from about El Capitan south, so I'm familiar with the mountain country and its hazards. I had heard folks were moving in up here, and I thought a trading post might be worth investigating."

Shorty couldn't keep quiet. "So, have you seen many people?"

Gideon shook his head. "Not enough for a trading post yet. It's still too sparse, but it won't be long."

"Humph, sparse, you say. This country is getting overrun with folks. Why, we ran into a bunch of them army fellers down on the plains about three weeks ago."

Floyd changed the subject before Shorty could slip into one of his rants. "So, what happened to your glasses and your supplies?"

Gideon had just ripped off another bite of jerky and was chewing with gusto. He slid it to one side of his mouth. "You heard of some folks by the name of Akers? Got a mighty pretty young woman traveling with them. The old man says it's his daughter."

Shorty spoke up. "We dang sure heard of 'em. There ain't an ounce of good in them folks."

Gideon nodded. "Right you are. I wish I had ridden past their camp without stopping. The old man was all smiles and good-ness when I rode in. He was surrounded by big men who looked ready to do his bidding, no matter what evil he conjured up. The moment I was close enough to see their faces, I knew I'd made a mistake. They couldn't take their eyes off my mules. I had them loaded with trade goods. I imagine those thieves are living high on the hog right now."

Shorty's deep voice cut in. "That hog's about to get butchered. You reckon you could lead us to 'em?"

The trader eyed Floyd. "Are you looking for them?"

A grim smile spread across the young mountain man's face. "Yes, Gideon. We're looking for them. Can you lead us to where you last saw them?"

The older trader examined Floyd's face for only a moment. "Yes, I sure can."

"How far do you figure they are?"

"I suspect I've traveled about a hundred miles. I was told there's a Shoshone settlement this way, and was hoping to get there."

Floyd shook his head. "You were headed in the right direction, but I don't think you would've made it. You've got a long way to go across tough country. With the shape you're in now, it would have been almost impossible, but that's not important now. You're with us."

Gideon went silent, giving his complete attention to the jerky Morg had given him.

While Gideon ate, Floyd moved to the Colt ring rifle and examined it. Almost immediately, he saw the problem. Pulling his Barlow knife, he opened the blade and removed a smashed cap and dropped it into his hand. With the cylinder clear, he grasped the ring and pulled aft. It moved with no problems. He reloaded the two fired cylinders, capped all three, checking the others were secure, and shoved the rifle back into its boot. "We had best be moving out of here. We've been here too long as it is. Should the Blackfoot decide to try us again, I don't want them to catch us here."

Floyd had switched his gear to Rusty. He swung into the saddle. "Gideon, why don't you ride with me for a ways? I'd let you ride Buck, but he took a Blackfoot arrow through his neck, and I imagine he'll be feeling it for a while." He held his hand out.

Gideon grasped his hand, stepped into the stirrup, and swung up behind him. "This'll be like riding the cushions after walking all over these mountains. I'm much obliged."

At the bottom of the beaver pond, the stream narrowed. They crossed it and headed up the side of the canyon along a much-used, meandering elk and deer trail. The horses climbed steadily until they were over the rim. Reaching the top, and after slipping back into the concealment of the tall pines, Floyd pulled Rusty to a halt. From their position, it was possible to keep a lookout on the opposite side of the canyon and the trail they had used to drop down to the beaver pond. Shorty and Morg eased their horses to each side of him. His voice low, Floyd said, "I want to wait here for a bit to see if any company shows up. Gideon, why don't you continue your story while we wait? Once we get moving again, we want to hold the talking to a minimum. There's no telling when we might run into Blackfoot." With his last statement, he gave Shorty a pointed glance. It was returned with a frown, but his friend made no reply.

"Sure enough. The old man invited me to get down, and I could see there was no other choice. If I'd tried to ride out of there, I woulda been a dead man. So I swung down, and that was almost the end of me. That pretty young thing sidles up to me, takes my arm, and leads me to a log by the fire. Old man Akers, he sits across from me, so he can keep an eye on me, while a couple of his boys sit next to me."

He shook his head. "I knew I was a dead man. They must've mostly been kin, because they were calling the old man either pa or uncle. There was one other fella with them. He looked to be a mite uneasy about being there. I found out his name was Henry

Page. I also learned the whole bunch has a strong hankering to locate you." He nodded at Floyd.

"Yeah, I killed a couple of the old man's boys. They tried to ambush me and a young fella. It didn't go well for them."

"Well, ambush was never a word they used. Mostly, it was murder. I'll tell you, Floyd, they're a mean-looking bunch, and it ain't just looks."

Floyd nodded. "Yeah, that's why we're looking for them. Finish your story. We need to get moving."

"Well, it's like this. The old man offers to unsaddle my horse and mules. I know that's a bad idea, but there's nothing I can do, so I just tell him I'd be obliged. Several of those younger fellas head over to my animals, and while they're unloading my two mules, they start going through the packs. I said something and stood, and the young fella sitting on the opposite side of me grabbed my shoulder and slammed me back on the log. The next thing I know, he's drawn this long double-edged blade and shoved the point into my nose." Unconsciously, Gideon rubbed his nose with a forefinger, then went on.

"I smelled blood on that knife for sure, and I knew it was my time, but then he just wiggled the blade, laughed, and eased it away. But just when I felt safer, this lovely girl leans toward her pa and says, 'Tell Cooter to stick him, Pa, like he did that drummer, and we can watch him squirm.' Talk about chilling, to hear that soft and what should've been sweet voice asking her pa to have me killed, um, um, um. She is one sick woman."

Floyd had had enough. They had been watching their back trail long enough. It was time to move on, even if the story wasn't finished. "Gideon, we've got to get out of here. Why don't you hold the rest of the story until we stop again?" He looked at Shorty and Morg. The tall mountain man nodded and nudged his mount forward, but Shorty shot him a frown for interrupting the story. Floyd ignored him and bumped Rusty. They were off on a slow walk through the timber, moving southeast, with Gideon Billings pointing the way and chewing on jerky.

Every couple of hours they would switch Gideon to another rider, who would take the lead until it was time to switch again. The timber had thinned a ways back, but they kept to it as long as possible, until they were about to be forced onto the plains. It was getting late, so Floyd opted to stop while they still had a few trees for cover and make a cold camp.

After taking care of the horses and Browny, Floyd began searching through one of the packs Browny had been carrying for some seal-tights he had originally bought at Bent's Fort. As he searched, he would glance up and scan the prairie. He felt the cans near the bottom of the pack, and reaching deep, his eyes drifted up to the plains again, and there it was, exactly what he didn't want to see, a column of dust. It was faint, but it was there. He straightened from the pack. "Morg, Shorty, look to the southeast. Unless my eyes are lying to me, I'm seeing dust, and it's coming this way."

Instantly, everyone was on their feet. Floyd closed the pack, walked to his saddlebags, and retrieved his telescope.

Shorty spoke first. "Dust for sure. Can't tell if it's moving towards us or away, but it danged sure ain't moving to either side."

Morg's big head nodded. "Shorty's right."

By this time, Floyd had the telescope up to his eye and focused. It was dust, and it was coming toward them behind a large detachment of cavalry. Floyd shook his head. "That's the last thing we need."

Morg said one word. "Blackfoot?"

Floyd shook his head. "No. Army."

Shorty looked down at the ground. Picked out a rock and kicked it. It flew in a high arc before crashing down. "Why don't they mind their own business?"

Morg gave a barking laugh. "You weren't singin' that tune when that army sawbones doctored the hole in your leg."

Shorty ignored the comment. "You think it's the same bunch?"

Morg shot a look at Shorty that clearly questioned his sanity. "Of course it is. There ain't enough of them soldier boys out here to send out two patrols that large."

Floyd continued to watch. They were closer, and the amount of dust was growing. He could make out two wagons behind the troopers. He let out a sigh of disgust. "They couldn't come straighter here if we had a string tied to them."

Shorty exploded. "What the blue blazes are they doing out here? They'll just stir up the Indians and make it worse. They're in hostile country, don't they know that? Look at all that dust. There's not an Injun within fifty miles who don't know they're here. Them soldier boys don't have a lick of sense."

Floyd watched them grow.

A voice from his side asked, "May I take a look?"

He watched for a moment longer. They were closer and not deviating in their track. They were coming straight to the camp. He handed the glass to Gideon. "It looks like you may get a hot meal tonight, Mr. Billings. They're bringing two wagons. Odds are one of them wagons is loaded with food."

Gideon Billings adjusted the telescope to his eye, looking for only a moment before exclaiming, "Why, that's the fellows I met on the way up."

Shorty walked over. "Let me take a look."

Gideon handed him the telescope. After only a few seconds of watching, he jerked it from his eye and handed it back to Floyd, who was relieved to have it back in his hands. He normally didn't let newcomers use it. Slippery hands had a way of dropping the glass, and the last thing he wanted was to have it broken. The telescope was a useful tool out here. It could be a lifesaver. He swept three hundred and sixty degrees. Seeing nothing but buffalo, deer, and the cavalry troop, he closed it, slid it back into the leather case, and carefully replaced the case in his saddlebags.

The trader cleared his throat. "You're not excited to see the army?"

Floyd said, "No, we're not. We've got the Blackfoot on the warpath, no telling how many other tribes out hunting buffalo, and now we have a big dust signal letting them know exactly where we're located. Unless we're really lucky, this camp will be under attack by morning."

"Floyd," Morg said, "we could pack up and pull out before they get here."

Floyd shook his head. "No. They'd be here before we could get loaded, and the animals are tired, not to mention us. At least we should get a good night's sleep, with so many men to pull guard duty. We'll just have to face the music and be prepared to fight whatever comes our way."

Shorty, his jaw muscles working, stared at the riders, near enough now to recognize them as soldiers with the naked eye. "I'll tell you what's coming our way. We're gonna wake up in the morning to a passel of Blackfoot out there intent on freeing us of our hair. That's what'll be comin' our way."

14

Captain Phillip Marsden was older than Floyd expected. He halted the troop in front of the four men, dismounted, and called, "Dismount the troop." The order was passed back until a crusty first sergeant yelled, "Dismount!"

Floyd almost cringed at the noise, the yelling, the squeaking of saddles, and the clanging of sabers against leather and bodies. To the listening ear, these sounds would carry almost a mile across the prairie. Morg and Shorty responded in the same manner. Their eyes tightened, foreheads wrinkled, and lips pursed.

The captain stepped toward Floyd while removing his gauntlets from his hands and folding them over his belt. He extended his right hand. "Good evening. I am Captain Phillip Marsden. I apologize for the noise. That is one of the necessary evils that accompany soldiers. The other is dust. In this part of the country, we send out a signal of our arrival long before we meet our opponents or friends, whichever the case may be."

Floyd took the extended hand and received a firm but friendly handshake. *At least he's aware of their shortcomings,* he thought. "Evening, Captain Marsden, I'm Floyd Logan, the tall fella is Morgan James, and the not-so-tall one is Shorty Zebulon the third. He turned to Gideon. This gentleman is a new member of our party. He's Gideon Billings, a trader who has run on hard times."

"I know these men, Mr. Logan. In fact, I feel like I know you, from all the stories I've heard. Would you gentlemen join me for supper? It shouldn't be too long before it's ready."

Floyd glanced at his friends, and they were nodding, along with Gideon. "Yes, sir. That would be a pleasure."

"Good." He shook hands with the other two mountain men. "Morg, it's good to see you again. Shorty, it looks like your leg has healed quite well."

Shorty beamed at the captain's interest. "It shore has. Yore Dr. Blaisdell did a fine job."

"Excellent. He is quite good, and I'm glad to see you're well over that Pawnee arrow." He turned back to Gideon, eyes widening as he examined the man. "Mr. Billings, my goodness. You have lost a tremendous amount of weight since last we met. Lieutenant Blaisdell should take a look at you." He looked over their animals. "I don't see your pack mules."

Gideon Billings shook his head. "No, sir. My pack mules are gone, which goes along with my weight loss, but I can explain all about it at supper."

The captain nodded. "Fine, but I want you to be looked at by Lieutenant Blaisdell."

The lieutenant immediately stepped forward. "Good evening, Mr. Billings. It's good to see you again." He waved toward one of the wagons. "Please come with me to the medical wagon. I want to check a few things. You are looking quite thin. Maybe you can tell me what has happened since we last met."

Gideon began his story again from the beginning, and the two of them walked toward the wagon.

"Mr. Logan, is there water here?"

Floyd shook his head. "No, sir. We pulled up to make a cold camp before starting across the prairie."

"That's too bad, but we're prepared. We carry our own water inside the two wagons for just this occasion. We'll be glad to include your animals in the ration if you wish."

Floyd's forehead crinkled in concern at the captain's free use of water.

"It's not a problem, Mr. Logan. We refill every time we strike water. Do you know if any is nearby?"

Shorty spoke up. "Depends on what you call nearby, Captain. 'Bout a mile west is a nice little creek. Good fishing if you have a mind."

"Good, thank you. Now, if you gentlemen will excuse me, I need to check on my men." With his last statement, the captain marched to a lieutenant and a sergeant with so many stripes there was little room remaining on his sleeves.

Floyd stepped to Morg and Shorty. "So what do you two think of our captain?"

This time Morg beat Shorty with the first word. "The man seems to know what he's doing, but I ain't too sure he's aware of what he's gettin' himself into. We're still south of Blackfoot country, but I'm not tellin' you anything to say they've been known to venture south of their home ground. With him this close, they could take offense or leave him alone, but I'm not really convinced the Blackfoot will leave anything alone, much less a bunch of blue uniforms."

While Morg talked, Floyd watched the army at work. *I've got to say,* he thought, *they're efficient. They've already got a pretty good breastwork thrown up, almost completely around the camp. The cooks have dug trenches, soldiers are chopping wood, and others are feeding and watering horses.* He watched the captain's tent being set up. It was a high-sided canvas structure, and the sides had been rolled up. There were several tables placed end to end, and a white tablecloth was placed over them with plates and utensils to hold it down. *I hope they're as efficient fighting as setting up camp.*

"Floyd," Shorty said, "they're feeding our horses."

He turned to where the horses were tied. They were getting grain, just like the army's mounts. "That's mighty nice of them."

Shorty shot back, "What do they want? They've got to want something. Why are they feeding and watering our animals and about to do the same thing for us? The government don't ever give you anything for nothing. You know that."

Floyd thought about it. "What could they want? We don't have anything they could use. Maybe we've just got a captain who's a mighty nice fella."

Shorty stared at Floyd as if he were a crazy man.

He shrugged. "Well, you tell me. What do they want?"

Morg pitched in, "Guides. You notice there ain't nary a guide or scout with 'em? Without a guide, it makes them naked out here. They could be hit from behind the next rise or creek crossing. Those soldier boys are blind."

Shorty spoke up again. "Bub Leach was with 'em when the sawbones fixed me up. But I don't see hide nor hair of him now. What do you suppose happened to him?"

The tall mountain man nodded emphatically. "Yep, Bub was with 'em, and he ain't here now. That's what they're after. He's plenty savvy. There ain't a soul who could slip up on Bub. He's too tough and ornery."

Shorty shook his head. "Ole Father Time could. Bub's gettin' plenty old. He coulda out and out died."

Morg looked down at his friend. "You think?"

"Shore I do. You remember how he was coughing, and it ain't even winter yet. I think he caught a bug that killed him."

Gideon, having just returned from the doctor's examination, heard the last of the conversation and jumped in. "Or the Akers bunch could have happened to him."

Shorty shook his head. "Nah, not Bub. There ain't no back-woods hillbilly that could put it over on Bub."

A corporal nodded while hurrying past.

Floyd nodded in return. "Excuse me, Corporal, do you have a moment?"

The young man paused. "Only a moment, sir. What do you need?"

"What happened to Bub Leach? I don't see him around. Is he off scouting?"

The corporal shook his head. "No, sir. At least I don't think so. He rode out a week ago and never returned. We ain't seen hide nor hair of him or his horse."

"Thank you, Corporal."

The man nodded again and hurried on to a crew who had stopped chopping and were leaning on their axes. Arriving, several strong hand gestures followed, accompanied by a young but commanding voice, and the men immediately went back to chopping.

Shorty said, "That's not good."

Gideon added, "I tell you, it's the Akers. He must've stumbled on them or their camp, and they killed him."

Morg shook his head. "That's hard to believe. Bub is a sly fox. I can't imagine them fellers, no matter how bad they are, puttin' anything over on him."

Gideon shook his head. "It's the Akers. You've gotta believe me. They're mean and devious. The way I figured them, they won't let anyone past them who could tell you"—he indicated Floyd—"anything about them."

Floyd finally nodded. He stared out across the plains, thinking, *If I had stopped them in Independence, this wouldn't be happening, but like Pa always says, you can't control the past, but you can sure make a difference today.* He turned to his friends. "I want to find this Akers bunch. With Gideon's help, we can put an end to this killing."

The other two mountain men nodded, then both heads turned toward the cooking fires. Fine aromas drifted in their direction.

Captain Marsden waved to them. "Come on over. Get in line, fill your plate, and join us at the table. Don't be bashful. There's plenty for everyone."

With the invitation, Gideon was the first to arrive at the table where the food was being dished. Two young men stood on the opposite side, one with a large fork, and the other a massive ladle. Floyd watched the first private stab a thick steak and drop it on Gideon's plate. The second private scooped a ladleful of potatoes from the pot and plopped it on the plate next to the steak. Meat and potatoes, his stomach let out a long growl.

Morg's echoed it.

Shorty couldn't resist. "Sounds like you boys are tuning up. You gonna sing us a duet?"

Morg stepped out of line, following Gideon, and shot Shorty a disgusted look. "Floyd, would you listen to what I have to put up with? All these years, and he's just as obnoxious as when we first met."

Captain Marsden was already seated. He waved his fork across the table. "Sit down, men. I'm sure it isn't often you can have supper around a table."

"No, sir, Captain Marsden," Floyd said, "this is mighty nice. Who would expect a tablecloth in this country?"

"Thank you, Mr. Logan. I believe a little civilization is always good for the spirit." He looked around the table. "Get to it, men. I know you are all hungry."

They had been joined by Lieutenants Blaisdell, Parrish, and First Sergeant Barney. From the two officers and the NCO came, "Thank you, sir." Silence wrapped the table as those present concentrated on making their food disappear.

Finished, the captain nodded, and the orderly stepped up with a coffee pot and filled his cup.

"Thank you, Mac. Would you gentlemen care for a cup?" Heads nodded around the table.

After the orderly poured Floyd's, the mountain man responded with, "Obliged."

Thanks were addressed to Mac from all. He responded to each with a nod.

The captain leaned back and, between sips of his coffee, asked Gideon, "So, Mr. Billings, perhaps you could share with us how you lost so much weight and your mules."

Gideon gazed around the table, making eye contact with each member of his audience. "Captain, first, I must say the buffalo steaks were about the best I've tasted."

Everyone agreed.

"Thank you, gentlemen. First Sergeant Barney found us a master chef before we left the fort. He is an excellent cook, but unfortunately he has a vile temper. He's been busted to private several times. Isn't that right, First Sergeant?"

"Right for sure, sir, but he makes magic with food."

The captain nodded. "He certainly does. Now, Mr. Billings, please continue."

Gideon nodded. "Yes, sir. There is a family of malcontents from back in the Tennessee mountains who are responsible." With that introduction, he began his story and covered all the details Floyd had already heard, taking just as much time.

The light was fading, and they were nearing the end of the second cup of coffee, when Marsden stopped Gideon with a raised hand. He then addressed Lieutenant Parrish. "Mr. Parrish, the perimeter is set along with the watch for the evening?"

"Yes, sir. I have examined the men's efforts. We are well shielded. The watch will be four shifts at two-hour intervals. It should allow all the men to get plenty of rest tonight. We saw no signs of Indians today, so I doubt we'll have any problems."

The lieutenant was doing fine, Floyd thought, *until his last comment.* He looked at Morg and Shorty. Both men's eyebrows had risen at the young man's last statement, and the captain hadn't missed their reaction.

"Mr. Logan, do you or your friends disagree with Lieutenant Parrish's last statement?"

"Captain, you seem to be familiar with the west, though I doubt with the country you're riding into. I'm sure you know, when you're not seeing Indians is when you worry. We're in Sioux country, though last I heard, they were still peaceable. Howsoever, there are Blackfoot about. I know this because I got jumped by a bunch of them yesterday, and if it hadn't been for Shorty and Morg, my scalp would be hanging on one of those fellas' lances. Were I you, I'd be operating under the assumption that sometime between right now and sunrise, I'll have a fight on my hands. It could happen anytime with the moon as bright as it is."

The captain had clasped his hands and steepled his fingers. The tips were resting against his mouth as Floyd talked. When the mountain man finished, he took a deep breath and locked his lieutenant in his gaze. "Well, what do you think of that assessment?"

The young officer hadn't been out west long, but he'd been out long enough to recognize a mountain man confident in what he was saying. "Sir, Mr. Logan has considerable knowledge of this country. I'd recommend doubling the watch and ensuring the men have plenty of powder and ball. Those asleep should sleep with their sabers close."

The captain gave a definitive nod. "I agree. First Sergeant, would you give the lieutenant a hand in ensuring the men are prepared?"

"Yes, sir." The first sergeant rose with the lieutenant, and the two men departed.

The captain stood. "Mr. Billings, I am sorry you didn't have time to finish your story, but I get the drift. This Akers bunch is crafty and dangerous, and we will certainly keep an eye out for them. Now if you will excuse us, I need to have a word with Mr.

Logan and his friends. Have a good night, and keep your weapon close. In fact, I noted that you have no rifle. If you would like one, we have extras. Check with Lieutenant Parrish, and tell him I authorized you to be given one of our weapons, powder, and ball. He will oblige you." He gave an abrupt nod, dismissing the trader, and turned to Floyd.

"Mr. Logan, I'll get right to the point. I need help."

In the failing light, Floyd saw the slight nod Shorty gave. *Both you and Morg were right, Shorty,* Floyd thought. *The captain is in a tight spot without scouts or a guide, and he sees us as a remedy to his situation.* "Before you ask, Captain, there's no way we can assist you. We're in pursuit of Akers and won't be changing our minds until that bunch is no longer a threat to innocent folks."

The captain's back straightened, and his face stiffened. "Mr. Logan, you do not understand. My guide, Mr. Leach, has been gone for over a week. I fear something dreadful has befallen him. After three days passed and he didn't return, our three scouts disappeared. They just faded into the trees. I have been ordered to make my presence known throughout this country, and it cannot be done without eyes. I need a man, or men, familiar with this wild land who can assist us."

Shorty spoke up. "We're right sorry, Captain Marsden, but this Akers bunch is bad clean through. They've got to be stopped. They kill whoever they run into, man, woman, or child, white or Indian. It don't matter to them. Their purpose is to find Floyd and kill him, which is just fine, 'cause our goal is to kill them."

The captain looked at Shorty, then Morg, and finally Floyd. "Is this some kind of personal feud?"

Floyd thought for a moment before responding. "No, sir, not on my part. I killed two of the leader's sons back in Tennessee when they ambushed me and a friend in attempted robbery. Now, the old man is dead set on killing me, and as many as it takes to get to me. I'm sure you can see I have no choice but to stop him."

The captain paced in his tent. "There has got to be some way to solve both of our problems."

Floyd stepped closer. "There is. You say your job is to make the U.S. Army known in this part of the West. You've done it. I guarantee tribes know you're here. Now's the time to turn around and head back, and on the way, we can combine forces and remove the vermin that's running loose out here."

Marsden had stopped pacing while Floyd talked. He thought for a minute, then began again, shaking his head. "My orders are to proceed west and make my presence known. I can't turn around, and with your help, we can continue west. Another week, maybe two, and our mission will be completed."

Floyd shook his head. "We won't be going west. You turn back east or southeast, and we'll be glad to help. We'll stick with you until we find the Akers bunch." He glanced at Morg and Shorty. They both nodded. "See, we agree. You've got our help if you turn around."

The captain stopped again. The moon, high above the pines, cast a pale shadow through the front of the tent, giving the captain's face an eerie, almost deathly appearance. He shook his head again. "No, I can't do it, and if necessary, I shall conscript you."

Floyd laughed. "Captain Marsden, you want us as guides. Guides ride ahead and to the sides of your columns. We could ride away anytime we desired."

"I know your type, Mr. Logan. What you described is something you would not do. I'm sorry, but I need you all, and I need you now. I'll brook no disagreement. You must stay."

Floyd felt his anger rising. The anger Lontac, his old Filipino teacher, had taught him to control and use for his own good. He took a deep breath and pulled it back. "Good night, Captain. Thank you for a fine supper." With Shorty and Morg behind him, he left Marsden's tent.

The waxing gibbous moon cast a broken, eerie pall over the

campsite. Its light intruded between the tall scattered pines, providing a haphazard pattern of light to the scattered brush and sleeping men. Reaching their gear, Shorty spoke in almost a whisper. "I ain't likin' the feel of this place. If these soldier boys weren't here, I'd be for mounting up and hightailing it out of here."

Morg nodded. "It ain't often I agree with Shorty, but this is one of those times. My skin's been crawling since the sun went down. I didn't like the feel of this place when we stopped. It gives me the creeps. I'm thinking this is a fight we oughta be runnin' from."

Floyd had been in many a fight, but he, like Morg and Shorty, didn't like the feel of this one. "I'm a bit edgy myself, but we're locked in here. If we try to ride out, you can bet the captain will stop us, and as much as I'd like to move on right this minute, we can't leave these boys in the lurch. But beyond that, I think it's too late to be trying to pull out. I think the Blackfoot are already out there, just waiting. Reckon we oughta make sure all our weapons are ready, and like the lieutenant's, make our watch every two hours. That'll at least get us a little sleep. I'll start off."

Gideon had returned with a rifle during the last part of their conversation and moved close. "Then you are expecting an Indian attack tonight?"

Shorty eyed the trader and his new weapon. "Danged right, and you best make sure that thing is loaded for bear, 'cause it won't be long in the making. I'm getting some sleep."

15

Floyd was tired. The long trip from his distant Leotie had drained a good portion of his weight and strength. Another fight with the Blackfoot was the last thing he wanted. His perfect day would be running through the long grass with his Shoshone wife, the warm sun on their backs. He had loved her when they had married almost eleven years ago, but it was no comparison to his feelings for her now. His love had grown every day. He could feel her warmth, the touch of her hand on his face . . . Floyd's head snapped up, eyes flying open. *Sleeping,* he thought, *when you're supposed to be on lookout. That will get you killed, boy,* he thought. He blinked the desirable but unwelcome sleep away.

Without moving his head, his eyes examined all they could see from his position. He slowly turned his head, first left and then right. The camp was quiet. He had taken a seated position in the shadows against a tall pine so his silhouette would be hidden. The Colt Paterson in his right hand and long-bladed fighting knife in his left felt reassuring.

It was past time to wake Morg, but they were all tired. His tall friend could use the extra sleep. He'd wait just a few minutes longer. He expected the attack to be closer to the daylight hours anyway, when the soldiers would be at their foggiest. It would be a surprise to him if they attacked this early in the night. *But, surprise is where the Indian is most adept, especially the Blackfoot.*

Silently, to his left, a moccasined foot appeared from behind the tree he was resting against. It lowered ever so slowly to the pine needles, creating not even a crinkle or whisper. *He's on my left, dang it,* he thought, *and my knife's in my left hand. There's no way I can get it into action fast enough from this angle.* He raised the Paterson and waited. He had cocked the weapon when he sat down, so there would be no telltale clicks when pulling the hammer back.

Slowly the Blackfoot appeared from behind the tree. In the man's right hand was an ugly-looking war club, and his left held a fighting knife. From Floyd's position, since he was seated, the Indian towered over him. Any shot he made would slant up. He tilted the muzzle slightly and pulled the trigger. His night vision was burned away in the brilliant white, yellow, and red flames leaping from the muzzle of his revolver. But in the flash, a neat round hole appeared under the brave's chin. The Blackfoot collapsed, stone-cold dead, and Floyd remained seated.

He'd do no good standing and flailing around in the dark. Bloodcurdling yells split the darkness, combined with screams of pain and dying. His shot had alerted the camp. Man-on-man battles were taking place everywhere. Grunts and yells of men fighting to survive filled the pine grove. His sight was returning, thanks to the bright moon. He arose and started forward.

A viselike hand grabbed his right biceps and spun him around. He allowed his body to spin with the yank and drove his knife deep into the chest of a massive Blackfoot brave. The man's arm was drawn back with a fighting club held high, about to crush Floyd's skull. In the moonlight, he could see the big Indian's surprise as the point of Floyd's knife skewered his heart. The club fell to the ground. Floyd yanked hard to pull the knife from the bone and flesh as his opponent followed the club.

Floyd shoved the muzzle of his revolver into the armpit of a Blackfoot tussling with the first sergeant. He pulled the trigger and smelled the sweet odor of burning flesh accompanied only by the roar of the revolver. The flash was completely blocked because he had shoved the weapon so hard into the Indian's side. Floyd could see the first sergeant's nod of gratitude, and instantly they were both jumped by two more attackers.

The brave grabbed Floyd's gun hand, twisted, and pushed. Floyd stepped back, pulling the Indian with him, and struck with his knife, only to be blocked by his enemy's blade. The two men grappled across the camp. Each man tried to gain leverage for a thrust with his knife. The warrior was strong. Floyd, especially in his weakened condition, could not bring the revolver's muzzle in line with any portion of the brave's body. It was all he could do to block the rain of thrusts. One sliced his shirt across his stomach, but thankfully, he had jumped back far enough to keep the blade from reaching his flesh. Suddenly, a long, thin silver bayonet appeared in the brave's chest. He stiffened, throwing his head back to yell, but emitted only a gurgling sound. The soldier stepped back, yanking the rifle hard and pulling the bayonet from the man's body.

Floyd could make out the features of the young soldier in the pale white light of the moon. His lips were locked closed, drawn into a straight line. Eyes were wide, blank, and his forehead wrinkled with determination. Floyd swiftly checked the immediate area surrounding him and the young soldier. It was clear. He took a deep breath and examined the camp. The attack was over, but with the sound of battle gone, the moans from wounded and dying men became clearer, and the odor of blood drifted on the wind.

The young soldier turned his back on Floyd, bent over, and heaved what must have been all the steak and potatoes he had eaten for supper. Floyd stepped forward and laid his hand on the soldier's shoulder. "Taking another man's life is a hard thing, and not something a man comes to naturally. If you hadn't killed the Blackfoot, he was well on his way to killing me. I thank you."

The fella straightened, wiped his mouth with the sleeve of his blouse, and stared at Floyd. "They just came out of nowhere. One minute, it was dark and quiet. Next, a gun fired, and they were all over us. I've never seen such a thing."

A soft call came from the first sergeant. "Alright, men. You did a good job. They're gone for now, but they could come back. Check your ammunition and get it replenished if necessary. Sound off if you're wounded or near a wounded man. The doctor or his helper will be along shortly. Help as you can, but be ready for another attack."

Lieutenant Parrish's strident call sounded. "Lieutenant Blaisdell, the captain is hurt. His quarters!"

Men started moving toward the captain's tent. First Sergeant Barney sounded off. "Mind your duty! The doc will take care of Captain Marsden. Your job is to be ready. Now get to it!"

The men stopped, murmured, and went about replenishing their supplies or getting a much-needed drink of water.

Floyd moved quickly to check on his friends. Nearing, he could see the tall frame of Morg, the short bulk of Shorty, and Gideon standing next to Morg. He breathed easy and turned back for the captain's tent. Reaching it, he remained outside. Inside, four bodies stretched on the ground. Two were Indians. Blaisdell shook his head and stood. Seeing Floyd, he motioned him into the tent.

Blaisdell stepped to Floyd's side as he entered. "The captain is dead, and so is Mac, his orderly. I don't know how many Indians targeted the tent, but definitely more than two."

Floyd could see one of the dead braves had been impaled by a saber. The other shot.

The doctor continued, "It looks like Mac killed one with the saber, and Captain Marsden shot the other. They were then over-powered, and Mac's skull was crushed. The captain sustained several knife wounds. Both were scalped. It looks like they concentrated their attack on the tent area. The captain and Mac never had a chance. To make matters worse, they made off with the captain's saber."

Floyd shook his head. "Who's in charge now, Doc?"

"Lieutenant Parrish. He's the ranking officer."

At that moment, Parrish entered the tent and strode to the doctor. His eyes were fixed on Captain Marsden. "Dead?"

Doc Blaisdell nodded. "Yes, sir, both men. The captain was still alive when I reached him. He gave a last command. End the mission and return to base."

"That's it?"

"I'm sorry, but yes. That is all he said. It's like he was hanging on to get those last words out." The doctor let out a long sigh. "But now I've got to go see to the others."

"If you see the first sergeant, send him in."

Before the doctor could answer, the gruff-voiced first sergeant responded, "I'm here, sir."

"Good, do you have a count for me?"

"Yes, sir. We came out pretty well, thanks to the warning from our guests. Only three were killed and five wounded. We were very lucky. The Indians left twelve dead and no wounded. Plus, they only got away with three horses."

"Thanks, First Sergeant. Tell the men well done, especially those on horse guard. I'd hate to think what it would be like to be marooned in this country with no horses. If Mr. Logan and his friends hadn't corrected my erroneous assumption, that's exactly what would have happened."

The first sergeant elected to make no comment. "Your orders, sir?"

"As soon as possible, reinstate the watch. Let the men get a little rest, even if they can't sleep, but make sure they are supplied and ready for another attack."

Floyd stepped forward. "Lieutenant Parrish, feel free to consult with my friends on what I'm about to say, but I'm pretty sure there won't be another attack. I'm figuring this attack comprised all the Blackfoot in this part of the country. We're quite a ways south of where they normally range. Of course, stay alert in case I'm wrong, but they attacked as soon as they figured we were asleep. It's still over five hours until daylight. If we had a large bunch of them out there, they would've waited to attack until shortly before daylight and then hit us again while we were licking our wounds. Plus, they lost twelve men. That's a major loss for a tribe all at once. No, I reckon those braves will head north, and they won't be bothering you again, especially when they see how little they hurt us. That doesn't mean another tribe won't attack, but not this bunch."

Shorty stepped up. "He's right, Lieutenant. Yore men did a good job. The Blackfoot might hang around to gather their dead once we're gone, but like Floyd said, you still want to be ready."

Morg nodded his agreement.

"Thank you, gentlemen. Had you not spoken up at supper, there might have been a different outcome to our little fracas tonight. Now, to another matter. I need your help. As the captain stated, without Bub Leach, we are blind. We need men who know this country and how to read it. I'm asking you whether you would assist us."

Floyd scratched a dried piece of blood from his cheek and flicked it into the night. "Lieutenant, are you following your captain's orders and turning around?"

"Yes, Mr. Logan, this is as far west as we will venture. We will be returning to Fort Leavenworth."

"Would you entertain assisting us in bringing the Akers bunch to justice? Gideon believes the Akers are the reason your guide never returned."

"I cannot commit to your request. Let's get moving back east. If things are going well when and if we near their camp, then I will reconsider."

"Lieutenant, we can't guide you all the way back to Fort Leavenworth. That would put us in deep winter, trying to return to our homes out here in the mountains. Whether or not you help us, we can't travel that far, and, I'll tell you, neither can you. Your supplies won't last, and your animals will die. Look how worn and tired they are now. We, you, would never make it."

The young lieutenant's frustration showed. "Mr. Logan, I can command you to help us. As the captain was saying, you would be forced to assist."

Floyd shook his head. This young fella was as stubborn as the captain lying on the ground. "Lieutenant, you wouldn't want to do that. Ask your first sergeant. He'll tell you if your animals can make the return trip from here."

First Sergeant Barney shook his head. "Sir, the animals are almost whipped right now. They need several weeks to rest and eat. With rest and food, they can return to their original strength, but not if we keep pushing them."

Morg stepped forward. "Floyd, Lieutenant, let me make a suggestion. What about Fort John? It's on the Laramie River, and it ain't more'n about a hundred miles from here."

Floyd considered the suggestion. "Morg, have you and Shorty been there?"

Shorty responded, "Sure as shootin', we have. It's actually a pretty nice fort." To the lieutenant, he said, "Last we were there, they had plenty of fine-looking horses, and there's always a passel of guides around. I'm bettin' there'd be several willing to tie up with you and get paid to go back east."

The doctor returned with several men to take the bodies. He knelt next to Captain Marsden first and removed his personal items, placing them in a box with multiple compartments. Next, he knelt beside the orderly, doing the same thing for him. With the items gathered, he stood and motioned the men forward.

Lieutenant Parrish shook his head. "I wish there were time for an honor guard and a decent burial instead of all these men going into a common grave."

First Sergeant Barney replied, "The men looked up to Captain Marsden, sir. They will treat him with respect, but we need to get this done and be ready to be on our way in the morning."

"You're right, First Sergeant. I was just thinking out loud. Go ahead, men." The captain was placed on a sheet, as was the orderly, and their bodies were carried from the tent.

Lieutenant Parrish came to attention as the captain's body passed, and gave him a hand salute, then spoke to the corporal in charge of the burial crew. "Call me before closing the hole, and I'll read a few words."

The man nodded. "Yes, sir." Turning, he led the burial crew from the tent.

Silence fell on the occupants of the tent until the first sergeant spoke. "Sir, I think these men have an excellent idea. I have been to Fort John twice. I did not know we were this close. Both times I was there, they restocked our horses and supplies, and there were several men to choose as guides. I'm sure our current guides will make recommendations."

Lieutenant Parrish thought about the suggestion for only a second. "It is an excellent idea." He turned to Floyd, Morg, and Shorty. "If this is agreeable to you gentlemen, I will write a contract good only until reaching Fort John. This way, you can be paid and released at the fort. Also, the records will show you as having been guides for the army, should you ever desire to ride for us again."

Floyd looked at his friends, who both nodded their agreement. He thrust out his hand. "Lieutenant, you have a deal. With no more problems, we should be at the fort in four days."

The lieutenant grasped Floyd's hand, shook it, and moved to

Shorty and then Morg. "Good. I'll have the papers done before we pull out in the morning. Thank you, gentlemen. I'm sorry we won't be able to help you with your quest, but I appreciate your willingness to render aid."

The mountain men exited the tent and returned to their gear. Shorty was the first to speak. "And the government takes advantage of us again. We get to ride northeast to Fort John, putting us farther away from the Akers bunch, and they don't help us even a little. Just once, I'd like to be in a deal with the government and come out ahead."

Floyd chuckled. "Shorty, this may work out better than we thought. We'll be able to resupply, and we'll be getting rid of the army. You know how they draw hostiles. Also, if we caught old man Akers and his kin, the army would want to take them back to Leavenworth for trial, and they'd want us for witnesses. I don't know about you, but I'm not going that far east for anybody. How about you?"

Shorty thought for a moment. Then he let out a low, "Heh, heh, heh. Floyd, I ain't never thought of that. The last thing we want around us out here is the army. Good thinking, boy. Good thinking."

16

The Laramie river bent around Fort John in a protective curve. Buck, Rusty, and Browny lapped at the water flowing past their feet.

Once the fort was in sight, Shorty never stopped talking. Floyd longed for the mountains, his teepee, and sweet Leotie at his side, quietly enjoying their life. Though the stocky mountain man had been a good friend for years, Floyd couldn't be around him for too long, and he felt the time had long been exceeded. Shorty never shut up, but it didn't seem to bother Morg.

"Now ain't that about the prettiest sight you ever saw," Shorty allowed. The fort awaited them on the other side of the river. "Why, I can't think of a better place to plant me a fort."

Horses and cattle grazed on the opposite side of the river, between the river and the fort. An abundance of green grass provided excellent grazing for the stock.

Floyd turned in the saddle to check the troop following. They had encountered no more problems once pulling out of their battleground. Before leaving, they had laid the slain Blackfoot in a row, arms folded across their chests. He knew they were being watched, and impressed upon the soldiers the importance of treating the bodies with respect if they wanted to safely make it to the fort. After riding away, and before they were out of sight, a group of Indians, too far to identify, rode to the bodies and began tying them on their horses. *It'll be a grim day,* Floyd had thought, *when they ride back into their village.*

With Shorty still chattering, they forded the river, climbed the opposite bank, and rode toward the open doors of the fort. "Now look at them wide-open doors. They're just askin' for trouble."

Morg, knowing better, responded, "That's so they can get the livestock in quickly if need be."

Shorty turned to his pardner. "You don't say. Well, thank you, Mr. Mountain Man, for enlightening this pore, stupid greenhorn. Morg, sometimes you amaze me. Of course, I know why them doors are open." And Shorty continued his harangue.

Floyd examined the fort as they neared. It wasn't big. He guessed it to be only a hundred feet long and maybe eighty or ninety feet wide. The walls looked to be made of cottonwood logs standing about fifteen feet tall. For fur traders, it wasn't a bad fort. For the cavalry, they'd have to camp outside.

Nearing, he could hear a piano banging. Of course they would have a saloon. He glanced at Morg. The big man was sitting more erect in the saddle, listening to the call of the piano. Floyd thought, *We'll need to be out of here in a couple of days. Hopefully Morg will be ready.*

They rode through the big open doors, and immediately Floyd heard his name called. "Floyd Logan, you old son of a gun, what got you so far north? I didn't figure I'd ever see your carcass up here." He recognized Abel Martin, a trapper he hadn't seen for at least six years. Floyd had met and grown to like him at the rendezvous. He waved to the man and pointed to the saloon. Abel waved back and began walking toward the building. Several other men had called to Shorty and Morg. The gathering at the saloon was like an old family reunion. Back-slapping, name-calling, laughing, it was the greeting of men who shared the life-and-death experiences of the Rocky Mountains.

Every day could be their last, but they loved this mountain country. Though they might curse the cold, that was the time the pelts were the thickest. Many had lived through the years of the beaver, before silk came along and displaced beaver hats. They had waded through beaver ponds to set traps, thrusting their hands into the ice-cold water repeatedly. Living in tiny cabins alone, with snow up to the eaves, and wondering if they'd survive the season, and always hoping the price of pelts would be high that year.

It was a life Floyd had loved, though he had only lived it for a few years at the very end of the era. He was one of the fortunate ones. He had found a wife who loved him, and he would never leave the mountains. As soon as he delivered justice to the Akers clan, he'd return to his Leotie and live his years out with the Shoshone. Laughing, with his arm around Abel's shoulders, he walked into the saloon and stopped short.

Across the room sat GentAkers.

Though they had never met, Floyd immediately recognized him. *They all look alike,* he thought, *with the prominent forehead and deep-set eyes.*

Abel, surprised at the sudden stop, turned to look at Floyd. "You all right?"

"Yeah, I'm fine. Do you know that fella whispering into the blonde girl's ear?"

Abel shook his head. "Nope, never seen him before he drifted in this morning with some supplies and a couple of mules he wants to sell."

Gideon was right behind Floyd with several men he also knew. Talking, he was much like Shorty in that vein.

Floyd turned around. "Gideon."

The man stopped talking and looked at Floyd. "Yeah?"

He nodded toward Akers. "You know him?"

Gideon's answer was the swinging of his rifle. He tried to get it to his shoulder in the crowd of men. "Gent Akers. I'll kill him where he stands!" Gideon shouted.

The shout, rifle, and men scattering tore Akers's attention away from the hefty blonde he was concentrating on. His eyes locked on Gideon and the rifle he was trying to get to his shoulder. He leaped to his feet, yanking the woman's substantial bulk between him and Gideon, shoved her toward the men, and made a dash for the side door.

"Stop that man!" Floyd shouted.

The room was crowded, and several of the frontiersmen responded, leaping toward Akers. He whipped out his deadly-looking pig-sticker, but he wasn't in some town in Tennessee. Every man in the saloon had fought for the right to walk this countryside, and a lone man with a knife didn't faze them. An older man with a thick walking stick slammed it across Akers' wrist. The knife thudded to the dirt floor. Three other men grabbed him.

Floyd had grasped the barrel of Gideon's rifle and thrust it high. Catching Gideon's eye, he shook his head. "We've got him. You don't want to be shooting that thing in here."

The older man's face, intent on his quarry, took a moment, but then, returning to sensibility, he nodded his understanding.

"You alright now?"

"Yeah, Floyd, I'm fine. I just reacted."

"I don't blame you, but why don't you lower that thing so folks in here can relax?"

"I'll do that." He dropped the butt of the rifle to the floor, and there was an audible sigh in the saloon.

"Good, so I take it you know him?"

"I know him all right. He's one of the bunch who tried to kill me and stole my mules and supplies. That there is Gent Akers, one of them who came west to kill you."

Floyd smiled. "Thanks, Gideon." He strode to where Akers

was being held. The man had stopped struggling and eyed Floyd as he neared.

"Are you Gent Akers?" It was a question tinged with icy anger.

At Floyd's approach, the three men holding Akers released him and stepped away from the man.

Akers stared defiantly at Floyd. "Who wants to know?"

Approaching, Floyd could see Akers focus on the knife scar that ran from his left cheekbone to just past his lip line. The man's eyes flared wide momentarily, and in that second Floyd saw recognition and gut-wrenching fear. Reaching Akers, he slapped the man. Not a little smack, but an open-handed blow that began at his hip and carried all the power, weight, and frustration Floyd could pack in his right hand.

This was one of the men who had attacked Salty, almost killing him, and they had disrupted Floyd's life, driving him away from his wife and nearly getting him and his friends killed by Pawnee and Blackfoot braves.

The strike sounded much like a handgun discharge. Akers staggered and would have fallen if the men who had initially stopped him from leaving hadn't caught his stumbling body and thrust him upright.

Once Akers was steady on his feet again, Floyd, his voice cold and emotionless, repeated his question. "Are you Gent Akers?"

Before Akers could speak, Gideon stepped around Floyd in full view of Akers. The man's eyes widened in astonishment, then went back to their hooded arrogance.

"Yeah, I'm Gent Akers."

Floyd smiled. "I'm Floyd Logan, *Gent.*"

At the mention of his name, a murmur traveled among the rough frontiersmen in the saloon.

"I understand you and your family are looking for me."

Here it was. The chance for Akers to stand up for what he and his clan were doing, an opportunity for him to proclaim a righteous cause. "Logan?" Akers cocked his head and looked up at the ceiling, then shook his head. "Don't reckon I know you."

Floyd wasn't surprised. He had taken the measure of this man when he'd first seen him, and over the years, he had learned to evaluate a stranger quickly. Sometimes his life depended on it, and this man was a coward. He'd do anything necessary to save his own skin, even betray his family.

"Akers, I've spent the last ten years with the Shoshone. As tribes go, I couldn't have picked better. They're an easygoing, live-and-let-live type of folks. But when someone tries to harm one of their own, they are especially effective at delivering pain in such a way that their victims last a long time and suffer immensely. I've learned most of their tricks, especially with a knife." His right hand swung back and slipped the long knife from its scabbard.

The knife had been a gift from his brother Nathan, who'd had a genuine artist of knives in Tennessee make it special for Floyd. The blade was a little over eleven inches long and carried an edge on both sides. A thick brass hand guard separated the blade from the antler handle. The handle had come from a big deer, and fit his hand perfectly. He had lost it once, but had it returned by a Blackfoot brave. He always thought of his brother Nathan when his hand closed around the handle.

The shiny, threatening, double-edged blade slid into view. The smooth motion of the draw, practiced thousands of times, made it appear almost by magic. Akers's body involuntarily retreated. He took a step back as the blade lifted in front of his eyes.

"Look at the edge, Akers. It's so sharp, you feel no initial pain when it slices through your flesh. But then the burning starts. It's like dragging hot coals through your body, except worse." Floyd watched the man's eyes widen and follow the movement of the swaying knife.

Floyd guided the point of the blade toward Gent's neck. Akers tried to dodge the big blade, but Shorty and Morg had moved next to him and grabbed his arms, holding him in place. Floyd continued the knife's movement until the tip touched the killer's neck.

The man stiffened and tried to pull away from the blade. His voice was tight. "Wait, wait. What do you want? Just ask me, I can tell you. You don't have to do that."

Floyd pressed only lightly, and the tip drew a single drop of blood. Akers yelped. "I'll tell you whatever you want. Don't cut me. Please."

The tough frontiersmen frequenting the saloon, several having survived torture, shook their heads in disgust.

Floyd eased the pressure on the knife ever so slightly. "Where's your pa and brothers?"

Akers couldn't get the words out fast enough. "Not far from here. They're in camp, waiting. I'm supposed to sell the mules and supplies . . ." He stopped, and his eyes snapped to Gideon's face.

Floyd said nothing, but applied a bit more pressure to the knife point.

Akers' voice rose. "I'm supposed to sell the supplies and mules, get what we need, and take the money to Pa. He's waiting for it."

"Where, Akers? And don't dally. I'm losing patience."

"I don't know the name of the place. It's on a little creek about five miles south of here, in a bend with three big cottonwood trees."

"What then?"

Akers's wide pale blue eyes jerked from one hard face to another, as if looking for a friend, but finding none, they settled on Floyd again. "He's lookin' for you. He wants to kill you for what you did."

Floyd removed the knife point from his neck, wiped the blade on Gent's shirt, and shoved it into its leather holster. *Just in time,* he thought, for he heard the troop pulling up in front of the saloon. Moments later, Lieutenants Parrish and Blaisdell, along with First Sergeant Barney and a big man Floyd did not know, marched into the saloon, accompanied by a cloud of dust from the troop's arrival.

Gideon, a grin splitting his face, and his right hand thrust out, stepped forward to greet the newcomer. "Fletcher, you old reprobate, you don't look a day older since I last saw you in Santa Fe seven or eight years ago."

The big man grabbed Gideon's hand and yanked him forward, wrapping him in a bear hug while pounding his back with his free hand. "Gideon Billings. I heard them Utes down south had separated you from your hair." He pushed the trader back and stood with an enormous hand covering each of Gideon's shoulders. "I can't tell you how happy I am to see it was all a yarn. Maybelle is going to be thrilled to see you're alive. It's been a long time." His eyes moved from his friend to Floyd, Akers, and the blood on the man's neck. "Now, would you mind telling me what's going on at my trading post?"

Gideon, indicating Floyd, Shorty, and Morg, nodded enthusiastically. "I'd be glad to, Fletcher. This here is Floyd Logan, Shorty Leander Zebulon the third, and Morg James. These men saved my bacon. If it weren't for them, I'd be back in those mountains, dead."

Fletcher looked Gideon over from head to toe. "You don't look too good right now, Gideon. You could use some of Maybelle's cooking." He nodded to the others in greeting. "Glad to meet you fellers, and I want you to know I'm much obliged for you saving my friend here, but I'm most curious about who the bleeding feller is and why he's being held by you two." Using his right index finger, he pointed at Shorty and Morg.

Before Floyd could speak, Gideon again jumped in. "I'll tell you, Fletcher. That man"—he pointed at Akers—"and his kin stole my mules and supplies and tried to kill me. If I hadn't slipped away while they were drinking, I wouldn't be standing before you today."

Fletcher, his face turning grim, stepped forward, towering over Floyd's six-foot frame, and stared into Gent's face. "I don't hold with people who steal from and try to kill my friends, mister. What's your name?"

Akers, showing his hope for possible salvation in Fletcher, said, "Gent Akers, sir. I can't tell you how glad I am to see you. These men were going to kill me."

Shorty's gruff voice filled the saloon. "We still might."

Fletcher turned hazel eyes on Shorty. "No, sir. You will not. I am Fletcher Rose, and this is my fort. There will be no killing here. This man will go to jail and be tried by his peers."

Fletcher Rose turned, looked to the door at the three men who had come in behind him, and waved them forward. When they reached the gathering, Rose said, "Take him to jail."

Floyd spoke for the first time. "Mr. Rose, I'd like to continue my questioning of Akers, either here or in jail."

"Mr. Logan, it will not be here, but see me at the jail. Perhaps you can have access." He nodded to Akers and spoke to his men. "Go ahead. I'll be along shortly."

Floyd signaled Shorty and Morg to release him, and Rose's men took the thief and killer from the saloon. Morg immediately moved to the bar and ordered a beer. With the entertainment over, the piano player began, and the din rose.

Lieutenant Parrish finally spoke, raising his voice and addressing Floyd. "I see you have been busy, Mr. Logan. Am I to understand that man is one of the group who are intent on taking your life?"

"He is, but he was nice enough to give us some information, Lieutenant. What are your plans?"

Parrish glanced at Rose. "I need to first inform Mr. Rose of Indian activity, and then, with his help, we will resupply, get fresh horses, and be on our way." He turned to Rose. "You could help us?"

Rose nodded. "Yes, sir, Lieutenant. We can provide you with supplies, horses, mules, whatever you need. We have a standing contract with the army. All you need to do is sign a couple of pieces of paper, and I'll have you taken care of. When do you plan on leaving?"

"In the morning, bright and early."

"Excellent. I believe we can accommodate your needs. You can move your horses and wagons down to the corral and stable, and I'll be along shortly."

Lieutenant Parrish thanked Rose and turned to Floyd. "Thank you all for your help. As you heard, we will get resupplied and acquire new mounts. I'm sorry, but we cannot assist you in your endeavors, but I am deeply grateful for the aid you men provided us. It will be noted in my report. See me later, and I will pay you for your service guiding us here. You may consider your contracts terminated for now, but your services will always be welcome."

"Thanks, Lieutenant Parrish, and good luck getting back home. You've got a long trail to ride, and much of it will be through hostile territory. Mr. Rose will set you up with guides who know the trail and are trustworthy. By the way, leave whatever pay we have coming with him, and we'll pick it up when we return."

"Good hunting, Mr. Logan." The men shook hands all around, and the cavalrymen turned and headed out the door.

"Good men," Shorty said, watching Morg drain his second mug of beer.

Floyd saw it too. "Shorty, would you get him? We have men to catch, and I'd like to have him sober."

A man hurried into the saloon and moved quickly to Rose's side. They had a quick conversation, and Rose turned to Floyd. "My man tells me that Akers came in with two other people. A young, slim man, and a lovely young woman. The two left with

supplies while you were questioning Gent Akers, if that's important to you."

Gideon shouted over the noise, "They wouldn't have left Gent
unless they knew what he was doing. They'll leave. We've got to
get 'em."

Floyd knew if they didn't move now, they might lose them. He
addressed Rose. "We've got to get on their trail right now. We
need about six men to join us. I believe there could be ten in their
gang. I can promise there will be shooting, and there's a chance
some might not return. Is that something that could be
arranged?"

Rose gave a short laugh. "You bet it is. A lot of these boys are
bored stiff. They've been hoping for a little excitement. Hold on a
second." He waved at one lady carrying a tray and pointed at the
piano. She hurried over, said something to the piano man, and
the playing instantly ceased.

Fletcher Rose towered over most of the crowd. He began,
"Fellers, Floyd Logan here needs some help. There's a bunch of
Tennessee riffraff who tried to kill my friend here." He put his
hand on Gideon's shoulder. "I understand Bub Leach has disappeared, and it looks like they may have been the culprits, plus
they're killing anyone who gets close. They need to be stopped,
and Floyd Logan here, and his friends, think they know where
they are. "He needs six men." Hands went up all over the room.
"Six *sober* men." At the last statement, there were several moans.
"We don't want any drunks out there shooting the wrong thing or
person. So if you're sober and can follow orders, step up to Floyd
Logan and let him know."

17

An hour later, Floyd rode out with Shorty, Morg, and six sober mountain men, dead set on putting an end to the Akers bunch. Two of the men were friends of Shorty and Morg, and another was Abel Martin. Abel, along with several others, knew the exact location of the creek camp Akers had described. It wouldn't be long.

Floyd could feel the excitement building. The chase was about to be over, finished, and he could meet with Leotie, Mika, Jeb, and his family. He wanted this chapter closed. It was time the Akers reaped the reward of their bloody vengeance. He wanted to ride hard and fast, but Rusty was bone-weary. *I should've gotten a fresh mount when I left Buck and Browny at the stable.* But he hadn't, and neither had Morg nor Shorty.

Shorty almost had to drag Morg from the bar at gunpoint, but he finally consented after downing a third beer. The others were riding fresh horses and wanted to push ahead, but Floyd wouldn't let them. He knew the type these Tennessee hill-country men were. If they had enough time, they'd set up snipers and nail them riding in.

A yell went up. "Dust, straight ahead."

Spotting it at the same time the call came, Floyd thought, *Sure enough, they got the warning and pulled out.* "Slow down!" he called to the men. He waited until they had pulled their horses back to a walk. "Listen close. I'm guessing they left a couple of men behind to ambush us, and if they're as good with those rifles as I expect, we could have folks going back over their saddle. Keep a sharp eye out. If you see anything shout it out. Now let's take it slow."

The men walked their horses toward the creek, eyes searching. They were less than a mile from the campsite when, from a thicket, two puffs of smoke appeared.

Two horses dropped, shot between the eyes. Their riders leaped clear of their collapsing mounts. Once the big animals were down, the riders dropped behind their dead horses for cover and laid their rifles across them.

The air was filled with cursing. "Fall back," Floyd called. Two men rode up to the downed frontiersmen and gave them a hand up, then the posse dropped back to pull up behind a low hill.

Floyd knew the two men had lost trusted mounts they had probably been riding for years. A bond grew between a man and his horse. It was always hard when they died or were killed. He rode to the two who had lost their horses and spoke loud enough for all to hear. "We'll give 'em a couple of hours, then go get your gear. Sorry about your horses."

Shorty was beside himself. "Any no-good who'd shoot a man's horse don't deserve to live. When they die, I know they must go to a special place reserved for horse killers."

Shorty took a breath, and Floyd jumped in. "We're not going to get 'em today, fellas. It's just not in the cards. Look at that dust. It keeps getting farther away as we watch. In a few more minutes, it'll be out of sight. The only thing we stand a chance of catching is a bullet from those bushwhackers. One of you fellas feel like going for a buckboard? It'll be a lot easier to haul two saddles and gear on it."

One of the riders peeled out of the group. "I'll do it. It won't take long." He took off to town.

Floyd watched him go. "I knew better. Posses hardly ever work. Either the thief gets away, or he ambushes the posse, so it's a terrible deal all around." He looked at Shorty and Morg. "We'll get a few days' rest, give the horses a break, then take out after them. We can find out where they're headed from Akers and maybe slide down and be waiting for them."

Morg thought for a moment. "You think they'll come back and try to rescue Gent? He is the old man's son?"

Floyd shook his head. "They might come back to shoot him for spilling his guts, but assuming that old man found out about him telling all, he'll disown him for life. No, since they're headed south, they won't be back, and with them off in that direction, they must have no idea I'm anywhere around. They're still thinking I'm down south."

The time ticked by. Finally, the rattle of a buckboard drifted over the hills. Floyd, who had stretched out on the slope of the hill, sat up, watching the wagon draw near. "Reckon they've had plenty of time to take off."

Shorty, sitting next to Floyd, stretched. "I'd sure like to give them two fellers a big surprise."

Floyd stood, tightened the cinch on Rusty, and stepped into the saddle. Seeing him move, the men followed his example, and by the time the buckboard arrived, everyone was mounted. They eased over the hill and stopped. Floyd pulled out his telescope and examined every tree and bush along their way. Seeing nothing, he placed his telescope in the case, closed it, dropped it back into the saddlebags, and bumped Rusty. The horse stepped forward, and the others followed along with the buckboard.

Picking up the two men's gear was a little unnerving, but they did it without gunfire. In no time, they were headed back to Fort John. Reaching the fort, the posse disbanded with Floyd's thanks. The shadows were growing long, and he was tired and hungry.

Floyd had told Abel the army was looking for guides back to Leavenworth, and his friend had dropped off at Fletcher Rose's office to put his name in the pot. After talking with Floyd, he had a hankering to spend the upcoming winter with his folks back east. He hadn't seen them for quite a while, and this provided him safety in numbers and payment for the ride, a hard combination to beat.

Floyd stood in the doorway of the stable, gazing at the inside of the fort. There were several stores, their backs butting against the wall of the fort. Straight across from the stable, a restaurant of sorts was doing a booming business. It was a large tent, the rear used for cooking, and the front with tables and benches. Next to it was the frontier's answer to a hotel, and he swore he'd be dead before his body would find its way onto one of those filthy cots. Shorty and Morg stood next to him. "What are you boys up to tonight?"

Morg cleared his throat. "I'm trying to decide between food and beer." He had been eyeing the saloon.

Shorty stared up at his friend. "It's food for me. I haven't lost a thing at that saloon."

Morg, without further discussion, stepped out toward the saloon. "See you later."

Shorty, his disappointment showing, watched his friend disappear into the barroom. "Floyd, are you planning on eating tonight?"

The scent of cooking meat drifted across to the two men. Floyd inhaled deeply and chuckled. "If I wasn't, I am now, and when I'm done, I'm curling up in my bedroll and sleeping until next week."

"That's sounding mighty fine to me. When you planning on taking after that Akers bunch?"

The two men started across the square. Floyd rubbed his scar as they walked. "The horses need a rest, and I figure we do, too. In three days, old man Akers should be completely relaxed, figuring he outsmarted us again. I'm thinking we might catch up with or even pass them and see how they'd like an ambush."

Shorty nodded in agreement. "Yeah, three days sounds good. We'll be going crazy in this fort by then."

"Could be you're right, Shorty."

The two men found a spot on one of the benches, and Floyd's mind drifted to Leotie. *I'm finally coming back to you, my Flower of the Prairie, and I won't be leaving you again.*

ISTAKA STRAIGHTENED from skinning the buffalo. *This is not man's work,* he thought. *It is for women.* But looking across the prairie, he saw other braves helping their wives.

It was late in the season, and his failed search for the mountain man had cost them time. Because of him, they had needed to stay longer on the hunting grounds and follow the buffalo farther south. Now it would cost more time to return to their home many moons to the east. The tribe had had terrible fortune on this hunt. Three braves, two with families, had died so far, and that number didn't include all those who had been killed by the mountain men, though their deaths were not his fault. In fact, if they had listened to him and not stopped to celebrate and eat mule, they would still be alive. But the tribe blamed him and his incessant desire for revenge on the Pawnee Killer. He spat at the thought of the name. *If only the Pawnee Killer were dead, killed by the great Istaka.*

He was staring at his skinning knife.

"Istaka!" His wife had stopped her work and was glaring at him. "What is wrong with you?"

It was not the soft voice he had fallen in love with during the courtship ritual. Now it was sharp, biting. This was the voice he was hearing more often, and it was working on his nerves. He whipped around, raising his hand. It was unfortunate, the hand he raised was the one with the knife in it. Her eyes grew wide, those beautiful brown eyes. He saw fear. Fear from the woman he loved. He immediately dropped his hand and turned back to the buffalo.

When she spoke this time, her voice was softer, like a leaf drifting to the ground. "Istaka, you must stop thinking of this white man. He is controlling your mind, and you are frightening me. When you turned, you were so angry I feared you meant to stab me. Is that true?"

He longed to take her in his arms and comfort her, but he couldn't. Silently, he continued working on the buffalo, and finally she too went back to her labors. Istaka continued with his knife until the hide was free of the carcass. He was done. The women would take care of the meat and body parts.

Straightening, he saw Chayton talking to someone, then his friend leaped on his horse, turned the bay, and galloped toward him. Nearing, Istaka could see the excitement on his friend's face. Chayton yanked the bay to a stop. "Keme is with the chief. He has seen three white men moving south. It appears you are blessed with luck. He thinks it is the same white men who killed so many of our braves. The chief wants a war party to wipe these killers from the earth. He wants you to join it. Hurry."

Istaka raced to his horse. Reaching it, he leaped onto the animal's back and kicked it hard in the sides, driving the buck-skin forward until they were hurtling across the prairie. He ignored the thought of gopher holes, for he knew he would be protected. His nemesis was near, and after all these years, his opportunity to avenge his father was finally here. It took little time to reach the chief's lodge, but there were already at least twenty-five, maybe thirty braves armed, mounted, and ready to fight. The horses stomped and snorted, feeling the energy from their riders.

The chief stood, waving for him to hurry. *He has his bow,* he thought. *Is he leading this party?* He slid the horse to a stop nearly on top of the chief.

Jumping out of the horse's path, the chief shouted at Istaka, "The Pawnee Killer has been seen by Keme. Come, we are going to kill your devil and make sure he is dead at last. We will avenge the Pawnee people and bring peace to our tribe." He swept his arm over the excited men. "These brave fighters will ride with us, and we will bring back the white men's horses and supplies and their scalps, especially the scalp of Pawnee Killer. This will cleanse the evil spirit that has been tearing at you." He threw his arm up, pointed west, and swung aboard his horse. "Come, you will bring back the Pawnee Killer's hair!"

Istaka let out a chilling whoop, joined in by the others, and with Keme on one side of the chief and him on the other, pride swelled his heart. The sight of so many noble warriors riding with him was more than he had ever hoped for. They would at last see him kill the white man. *I am riding toward my destiny. Today is my day.*

Istaka and the Pawnee braves galloped west.

As usual, Shorty was busy expounding his opinion. This time, it dealt with the reason President Harrison had been in office for only a month. The new president's sudden death so soon after his inauguration had been a shock to the nation, but as usual, those who knew the least had the loudest opinions. Shorty was busy blasting his friends with his. "I'm telling you, Floyd, Tyler had President Harrison killed. It's one of those conspiracy things for sure."

Floyd grunted. Over the long time he had known his friend, who was a good friend, he had learned the best response to a Shorty opinion was a grunt. Anything more committal would dig the listener into a deeper conversation that would never end. He glanced over at Morg, who was half asleep, swaying in the saddle almost as badly as he had when they left Fort John. Floyd felt sure his friend would drink himself to death before he hit forty. But after a day of riding, he had gotten back to normal and showed no long-term effects.

They had been trailing the Akers bunch for almost two weeks and found themselves in the foothills of the eastern slopes of the Rockies near the prairie. Floyd preferred traveling in the mountains. The pines and aspen, brush and boulders provided excellent cover, but out here, he felt naked.

The prairie, especially near the mountains, wasn't completely open. Juniper helped break up outlines, and the creeks and draws usually had trees and other vegetation along them, so a rider wasn't completely naked on a flat plain, but Floyd never felt as secure as he did in the mountains. Granted, the Utes could hide behind the tall pines or thick aspen, but he still preferred the mountains.

He stretched his stiff muscles as Buck slogged along in the afternoon sunshine. The days were perfect now. Gone was the sweltering heat, replaced by cool, pleasant breezes. However, the nights were getting downright cold. He yearned for his teepee and the warmth of Leotie. *Soon,* he thought. *Soon.* He glanced at Morg again, and his tall friend was sound asleep with Shorty riding next to him, still talking up a storm. Floyd grinned, shook his head, and turned to check their back trail.

The sight sent a shock through him. Only five or six hundred yards behind them, a horde of Indians was racing toward them. "Morg! Wake up. Indians." He did a quick wrap of the leads for Rusty and Browny, and kicked Buck in his sides. The buckskin leaped forward.

His friends responded as quickly. Shorty shut up, Morg jerked awake, and both of their mounts leaped out alongside Floyd.

Shorty yelled, "Where'd they come from?"

Morg, whose tall frame now leaned forward over his mount,

the wind whipping his long hair, shouted, "Who cares? They're here now."

In the time it took to spot the Indians and accelerate, their pursuers gained a hundred yards on them.

Morg yelled, "Where to?"

"The boulders ahead and to the right," Floyd shouted. He had spotted a patch of red boulders about three hundred yards ahead. It looked to be a good defensive position, but good or not, they needed something, and they needed it now. Their horses wouldn't last long. The trip had taken a toll on the horses and mule, and they wouldn't last long. Floyd had been hoping this ordeal would be over soon and the animals would get plenty of rest and feed, but there would be no rest now.

They were closing on the boulders, but the Indians were also closing on them. Their pursuers had narrowed the distance to less than two hundred yards, and he could hear the whoops of confidence behind him. Floyd flipped the leather loops from the hammers of his Patersons draped in holsters across his saddle. A minute later, they dashed through a gap in the rocks.

The mountain men yanked their horses to a stop, leaped from them, and pulled their weapons from their scabbards. Floyd shouted, "Morg, tie the animals," while he was sliding the two Patersons on his saddle behind his pistol belt. His Colt ring rifle leaped to his shoulder as he turned toward the Indians, recognizing the tribe. "They're Pawnees. What the blazes are they still doing out this far west?" He wished he had pulled his Ryland. Their pursuers were still too far for the revolving rifle.

But they weren't too far for Shorty's Hawken. He had yanked the rifle from its scabbard before hitting the ground, and the instant his feet touched earth, it found his shoulder. Smoke blossomed, and Floyd saw one of the Pawnees' bodies snap erect, then drop to the ground.

Morg quickly tied the animals to a line of sagebrush and leaped to a boulder for cover near the horses, where Floyd and

Shorty had located. They couldn't take any chances of the Indians getting their mounts. Not like they had before. The Pawnees were still out of range for Floyd's rifle, but while Shorty was reloading, Morg threw the Hawken to his shoulder and fired. Another Pawnee fell, the bloody wound visible in the big man's chest.

Shorty, always the talker, yelled, "Two down, too many to go!" Once again, he asked, "Where the blazes did all them fellers come from? There must be a hunert out there."

Standing behind one of the boulders and reloading, Morg replied, "Thirty. You never could count."

18

F loyd pursed his lips and raised the ring rifle. They were in range now, turning their horses to circle the rocks and presenting side views, harder to hit but closer. He recognized the Pawnee who had shot him. The man had slowed his horse when he turned and had his rifle thrust high in the air. Floyd settled the front sight just below his armpit and squeezed the trigger. The rifle roared, sending the ball on its destructive mission. However, a moment before he fired, one of the Indians next to his target spurred his horse forward, and the bullet struck him at the point of his shoulder. Floyd could see the man topple as he pulled the ring in front of the rifle's trigger guard, cocking the hammer and rotating another cartridge into the ready position.

He took aim at another attacker. Shorty and Morg fired almost at the same time, sounding like an echo, except very loud, and one of the Pawnees rolled from his horse. Shorty immediately began berating Morg even as he was reloading his rifle. "You long drink of water, how many times do I have to tell you, don't shoot at my targets? Pick yore own."

The Pawnees had disappeared over a ridge.

Morg ignored Shorty while he reloaded and kept an eye out for attackers. "How many's that down?"

"Four," Floyd said, giving the animals a quick once-over. They were fine, pulling at the sparse grass and seemingly unfazed. He scanned the countryside in all directions, watching for any sign of his enemy.

ISTAKA WAS BESIDE HIMSELF. They should have continued the charge. With the number of men they had, it would have been simple, but the chief had swung them away and had now dismounted. Istaka dropped off his horse and stormed to his leader. "We must attack. Now. It will be over in minutes. There are only three of them. We will kill them, and it will be over."

The chief stepped close and shoved his face near Istaka's. "How many of our brothers have already fallen in this attack?"

Istaka stared at the chief as if he were crazy.

"Answer me, Istaka. How many have already died?"

Dust had boiled up around them when they pulled their horses to a stop and dismounted. The horses' sides heaved from exertion, and their bodies glistened. He could smell the dust and sweat of the animals. It was an odor he loved. He remembered riding with his father and smelling the same odor. His father used to tell him after running his horse, "Be sure to give him water after he has cooled, for horses sweat much when they are running." *My father was a great man,* he thought.

The chief leaned closer, his nose almost touching Istaka's. "If you do not answer me, I may kill you myself."

Istaka stood tall and stared at the chief. He shook his head defiantly as he spoke, his voice touched with scorn. "I do not know. I was attacking the white men."

"It is the duty of a leader to know. Four of your friends have died at the hands of the white men. Our number of braves is thinned even further. Would you have us attack again, knowing the white men will kill more of our brave men before they die?"

Istaka stared down his hawk nose at his chief. "Isn't it also the duty of a leader to win battles? It's only three scrawny white men."

The chief's eyes narrowed. "Your madness has blinded you. I will have no more braves die over this man. We will go home." He turned toward his horse.

Dumbfounded, Istaka's mind raced like a running buffalo. *He can't make us quit. We are so close. We can overrun them and kill them. Pawnee Killer will be dead forever. I will gouge his eyes out and cut his head from his body so he can never see again and will wander without sight and thought forever.* "No. Let me fight him. I have seen how he fights, and I can beat him. It is my right."

The chief turned and stared at Istaka. "You would fight this white man?"

"Yes, knives. I will fight him with my knife and will take his life from him, then I will gouge out his eyes and cut his head from his body."

He saw shock on the chief and on the faces of his friends.

The chief strode back to him. "Would you do this to another warrior?"

"Him. I would do it to him."

A single nod greeted his remark. "And you will fight him with a knife, you and him, no other. I will give the white men my word we will not attack them if you are killed. Do you agree?"

Istaka was tired of talking. His body ached for combat. He was ready. *I am at my peak,* he thought. *The white man will learn what it is to fight a warrior who cannot be tricked.* "Yes, yes. I agree. Let me fight him now. There has been too much talking." He turned to the braves watching him. "My brothers, I can kill this man. I have seen him fight. He killed my father by trickery, which will not work with me. However, if he should be lucky and take my life, let him and his friends go free, for I will be happy in having tried to avenge my father. I will greet him with pride." He turned back to the chief. "I am ready."

The chief's dark brown eyes examined him once more. "You are a willful, single-minded man, Istaka. But you are also a brave man. Mount your horse, and ride beside me."

He turned to the rest of the braves. "Ride behind us and do not raise your weapons. I do not believe these white men will shoot. If this man accepts Istaka's challenge, we will remain well away. We will not surround them, and we will harm no one if they agree to this fight, and if they do not agree, we will still not fight. We have lost too many braves. Each of those who are left must return to their wives and families." He made eye contact with every man. "I have spoken." With his last remark, he mounted his horse and, with Istaka alongside, rode over the hill.

Istaka sat tall in the saddle. Now that he had a plan, his heart was calm. If the white man shot him, it would be shown they were cowardly, and the remainder of the braves would overrun them. But with his chief, he believed they would hold their fire.

FLOYD WATCHED the band of Pawnees slowly appear from behind the hill. There were two in front, with the rest behind the leaders.

Shorty shook his head. "What the blue blazes is going on now?"

They closed the distance until stopping to sit motionless roughly twenty-five yards from the waiting muzzles. Their weapons were down with no threatening action from either of the two leaders or the braves behind them. The group sat stoic, waiting.

Morg lowered his rifle and looked at Floyd. "I swear I think they want to talk. It don't make sense to me. With the number of braves out there, we could be buzzard bait in a matter of minutes."

"Agreed," Floyd said, "but I sure don't have any idea what else it could be." He stood, handed his rifle to Shorty, and checked his pistols one last time. "Shorty, I've fired two shots out of this rifle, so it has six remaining. There's one in the barrel, ready to go. Just pull the trigger. All you need to do after that is pull the ring back and fire. If it doesn't jam, it'll fire all six before it's empty." He handed Morg the two Patersons in his belt. "You've fired these things. If it comes to it, pull the hammer back, and the trigger will drop. Five shots and you're done. Hopefully, you won't need them."

Morg examined the two pistols and shoved them behind his waistband. "As much as I like shooting these two hoglegs, I'm sure hoping I don't have to draw 'em this time, because if I do, we're all dead men."

Shorty, still sitting and his back against the boulder, looked up at his tall friend. "Morg, you are about the most negative feller I think I've ever met. Them Pawnee want to palaver. That's a good thing. They could be lifting our hair right now. Be thankful for what you got."

Floyd couldn't help but laugh. Shorty calling Morg negative was like a grizzly calling a black bear dangerous. Then he stepped into the open. "Morg, how's your Pawnee?"

"It's mighty good."

"Good. Mine's a little rusty. I might give it a shot, but jump right in if you need to. Now come on. Let's get this done. Luck, Shorty."

Morg looked down at his friend as if seeing him for the last time. "It's been a good ride, pardner." He stepped beside Floyd.

The two men strode to what could be certain death.

Floyd inhaled the fresh air. The breeze was at their backs, blowing the horses' dust away from them and bringing the tangy smell of sage and rabbitbrush with a hint of the distant pines. A puffy white cloud drifted across the azure blue sky. High above them, a lone bald eagle, wings set, sailed, always hunting.

Reaching the braves, Floyd stopped and watched the eagle, thinking, *You welcomed me to the mountains so many years ago.* A faint smile drifted across his face. *This is a good day, live or die.* He lowered his eyes to the older man, who was examining him closely. Floyd's face turned solemn, and he remained silent. *These fellas called this dance. They should start it.*

The silence had turned heavy when the older man, obviously the chief, focused on Floyd and said, "You are Pawnee Killer?"

Floyd gave a single nod.

The chief asked, "How did you get the name of killer of my people?"

Morg looked at Floyd. "Did you understand that?"

"He's asking how I got the name?"

Morg nodded.

Floyd began his explanation of being given the name by Comanche Chief Black Hand, but said in Pawnee, "I pee many times in the daylight."

At first, the chief frowned in confusion, and then his face went blank as he obviously strove to keep a straight face. Behind him, his warriors weren't so concerned. Several chuckled.

Floyd stopped and turned to Morg. "Is there a problem?"

"Why don't you let me translate? Yore Pawnee is a little rusty."

"If you think it's necessary."

Morg gave an emphatic nod. "I do." He turned to the chief and began speaking in fluent Pawnee while motioning to Floyd. "This here is Floyd Logan, and Chief Black Hand of the Comanche gave him the name after he told him how he received the long scar on his face."

The chief's mouth pulled down at the corners. Though he continued to hold Floyd's gaze, he turned his head slightly and spat. "Comanche, bah! So you did not make the name for yourself?"

Morg told him what the chief had said.

Floyd shook his head emphatically and began his explanation

in English with Morg translating. "I would not insult the Pawnee or any other great tribe by taking such a name. Once Chief Black Hand said the name, it spread like fire across the prairie. I could not contain it."

"Tell me how you received the scar."

Morg relayed, "I fought the brave Pawnee, who was much too good for my young skills. He would have killed me, for I was bleeding much from his many knife cuts."

As Morg translated, several of the braves nodded, for that was one way they had been taught to best an opponent who was equally good with a knife. Many cuts brought substantial blood loss until the opponent weakened and slowed to where a fatal thrust could not be blocked.

Floyd continued, "Only because of luck was I able to best him, but he left me with this." He slowly ran his finger down the long, thin scar on his left cheek. His mind returned to the fight where he had come so close to losing his life. The face of the brave he fought came back clearly, and he suddenly stopped, his head turning to the young brave sitting next to the chief.

The man was about Floyd's age, bigger, maybe two inches taller, and thicker in the chest and arms, especially since Floyd had lost so much weight. He was the same one who had shot at him and nearly killed him at the attack where the Pawnees had stolen their horses, and who had so doggedly followed him into the mountains. *It couldn't be,* he thought, *but it is.* Floyd nodded at the fierce, angry man. "You are the son of the man I killed."

Floyd could see the hate in the dark brown eyes that stared hard at him. *No wonder he has been so relentless,* he thought. *I would've been the same.*

For the first time, the man spoke. "I am Istaka, son of the brave leader whose life you took by a little boy's trick. If you are not a coward, I will fight and kill you this day."

Morg translated, but Floyd had already gotten the gist of the statement. The man wanted to kill him.

The chief gave Istaka a stern look and turned back to Floyd. "That is why we do not kill you and your friends. Istaka has the right to challenge you to a fight to the death. No matter who wins, your friends will come to no harm. You have my word."

Morg finished translating. "Listen, Floyd. You don't need to do this. We can take a bunch of these fellers with us. I can tell you Shorty and I don't want you fighting for us. Anyway, look at the feller. He's well fed and strong, while you've gotten scrawny as a rail."

"Thanks for the vote of confidence, Morg. Tell him I accept."

Morg hesitated.

"Tell him, Morg."

Istaka gave a grim smile when he heard his challenge had been accepted. The Pawnee chief nodded to him, and he threw his right leg over the saddle, jumped to the ground, and drew his knife.

Again the chief spoke, laying out the rules, which amounted to no rules at all.

Morg relayed the instructions to Floyd, who had passed him his gunbelt and hat and now pulled his shirt over his head. He tossed it to his friend. At the sight of the scars scattered across his head and upper body, an indistinct murmur coursed among the braves.

With Morg holding his gear, Floyd grasped the knife sheath on his belt and slid the fighting blade from its thick leather protection. Again, there was an indistinct murmur among the warriors.

Morg looked his friend over from head to toe. "You ready?"

Floyd grinned. "About as ready as I'll ever be. You can tell them."

Turning from Morg, Floyd faced the chief and Istaka, who stood next to his leader's horse. One of the other braves had ridden forward and taken Istaka's animal.

The chief made an abrupt closing motion with his hands, and

Istaka burst into a run toward Floyd. Lontac had taught him about sudden attacks, and Floyd stood with his hands at his sides, his knife hanging from his right hand. He watched the bigger man charge, closing the distance like an enraged buffalo bull. The first change he saw was the bunching of the muscles in Istaka's right shoulder. He told himself, *Right now, this fella is operating on adrenaline. He hasn't switched on his brain yet. If I'm going to kill him, now's the time, before he thinks, but I really don't want to kill him. I've harmed this family enough.*

Floyd waited until the last second and stepped clear of his opponent's thrust. The Pawnee brave's full right side was exposed. Floyd could have ended the fight with a single deep thrust, but his knife never moved from his side, still hanging straight down.

Istaka spun and charged again. This time, Floyd sidestepped to his left and, ensuring Istaka's knife was clear, drove his left fist into the side of the man's head, knocking him to the ground. Istaka slid close enough to a prickly pear patch to pick up some needles in his knees, but ignored the sharp thorns and leaped to his feet. He spun on Floyd. This was twice Floyd could have ended the fight, but he refused to make a killing thrust. The knife still hung in his right hand.

The Pawnee's chest rose and fell rapidly, sucking in the fresh prairie air. His eyes searched Floyd's face, no longer filled with uncontrolled anger, now calming, calculating. Knife hanging down like Floyd's, he began to slowly advance toward the mountain man. This time, Floyd could see the man was thinking.

In the Pawnee audience, a murmur again ran through them, and several of the older heads nodded. When Istaka raised his blade, Floyd, for the first time, raised his. There would be no trickery this time, only skill. Istaka began to move to his left, his knife making small circles in the air. *I need to go to work*, Floyd thought. *Keep him off balance.* He had made no attack thus far and could see from Istaka's movements, the Pawnee was expecting none.

He moved. Like a viper's tongue, the eleven-inch blade flicked out, leaving a long slash along the length of Istaka's forearm. Before the man could register the pain and surprise, Floyd struck again, this time marking the Pawnee with a deep slash across his left bicep. The blade was razor sharp on both sides, and Floyd lifted it a bit and, in drawing it back, left a red line along Istaka's neck. Stepping back, Floyd again dropped the knife to his side, waiting.

lood dripped from both of Istaka's arms and his neck. Floyd could see the shock in the man's eyes. He remembered Lontac's words during his first session with the small but deadly Filipino. Lontac had said, "I see your movements as if you are walking in mud." That was what he was seeing with the Pawnee. The man, so far, hadn't shown him anything other than understandable rage. Much like he had been when he began learning from Lontac. Floyd watched Istaka, motionless. Now he began moving, his eyes constantly evaluating his opponent. As he moved, he pushed Istaka into moving.

Floyd feinted another slash. Istaka was quick to block the move, but Floyd's knife was not there. The blade was busy slashing another long gash along his bicep. *I don't want to kill you, but you can't keep giving me this type of opening.*

Istaka was quicker this time. Blades rang as Floyd blocked what would have been a nasty jab if his blade had not been there. *You're getting better,* Floyd thought, *but you're bleeding quite a bit. I could just wait until you pass out.* But Floyd knew that in a knife fight, a fighter can't sit back and coast, or he'll be chewing on a steel sandwich.

He tossed his knife to his left hand and immediately went in low, drawing Istaka's blade down. Floyd hit him again with a horrendous right to the temple. The Pawnee dropped to his knees, falling forward, his forehead resting on the ground. He was out cold.

Keeping a wary eye on the man, Floyd turned to the chief. The chief's eyes were wide with surprise and maybe a touch of admiration. Morg stepped forward while two braves dismounted and jogged to Istaka's motionless, bloody body. Each man grasped an arm, lifted his limp form, and carried him to his horse. He regained consciousness as they neared the animal.

Istaka's head jerked up. He shook it and looked around. His arms and neck were bleeding profusely. Floyd could see the weakness setting in. The two braves tried to lift him into his saddle, and he pushed them away, turning to Floyd. The hate was still there, and unfortunately, Floyd could see the lust for his blood. There was no gratitude for being alive, only hate. The two men helping him had placed his knife back in its scabbard, but he yanked it out and yelled at the chief.

Finally, the chief spoke to Morg while watching Floyd. Morg, his head shaking, looked at Floyd. "Istaka wants to continue the fight. I ain't normally one to tell anybody what to do, but Floyd, you can't save him. Look at those eyes. That's pure hatred. My guess is you're gonna have to finish him. I think that's what the chief wants. From their conversation, I gather that Istaka's lust for killing you has cost the tribe plenty. What do you want to do?"

Floyd didn't have to think. He knew the only way to end this was to finish Istaka. "Tell him I'm ready." His knife had hung from his right hand throughout the fight, but now, turning to the Pawnee, he brought the bloody blade up. He had been kidding himself about saving this man. He was eaten up with hate, and Floyd had no desire for that hate to get near Leotie or Mika or, for that matter, the tribe.

Morg stepped out of the way, and Istaka strode to Floyd.

Blood covered most of his body. It ran along both arms and dripped from his fingers. *His knife hilt must be tough to hang onto,* Floyd thought. He prepared for the man's rush, but it didn't come. Istaka strode within striking distance, just out of Floyd's reach. The Pawnee stood motionless, knife up, point toward Floyd. He made a feint and slipped on a rock.

Floyd knew it was up to him to end this, but he had no desire to kill this son of the father he had also killed, but here was his opening. His opponent's knife swung back and away from the conflict while he struggled to maintain his balance. Floyd started forward with his knife, but jerked to a halt. The thought hit him, *I'm being suckered just like I suckered his father. Where is my mind? I should've seen that a mile off.* He rocked up onto the balls of his feet while, at the same time, snatching back the blade. Even as he began withdrawing his knife, the opportunity closed, and Istaka slashed down with his blade. His knife struck sparks as it glanced off Floyd's blade just in front of the guard. *Thank you, Lontac,* Floyd thought. *Another second in catching the ruse, and that blade would have severed my wrist.*

The Pawnee's face twisted in rage. He leaped forward, lifting his blade to slash across Floyd's throat. The last thing Floyd expected was for Istaka to try to leap at him from an off-balance position.

Their bodies were close together. Floyd dodged Istaka's blade and had time only to lift his knifepoint.

He was shocked. Tides could change quickly in a knife fight, but thanks to Lontac, Floyd would live to fight another day. The Pawnee had leaped forward and, in so doing, impaled himself on Floyd's knife. It was almost as if the man was trying to kill himself, and at the last, the Pawnee appeared to be seeing past Floyd. Gripping his opponent's arms, he laid the big man gently on the ground.

Several braves rushed to him, but the warrior was gone, and Istaka's last grimace of pain was combined with a smile, which remained on his face. Four of the braves who rushed over to him bent to lift him to his horse, but when they saw his smile, they stopped, looked closer, then turned to their chief and spoke.

The older man walked his horse until he could look down on the dead brave. He stared at Istaka. At last he spoke to the braves standing around the dead man, and they lifted him, laying him across his saddle. No one spoke a word. Silence reigned on the prairie until the chief finally spoke to Floyd. "Floyd Logan, as I promised you, with your friends, you are free to go. You have done Istaka a great favor. His was a troubled spirit. He yearned to be with his father. He is there now and is happy. I thank you for freeing his spirit, but this does not mean we are friends. The Pawnees will always be your enemy. If the Great Spirit smiles on us, we will take your hair before you grow old." He looked at Morg. "And any who rides with you, even if they are friends of the Pawnee, will also die." The chief wheeled his horse and walked him northeast, while the others, leading Istaka's mount, on which rode the brave's body, followed.

Floyd stood frozen to the spot, watching the Pawnee braves shrink into the horizon. Morg grabbed his arm, yanking him out of his trance of exhaustion, and the two of them walked slowly to the boulders. In his mind, Floyd could hear the Pawnee chief's promise playing over and over.

Reaching the boulders, Floyd stepped behind them and sank to the ground, exhausted. Shorty was at their sides, handing each man a canteen. Floyd turned his head up and felt the water cool his parched throat. After a couple of swigs, he looked at his friends. "Did you see his last move?"

Shorty was the first to speak. "I saw it clear as a mountain stream. That feller leaped right on yore knife. I never seen such a thing before in my whole lifetime."

Morg's head was bobbing up and down. "Shorty's exactly right. This is one of those times we agree. That feller jumped right on your blade, and Floyd, he had a smile on his face. I know it's crazy, but he was smiling and looking beyond you. I swear he was seeing into eternity." Morg looked first at Floyd and then at his partner. "I mean it. I know it sounds crazy, but that feller was seeing something besides us." He headed for his horse. Getting there, he unfastened one side of his saddlebags and pulled out a bottle of firewater. He looked back at Shorty and Floyd. "Sorry, fellers, I need a drink right now." He turned the bottle up and let the burning liquid pour down his throat. His Adam's apple jerked up and down three times before he brought the bottle down, shoved the cork back into the mouth, and slapped it tight. "Whew, that'll help."

Floyd knew it wouldn't help, especially when there were hostiles near, but he said nothing. The entire scene had spooked all three of them, and then the chief's promise, or curse. He shook his head and thought, *I was just a kid, defending myself, when those Pawnees jumped us at the old post office. I wasn't looking for trouble, but the Pawnees have been after me ever since that day, and it looks like for the rest of my life.* He took another swig of his water, closed the canteen, and stood. The afternoon was cooling, and they had to get moving. He gazed toward the mountains and smiled. *I guess a man's got to take a little bitter with the sweet.* A picture of Leotie drifted into his mind, and his smile widened. *I've got more sweet in my life than any man deserves.*

Shorty pulled the stopper from his canteen. "What the blue blazes are you smiling about? Wash that blood off yore arms and hands, and make it quick. We gotta get moving. Them Pawnees could change their minds any time."

Floyd held his hands out while Shorty poured. It took only a few pours, and he was clear of Istaka's blood. "Thanks, Shorty." He slipped his shirt over his head, picked up his gunbelt, and swung it around his waist. Once fastened, he picked up his knife from the grass, and Shorty poured water over it. As he cleaned, he admired the workmanship of the weapon. It had saved his life on several occasions. He owed Nathan more than he could ever repay. There was a small nick where Istaka's blade had slashed down on his. He ran his thumb over the rough spot. He'd have to take the whetstone to it when he had time.

The horses and Browny stood eyeing the water as Shorty poured. Floyd strode to Browny's packsaddle and lifted the water bag. "Shame on me for leaving you boys thirsty," he said to Browny, and poured water into his hat. The mule thrust its nose into his hat, almost pushing it from Floyd's hand as he drank. Floyd repeated his efforts with Buck and Rusty. When he finished with Rusty, he returned to Browny and watered the animals for a second round. Shorty and Morg were mirroring his efforts. In a short time, all of their animals had quenched their thirst. They would camp tonight along a clear mountain stream, and everyone could slake their thirst as often as they liked.

Floyd switched his gear to Rusty, pulled the cinch tight, tied it, dropped the stirrup, and swung into the saddle. Shorty and Morg were right behind him. The three of them rode to the edge of the boulders and scanned the countryside. Floyd turned to his saddlebags to unfasten one side.

Shorty shook his head. "Floyd, I swear, you use that there spyglass more'n you do yore eyes. What's the matter with you, boy, you going blind? We waste more traveling time while you look than any three mountain men I know."

Floyd grinned at his friend. "Yeah, but this *spyglass* has saved your bacon several times." Shorty spit, but said nothing as Floyd pulled the telescope from its case and extended it. He first swept the prairie, then slowly worked his way into the lower foothills. The telescope jerked to a halt, and Floyd leaned forward, his smile so wide his teeth shone in the sunlight.

Both men had been watching him, and when the telescope halted, they too leaned forward, squinting. Shorty couldn't wait for Floyd to relay the information. "Well, come on, Floyd, what are you lookin' at? More Indians?"

Floyd's smile widened even more into a huge grin. "How'd you boys like to sit down to a big buffalo steak tonight?"

A frown creased Shorty's face, wrinkling his brow. "Don't fun with us. What do you see?"

"I'm looking at the Shoshone tribe moving north."

Both of his friends let out a whoop. Morg was the impatient one. "What are we waiting for?" He kicked his horse in the flanks and tore out of the boulders, Shorty right behind him. Floyd brought up the rear. He felt his heart soar like the eagle he had seen earlier before the fight. In no time, he would see his beautiful Leotie. With thoughts of her riding with him, he clucked to Rusty, and his game red mustang bolted after Morg and Shorty.

They rode and rode, slowing their horses to a walk. *That's the thing about this open country,* he thought, *everything is farther away than it looks.* Finally, they drew close enough to see individuals and animals, close enough to confirm it was his family.

Pallaton had elected to travel north on the plains instead of cutting across the mountains. Though longer, it was definitely an easier trek. The masses of buffalo provided them the opportunity to constantly fill their larder as they traveled, but Floyd wondered about the chief's change of heart. Usually, when he made a decision, he stuck to it. A twinge of concern touched him. Had something happened?

He had also hoped they would be farther north. If they didn't maintain a good pace from here, winter would catch them, and the snow could get so heavy they would have to stop. He decided that for now he would think only good thoughts, for he would soon see Mika and his Leotie. Riders broke from the scattered mass of people and animals and sped toward them.

As they drew near, Floyd laughed out loud. Kajika led the group, and alongside him was Mika. In the past months, the boy had grown taller and filled out. He was only thirteen, but he was developing thicker shoulders already, and he rode with the abandon of youth. *Ah,* Floyd thought, *it is good to be home.* Then a touch of sadness found him. *But we have left home. We will no longer live in my beautiful valley.* Floyd knew, whether from a medicine man's dream or not, it made sense for the Shoshone to live together, but he suddenly realized he didn't like it. He loved his valley and had no desire to leave it. Tucked between the Sangre de Cristos and the Greenhorn mountains, it was the perfect home place.

He pushed the thought out of his mind. Mika galloped to him, yanked his horse to a stop, leaped off, and ran the remaining ten yards. Floyd leaned, kicked his foot from the stirrup, caught his bounding son, and wrapped him in his arms.

His heart sang with the closeness and smell of the boy. He had missed him almost as much as his mother.

Mika, arms around Floyd, pounded on his back. "You have returned. You can now be with us on our trip."

Floyd shook his head and pushed the boy back so he could look at him. "No, we're not finished yet, but soon." He watched the boy's face cloud over, his excitement replaced with a frown. Changing the subject, Floyd continued, "Look at you. You're looking more like a man every day." He grabbed a thickening shoulder. "What have you been doing? Look at those shoulders."

"I have been helping much in our preparation and travels. Chief Kajika has shown me many things. Oh, I must tell you about my coup celebration. I—"

Kajika, leading Mika's horse, rode close. "Mika, I need to talk to Igasho. You can tell him later about the celebration. Mount up."

Mika, a bit deflated, gave Floyd a parting grin. "I will tell you later. Now I will tell Ma of our meeting." He jumped to the ground, ran to his horse, leaped onto its back, and raced back to the tribe.

Floyd watched him for a moment and extended his arm to Kajika. The two friends shook hands, enjoying the moment of greeting.

Kajika looked to Morg and Shorty. "It is good to see you. You have been on a long trail."

Morg nodded. "Howdy, Chief, hopefully not much longer."

Shorty, unlike himself, only said, "Howdy. What's Jeb up to?"

Floyd asked, "Where is your father? I would expect him also, unless he is busy."

Kajika's face grew solemn. "He is dead, killed by the Apache shortly after you left. I believe they were part of the group that was after Wirasuap when you rescued him. They too are dead now. My mother died a few days later. It was her wish. She wanted to be with her husband."

Floyd felt a deep loss, for it was Pallaton who had brought him, an injured man, to their village after he had killed the bear, and it was Nina and Leotie who had doctored him when he was delirious with fever from his injuries. "I am sorry."

Kajika nodded. "As am I. We still needed her, especially for this long trek, but without my father, she lost her will to live. She stopped eating. We could barely get her to drink. It did not take long before she was gone, but she is happy now, and I am happy for the two of them. The time will come when I too will join them, and we will hunt and fish together again."

They rode toward the tribe in silence, then Floyd turned to his friend. "Who is the tribal chief?"

Kajika gave a small tilt of his head, and a grin hit his lips for only a moment. "I am. The committee elected me."

The Shoshone had turned their horses around, and the group walked the animals toward the approaching tribe. Kajika and Floyd rode side by side. Floyd grasped Kajika's forearm and squeezed. "Good. You will be a fine chief."

"I will think about what my father would do. That will help me, and I have the shaman for advice, and the elders."

Floyd nodded. "But only one can decide."

"That is true. Father taught me to listen to advice from those who know, but decide for myself. I wish I could have told him how much I respected him."

"He was a great man. I owe him more than I can say, but you are a great man and will become a great leader."

Kajika's wide chest expanded with a deep breath. He exhaled and looked across the prairie. "Shorty asked about Jeb. He is trailing the men you hunt."

20

Floyd abruptly pulled Rusty to a stop and stared at Kajika. "What? They've been near the tribe? Did they harm Leotie? Is she safe? Where can I find them?"

"Slowly, my friend. Leotie is safe, and they did not harm her, though they do know her name and know about her. Later, we can talk, and I will tell you how we found out."

Floyd's heart beat so hard it felt like it would explode. *If any harm comes to Leotie or Mika because I shirked my duty and didn't take care of the Akers back in Tennessee, I'll never forgive myself.*

They were approaching the tribe when Floyd saw a figure running toward them, her skirt flying. He handed the lead ropes for Browny and Buck to Morg and clucked Rusty into a gallop. His mind was consumed with the slim figure, arms out, racing toward him. Nearing her, he slowed Rusty to a fast lope and aimed slightly to Leotie's left. *She's beautiful,* he thought, her pitch-black braids bouncing with each of her running steps. He leaned to his right. At the last minute, the thought dashed through his mind, *I hope I still have the strength for this.* He kicked his right foot from the stirrup, flung his right arm under her left, and swung her up and to him. Her foot slipped into the stirrup, and her lips found his.

I'm home, he thought. *Wherever she is will be home.* He slowed Rusty and brought him to a stop, turning his body to face her, and wrapped both arms around her, crushing her to him.

"My husband," she gasped, "I can't breathe."

He relaxed his grip, but held her close.

She gave him an impish smile. "You are happy to see me?"

They both laughed. She leaned back to look at him, and her sunny smile died. Concern brought a frown to her smooth brow. "You have lost much weight. Have you been sick?"

"Just a lot of hard traveling. The horses have lost more than me."

"I do not worry about the horses as I worry about you." She noticed dried blood on his cheek. Her slim fingers flitted to the spot, and first the pad of her finger ran lightly over it, then, using a nail, she scraped it from his cheek. "Another's?"

"Yes."

"Good, you can tell me later." She kissed him again.

Jeb's wife, Aiyana, rode past with her baby son, Matto, a knowing smile spread across her full lips.

Floyd nodded to her. "Hello, Aiyana."

"Welcome home, Flo-yd. Mika can stay with us tonight."

Leotie returned the smile. "Thank you."

Kajika rode back with his braves, Morg, and Shorty. He gave the order to halt and set up camp. It was early, but there would be a celebration tonight for Floyd's return.

Floyd slid forward in his saddle, and Leotie swung her long left leg over Rusty and dropped into the saddle behind Floyd, wrapped her arms around her husband, and pulled close. He felt her warmth against him and for the moment was consumed with thoughts of her. She lay her head on his shoulder, and the scent of her hair made him want to turn and wrap her in his arms again, but he rode on. They rode in comfortable silence, each in their own thoughts.

Finally, she released him and pointed toward a teepee-loaded travois. "That is ours."

He swung toward the dun drawing the load. Mika was there and had already begun unloading the horse. Floyd pulled up, gave Leotie a hand down, and swung out of the saddle. Morg and Shorty arrived and pitched in. In no time, the structure was erected, with the entrance facing east for the first glow of morning.

Kajika joined the group. "Morg, you and Shorty will stay with me tonight."

Shorty's face worked into a devilish grin. "Why, thanks, Chief, but we had a hankerin' to stay with Floyd and Leotie tonight. It's been so long since we've seen her."

Leotie looked up and gave Kajika a sweet smile. Morg and Shorty were good friends and had helped to rescue Mika from the Blackfoot. She loved them dearly, but not tonight. "I would not be in trouble if I slit two trappers' throats tonight, would I?"

Kajika thought for a moment, shook his head, and said, "No, I think it might be warranted."

Shorty didn't miss a beat. "On second thought, Chief, we'd be mighty pleased at spending the night in yore teepee."

Floyd spoke up. "That's good, boys, because if she didn't, I would. I can't stand Shorty's snoring."

Shorty frowned. "Now that was uncalled for." He turned to his horse and began talking to it.

Morg grinned. "He's a mite sensitive about his snoring." He glanced at Kajika. "But you might want to make him sleep in the bachelors' tent. He's mighty loud."

Kajika laughed. "Then I might slit his throat."

Everyone laughed but Shorty. He continued unloading his horse in silence.

Kajika grew serious. To the three men, he said, "We need to talk. I have word of Jeb."

Floyd hugged his wife close. "I'll be back."

"Go, husband. I will be waiting."

Mika stepped up and waved his arm, encompassing all the animals, including Morg's and Shorty's. "Pa, I can take care of the horses."

Floyd placed his hand on his son's shoulder. "There's too many for you. We'll be back soon and give you a hand."

"Do not worry. I too have friends. We will give the horses good care."

Floyd squeezed Mika's shoulder. "Thanks, son. I'll see you after a while." He smiled at Leotie over Mika's head and turned to join Kajika, Morg, and Shorty.

The chief's tent had been erected, and he stood aside as they entered, followed, and dropped the flap.

After they were seated, Kajika began. "Jeb is following the Akers. They showed up here two days ago. There were seven of them, including a woman. The leader is an old man. I do not know whether he is crazy or stupid. They rode into camp, and he declared he was looking for Floyd Logan. Leotie stepped forward and said she was your wife. The old man said he was going to kill you and every Logan he could find."

Floyd was leaning forward, anger burning through him. "Did he attempt to harm Leotie?"

Kajika shook his head. "Attempt, yes. Harm, no. You have a brave woman. She stood there defiantly. The old man swung his rifle toward her, and I signaled our braves. Arrows were drawn and hammers cocked throughout the village. Jeb, holding one of the pistols you brought back, stepped from his teepee. He told Akers that if he raised his rifle, he would die. The old man said nothing. He stared at Jeb, lowered the rifle, and rode away. Henry Page was with them. Jeb followed. I wanted to send braves with him, but he declined. He is expecting you."

Floyd began to rise. "We should go help him. We need to finish this."

Kajika placed his hand on Floyd's arm. "Wait, my friend. It will be dark soon. There will be no tracking of Jeb in the dark. Wait until morning. You will have plenty of time."

Shorty leaned toward Floyd. "That's good advice. We won't get anywhere this late. Take the night off. Forget the whole thing. You and Leotie enjoy being with each other. There'll be plenty of killing tomorrow or the next day."

Floyd's legs relaxed, and he returned to a sitting position. "You're right. Jeb will be fine, and we won't find him in the dark."

"Good," Kajika said. "We will celebrate your return tonight with food and dancing. Tomorrow, many braves and I will ride out with you. We will end this chase so that you can return to us and enjoy life."

Floyd shook his head. "Kajika, I would love for you and your braves to join us, but you cannot."

Kajika's brow wrinkled, and his lips tightened. "You tell me I cannot? You are my friend, but do you forget yourself? I am chief of the Shoshone."

A quick thought slashed through Floyd's mind. *I did forget. I'm dealing with a chief now. He's my friend, but I had best be more diplomatic.* "You are right. I say this as advice to a good friend. I do not intend to insult." The tension went out of Kajika's features, and Floyd continued, "The army is becoming more involved in what happens in the west. If word got out that the Shoshone had attacked and killed a group of white men, no matter how bad the white men were, the army would send soldiers. You do not want that. You remember our conversation with Jeb, the shaman, and your father? The Shoshone are known as friends of the white man. Let's keep it that way. Let us take care of this Akers bunch. We'd love your help, but I believe this way would be better."

Kajika solemnly nodded his head. "I see the truth in what you say. I am sorry it is so, but you are right."

Floyd relaxed and grinned. "You mentioned enjoying life. When are you planning on getting married?"

Kajika shook his head. "I do not have time. Maybe after we join our brothers."

Floyd looked at Shorty. "Don't wait too long, my brother. You might find yourself too old and crotchety for any woman to have you."

Shorty watched Floyd. "Are you hurrahing me, boy? You don't want to mess with this old and crotchety man."

Morg snorted and poked his friend in the ribs. "Did you watch the same knife fight I saw?"

Kajika said nothing, but Floyd could see his friend was curious. "Pawnees jumped us, and I killed one. There are Pawnees hunting buffalo to the northeast of here. I don't know how far, but it's close enough that they spotted us, although I don't think they'd be hitting a band of your size."

The chief nodded, waiting for more of the story, but none came.

Shorty couldn't stand it. "Floyd, you're about the worst story-teller I've ever known. Tell Chief Kajika the entire story."

This time, Floyd was seriously irritated. Turning, he shot Shorty a dirty look.

"Don't look at me like that. If you don't, I will."

Floyd turned back to Kajika. "You have a celebration to prepare, right?"

"No. Others are taking care of it." He waited.

Finally, Shorty could wait no longer. He let out a long sigh. "Well, it seems the son of the feller—"

"I'll tell it," Floyd interrupted, and began the tale.

LIGHT from the moon shone through the teepee's smoke hole and played on the buffalo-hide floor. A relaxed Floyd Logan watched the circle of light, thinking how great life was. Leotie's head lay on his chest, her finger drawing circles in his chest hair. "I am a lucky woman, Igasho. You bring big medicine to my teepee."

He chuckled. "I don't know. It was your big medicine that saved my life so many years ago."

A melancholy smile drifted across her face. "Yes, mine and Nina's."

Floyd was sorry he had mentioned her healing him, for it brought Pallaton's and his wife Nina's deaths into their happy presence. But he thought, *Why not? They were a big part of our lives when they were alive, and Pallaton would probably influence him for the rest of his life, much as Nina would Leotie.*

She pressed her face against his chest. "It is hard for me to think of her and Pallaton gone. Oh, I know death comes to us all, but it was so sudden, and I never would have thought Nina could ever just stop living. She was such a strong and vibrant woman as long as Pallaton was alive."

"Did she give up?"

Leotie raised her head so she could look into Floyd's eyes, and shook her head violently. "No. She would never give up. I talked to her. She said she had married her husband to be with him, whether here or in the spirit world, and that's what she was going to do. It wasn't a matter of giving up. It was a choice."

Floyd started to respond, and she laid her finger against his lips and whispered, "No more about Nina and Pallaton or the tribe or even Mika. You leave in the morning. The tribe has celebrated your return, and now it is my turn to continue the celebration." She slid up to him and laid her soft lips against his. The kiss was long.

When they stopped, he grinned at her. "You talked me into it. No more talking about anything or anyone."

~

FLOYD HAD PROVIDED fresh horses for everyone out of his remuda. Over the years, he had increased the number of his animals, and now he had a fine herd. Buck, Rusty, and Browny could take a break and work on adding weight. The march of the village would be slow enough to allow them to graze and recover. Browny stared at Floyd, appearing to accuse him of betrayal, but the poor mule had worked harder than any of the horses. Though the horses had been changed out, Browny had been loaded day after day, and the mule's weight loss confirmed it. The mule was still willing, but Floyd knew Browny was about done in.

He picked out a heavily muscled, steel-dust-gray mustang he had named Steel.

Now, the four of them traveled south, following Jeb's signs. Floyd knew them and could pick them out as he rode along. This was their second day of travel since leaving the village. Floyd had first established the direction the Akers gang was traveling, which was almost due east, then he rode back to Jeb's first marker, a rock and a stick, with the stick appearing to have fallen naturally pointing south. He knew Jeb was circling the Akers bunch, and followed his friend.

They had dropped into a wide, dry wash. It was at least eighty feet wide and fifteen deep and weaved its way southeast. Leotie rode next to Floyd, their knees occasionally touching. A big fight had ensued the night before they left, when she announced she was going with them, and Floyd absolutely forbade it. He gave a snorting laugh now and thought, *A lot of good that did.* At the laugh, Leotie turned to gaze at him, a smile across her face.

Early in the morning before they left, she woke him. He remembered it clearly. The village was silent except for the night sounds. She had said softly, "Flo-yd, are you awake?"

Since a boy, Floyd had always awakened with a clear mind, ready for whatever might come. "I am."

"I have remembered something. I didn't want to ruin our evening, so I waited to tell you." She paused, drawing her face close to his so she could see into his eyes. "You know Akers and his men came to our camp?"

He nodded.

"Henry Page was with them."

He nodded again, waiting.

"When I saw him, a memory suddenly flooded into my mind from when I was captured and in the cabin."

Floyd didn't like the way this was sounding, but he remained quiet. He felt her shudder and slipped his arm around her.

"The memory was of him getting off me and pulling up his pants as I was waking from being knocked out by McMillan."

Floyd's entire body tensed. He felt a knot the size of his fist in his chest and pulled her close. Her face was next to his, and he felt a tear transfer to his cheek. In his mind, all he could see was Page's face swearing he had done nothing to her, that it had just been McMillan.

"I'll take care of him this time. He will never cause any other woman the pain you have endured. I promise you." He wanted so badly to feel Page's neck in his hands.

Her soft voice came out of the darkness. "Flo-yd?"

"Yes?"

"I am going with you. I must see him die. I must know. I need that."

Halfway through her sentence, Floyd began shaking his head. "I'm sorry, but you're needed here. Nina is gone, and you are the only healer."

"The shaman is here."

She pulled away from him, and her voice lost its softness. "Husband, I am going."

In the morning chill, Floyd sat up. "No. You are staying here. It will be too dangerous out there. The Akers bunch are skilled woodsmen. I want you safe."

She yanked the buffalo robe around her and sat up, uncovering Floyd. His body, warmed by the robe and Leotie, was immediately slapped with the frigid mountain air. He grabbed his clothes lying next to him and dressed quickly, then stoked the coals remaining in the fire, dropping a few sticks on the red-hot coals, and then a couple of small logs.

In seconds, flames leaped around the timber, and he felt the warmth. He turned to see his wife still sitting, watching him, the buffalo robe wrapped tight around her, and her long black hair glistening in the firelight. Her eyes appeared to flash in the fire's reflection. There was no smile on her face. It had the same determined look as when she'd insisted she head north with them to rescue Mika from the Blackfoot. He had a moment of doubt, but then felt sure he was right. His job was to keep her and Mika safe, and she wouldn't be safe chasing after Akers and his brood.

Her dark eyes flashed when he turned back to her. "Safe? Was I safe when the Blackfoot kidnapped me and my little boy from our tribe? Was I safe when they sold me to those trappers at your rendezvous? Tell me, Flo-yd, was I safe then?"

He thought he'd try a softer, more persuasive tone. "Look, honey," and the conversation had gone downhill from there.

Steel's left front hoof rolled on a large rock. The horse stumbled but caught itself. The sound of horseshoe on rock was a loud grinding crunch, but the wind, which had picked up only an hour before, kept the noise from echoing off the tall walls of the wash. However, the lurch and sound yanked Floyd back to the present.

21

S horty glanced at him. "You sleeping? If it weren't for this south wind, them Pawnees could've heard that a mile away."

They swung around the next bend in the wash, and Jeb sat against the steep bank, drinking a cup of coffee. The pot boiled on the edge of a tiny fire that was producing only a thin ribbon of smoke, which, rising, the wind ripped and tore until nothing was visible above the walls of the wash. "I heard it. Floyd, I thought I'd taught you better."

If his friend was also surprised at Leotie being with them, he didn't show it. Floyd had to admit that Jeb's being here, making coffee, had startled him. Of course, he thought, *I shouldn't be surprised at anything he does. He has always been a surprising man.*

Jeb smiled at Leotie. "It's good to see you. Climb down and have some coffee. Howdy, boys, you're welcome, too. How's Aiyana and my son?"

Leotie swung down, flipped her reins around a piece of sagebrush growing out of the vertical bank, pulled a cup from her bag, and smiled at Jeb. "They're doing fine. Aiyana misses you and says to hurry home."

"Thanks." Jeb looked up at Floyd. "Took you long enough. What'd you do—go to Canada?"

Floyd tied Steel, grabbed his cup from his saddlebags, and tugged his hat tighter on his head. In the process, he brushed against Leotie. She smiled up at him and took his cup. *Thank goodness that's behind us,* Floyd thought. *At least I've learned how to prevent those kinds of confrontations. Just let her do what she wants.* He chuckled quietly to himself.

Jeb had been watching him. "Boy, what are you grinning at?"

Leotie had reached the coffeepot, and looked up at Floyd, her eyebrows raised. He winked at her and said to Jeb, "Nothing. How long have you been waiting?"

"Not long. Got here right after the wind started picking up. You fellers get a cup, then we've got a job to do. Our friends aren't far from here."

Floyd looked pointedly at the fire and the thin column of smoke being ripped apart.

Jeb shook his head. "Don't get your lather up. They'll never see it."

"Not to mention the Ute or Comanche smelling it. No telling how close they might be."

Jeb frowned and looked at Shorty. "When did he turn into an old woman?"

Shorty laughed. "Well, let me tell you, you mentioned Canada. We traveled all the way to the Snake."

Jeb shook his head. "Tell me later, Shorty." Jeb tossed the remains in his cup to the ground and shook it out. He set it next to him and picked up a long stick. "I want to show you boys where those fine, upstanding citizens are located. By the by, I hope you brought yore heavy underwear, 'cause I'm betting we're looking at a blue norther before the day is out. In fact, I'm hoping so. You'll see why in just a second."

Leotie poured coffee into Shorty's and Morg's cups and, holding the handles of both her and Floyd's cups, poured them about half full. She moved next to Floyd and squatted beside him, handing him his cup.

Jeb moved to one knee and smoothed out the dirt in front of him. As he smoothed, the lighter dust whipped away in the wind. He jabbed the point of the stick into the ground and rotated it, making the hole wider. "We're right here." He continued moving the stick in such a way as to form a single line, weaving and turning. "This is the creek bed. We'll stay in it until we reach a large dead cottonwood on the left. It's about two miles from here. There's a narrow wash that runs into this one at the base of the tree." He drew a line departing the large channel to the left. "We'll follow it for about three miles, and guess whose camp it leads us to."

He looked at Floyd and grinned. "There's a nice water hole right there, surrounded with plenty of brush and willows, all tall and green. It must be fed from an underground seep, because it doesn't look like the vegetation around this thing has ever had a water problem. The trees are tall, and the brush is thick. It's a great watering hole. Those fellers camped right beside it."

Floyd knew his friends were hating on the Akers bunch a little more for camping next to the tank. Their presence beside the waterhole would keep wild game from coming in to water. *Staying clear of a waterhole, unlike a running stream, was one of the first things Pa taught me and the boys,* Floyd thought. *He said you could tell a man's character by how close he camped to a single water source, especially in a dry area.*

Jeb tossed the stick down. "I counted six and a girl, and I think they're all related exceptin' for Page. He looks like the last thing he wants is to be here, especially with the Akers. With this wind, we'll be able to ride right into their camp. They won't hear a thing. I'm hoping it switches to the north before we get there. That'll help keep our scent away from their horses, but if it doesn't, we shouldn't have to worry. As hard as it's blowing, I don't think their horses will smell anything. He tossed the stick to the ground. So there it is, Floyd. It's all yours. You tell us how you want to take 'em, and we'll do it. The only suggestion I've got is to do it today. They've been lookin' a little antsy."

Floyd nodded to his friend. "Thanks, Jeb. I'm beholden for all you've done. Is the bank of the wash high enough to hide us and low enough to ride up all at once? I'd prefer not to come up single file. This bunch is from the Tennessee hill country. They may not know this country, but they're first-rate fighters. If we come up single file, they'll blow us out of the saddle one by one. Their normal reaction is to shoot first and celebrate later."

Jeb scratched his chin. "Reckon you could get three riders up at one time, but that would be all. Two would have to wait and follow."

"How far away from the creek bed is their camp?"

"Not far. If we didn't have this wind to cover our noise, we'd have to slip in on foot, but you've got room to ride horses up and onto level ground. When you pull them to a stop, you'll be only thirty feet from the farthest man."

Floyd thought on the problem. "Alright, here's what I'd like to do. The first three will be me, Jeb, and either Morg or Shorty. You two work it out between yourselves, without any fighting. The remaining two will be either of you two and Leotie. The reason I want to do it this way is to get firepower on those Akers. We've got the Patersons. We should be able to overpower them quickly."

Leotie spoke softly. "Flo-yd, if you want firepower, wouldn't you want me with the first group? You have given me two of the repeating pistols, and you know I can shoot them."

Floyd knew he was going to lose this argument. He didn't want to expose Leotie to the heaviest firepower, but other than the fact that he loved her and wanted to protect her, she was right. Silence reigned in the group. Floyd knew that because they all respected him and Leotie, no one else would say a word. He also knew she could shoot the Patersons and shoot them well, but she was his wife. He didn't want her to get shot. She watched him with those big brown eyes. Without saying a word, her expression was begging him to allow her to be in the first group.

Finally, he nodded. "Alright. I don't like it, but you're in. Jeb will be on the right, I'll be in the middle, and you'll be on the left. I'd like you to look for the girl. None of us are hankering for the opportunity to shoot a woman. If it has to be done, another woman might not hesitate the way a man would."

She nodded. "Thank you, my husband. I will look for the woman, but I will also look for Henry Page, and I can't guarantee I won't shoot him if I see him."

"Just look for her, and make sure she's not planning on shooting anyone before you go after Page. That's all I ask. The only other thing is, if they don't shoot, hold your fire. The goal here is to hang these killers. If we can't do that, then I guess we'll have to shoot them, but for now let's plan on taking them alive if they don't shoot. I think they will, but be ready either way. Any questions?" No one responded. "Good. Jeb, what say you lead us out of here?"

Jeb picked up the coffeepot and dumped it over the fire. A strong roasted-coffee smell surrounded them for a moment and was gone on the whirling wind. When he was done, he kicked dirt over the dead coals and headed for his horse.

Floyd walked beside Leotie. "Please be careful. I couldn't stand for you to get hurt. We're about done with these skunks, and we'll be able to have a good life together."

She slid her hand into his. "I'd like that, Flo-yd, and I ask you to also be careful. I would not like for you to get hurt."

He grinned at her. "I'll do my best."

The four mountain men and the Shoshone woman rode out on what each hoped would be the end of the killers. Floyd especially was tired of his long chase. He blamed himself for Roscoe Akers and his brood being out here and putting his family and friends at risk. But he was thankful they had exercised their vengeance on him and pursued him here, in his mountains, rather than harm his family in Tennessee. Floyd felt an icy anger burning deep in his belly. He was ready for this chase to end.

THE WORST DECISION of my life, Henry Page thought. *Why did I join up with these killers? Roscoe Akers must be crazy as a loon. That man rode right into the middle of the Shoshone camp and could have gotten us killed, but I got to see Leotie again. She's just as pretty, even with the scar, as she was when we had her in the cabin, but I didn't like the way she looked at me. It was almost like she knew what I did, but that's impossible. She was knocked out cold as a wedge. I've got to get out of here. I don't belong with these animals, and if she ever remembers, I don't want to be anywhere near Floyd Logan.*

Roscoe Akers tilted his bottle and swallowed twice. He pulled it from his lips, wiped his sleeve across his mouth, and belched.

Cooter sat on the cottonwood log next to Roscoe. "Come on, Pa," he said in a high-pitched, wheedling tone. "Don't drink it all. Me and my cousins want a sip."

Akers looked at him as if he were a roach and began to say something, decided against it, took another swig, and handed the bottle to him. He watched his son lift the bottle to his lips and tilt it high. "Cooter, blast you, don't drink it all. We ain't got but two bottles left." He looked at Mary Grace. "Ain't that right, girl?"

"Yeah, Pa, two bottles." She directed her attention to her brother. "Cooter, you gonna drink that or stare at it?"

Mary Grace's brother grinned at her. "Why, you thirsty, Mary Grace? You know it ain't proper for a lady to drink from a bottle." Roscoe laughed at his son's remark as Cooter turned the bottle up again, took another swig, and coughed. "Whew, that's strong stuff. I can feel it burning all the way down to my toes."

Mary Grace walked over to Cooter and stopped in front of him, her hands on her hips. She stared at her brother for a moment and, quick as a striking snake, yanked the bottle from him. "You heard Pa. Don't drink all the liquor." She tilted the bottle, took a drink for herself, and then handed the bottle back to Roscoe.

Cooter's eyes narrowed, and he reached for his knife. "You know better than to do that to me."

"Shut up, Cooter," Roscoe said. "Stop yore drinking. You need to get back to that Shoshone camp and do like we talked about." Cooter was slow to move, so Roscoe slapped his son on the back of his head. "Get goin', boy. You need to kill Logan's woman and her whelp. That'll show Floyd Logan what it feels like to lose his family."

"Pa, the weather's turnin' bad. How about I do that after it passes?"

Roscoe Akers raised his voice. "It don't matter, Cooter. It'll be bad here, too. Now get going."

Page had had enough of this bunch. He wanted to get out of here. He was used to living in hotels and eating at fine restaurants. Money had always been his friend and gravitated to him. Why he had elected to tie up with this pack of trash, he had yet to figure out. He would have already left if the chance had presented itself, but it seemed like at least one of the hillbillies was watching him every minute. *Why can't they just let me go?* he thought. *I've done my job. I've found the Shoshone. Floyd Logan will be there eventually.*

The horses were edgy with the wind. It had started blowing this morning and seemed to pick up through the day. At least it had warmed with the south wind. That was good enough for him. He couldn't stand cold weather, and the days had been getting cooler, another reason to get out of here. South, that was where he needed to go. New Orleans would be perfect.

Roscoe yelled, "Get away from those horses, Page. You planning on going somewhere?"

~

FLOYD COULD ALMOST REACH out and touch each of the tall banks in the narrow draw. But the bottom was soft sand, so, especially in this high wind, the horses made little sound. Rounding a bend, he saw the green of the huge willows and tall cottonwood trees. *This is a real oasis,* he thought. *I wonder how they found it. Page is the only one who's been west, and he has never ventured this far south.* He glanced over his shoulder and received a smile from Leotie. Floyd returned her smile and faced forward as Jeb pulled up and motioned to get ready. He reached for his pair of saddle guns, the two Patersons, before he realized Leotie was wearing them, and smiled to himself. They were in excellent hands.

Jeb had positioned them in the wash where there were several trails going up the side toward the camp. Floyd could see that there was room for three horses at a time. The horses would have their work cut out for them, for the bank was steep, but not so steep it would keep them from charging out. There were a lot of roots in the bank, which would help hold the dirt together, so the animals wouldn't slip.

Jeb mouthed, "When you're ready." He carried the pair of Paterson revolvers Floyd had purchased for him.

Floyd checked on Leotie. The revolver looked large in her small hand, but she was ready. Past her, Shorty and Morg had their Hawkens gripped in their right hands and resting across their saddles, with their single-shot pistols waiting in saddle scabbards. Everyone nodded. He heard yelling coming from above, but with the wind, he could understand nothing. He took one more look left and right, confirmed both Jeb and Leotie were ready, nodded, and kicked Steel. The mustang was used to traveling in this kind of country. He leaped forward and up, putting Floyd on top in two leaps. Leotie popped up to his left, but Jeb was nowhere to be seen. Floyd kept moving forward to allow Morg and Shorty room as well as Jeb, if he ever made it.

In the instant they broke over the top of the wash, Roscoe Akers went for his rifle.

Floyd shot him in the belly.

Mary Grace grabbed a nasty-looking double-barreled shotgun and was bringing it up.

Floyd didn't have time to address her because the fella who was sitting next to the old man already had his pistol up and was leveling it at him. Floyd thought, *This guy is fast,* and squeezed the trigger of his Paterson. The ball hit the man in the chest, and he fell across the log where he had been sitting. His pistol fell to the ground, and the man lay still.

Leotie's Paterson barked moments before the shotgun fired, and buckshot whistled over their heads. Morg and Shorty rode up as Gomer and his two brothers, Elmer and Jethro, leaped up. All three had rifles coming to bear on Floyd and Leotie.

Morg yelled, "I got the one on the right," and they both fired.

Gomer and his brother Jethro toppled over, both with holes in their foreheads.

In his peripheral vision, Floyd could see the last man standing halt his rifle's swing, and the big .50-caliber muzzle settled on him, but there was nothing he could do about it. He was busy firing at the fella next to the old man.

A pistol shot cracked from behind them, and the last man staggered, the muzzle dropping, but it started up again. After shooting the man next to the old man, Floyd swung his Paterson toward the man who had just been shot, but the same pistol fired again before either he or the man with the rifle could fire. The man staggered, released his rifle, and clutched his chest. He collapsed to his knees, swayed, and fell face first into the dirt, motionless.

Floyd immediately turned left to check on Leotie.

Eyes wide, she gazed back at him and mouthed, "I am fine, Flo-yd."

The only sound was old man Akers moaning on the ground. Excluding him, no one in the Akers gang moved.

Floyd turned in the saddle to see where the last two shots had come from.

Only Jeb's head and shoulders were visible over the top of the wash. In his right hand, the smoke from the Paterson's barrel whipped away.

"Thanks, partner. I figured I was a goner."

A wry grin pulled up the right corner of Jeb's mouth. "You almost were. I barely managed to scramble above the wash in time to take care of that feller. My horse got its front leg tangled in a root. I think it's from that big cottonwood. I've gotta get back down and help him. Everybody alright up here?"

Floyd surveyed the carnage and checked on Morg and Shorty. He received nods from both. "Yeah, looks like we're all fine." *That's the way it happens,* Floyd thought. *With all the trailing, planning, and anticipation, it's over in seconds.*

Roscoe Akers was down, moaning on the ground, with the other guy, probably Cooter, stretched across the log alongside him. By a count from Gideon's numbers, the only one missing was Henry Page. Unfortunately, the girl was down with a hole in her belly, much like her old man. Floyd glanced at Leotie. "Are you alright?"

"I am fine, Flo-yd, but I do not see Henry Page."

"We'll ask a few questions. Maybe we can find out what happened to him. Why don't you take a look at the girl? Good job, by the way. That shotgun could have taken our heads off if you hadn't stopped her."

Jeb finally rode out of the wash to join them. Fortunately, his horse wasn't limping.

Floyd swung down as Leotie stepped from the saddle. He headed for Roscoe Akers while Leotie ran to Mary Grace. Roscoe was on the ground, rolling and moaning. Floyd stopped a roll with his foot, allowing him to see the man's grimacing face. "You've been looking for me, Mr. Akers?"

"Help me. I'm hurting bad. You shot me."

"Yes, sir. I seem to remember you tried to shoot me. I asked you a question. Are you looking for me?"

"Who are you?"

"I'm Floyd Logan. You've been all over my mountains, killing folks and threatening others while you looked for me. How many folks have you killed since coming west?"

"You've got to help me. I'm hurtin' something terrible."

"First, maybe you can tell me where Henry Page went."

"Page? Who cares about Page? I'm hurtin', man. You've gotta help me."

Floyd said nothing.

Akers moaned again and squinted up at Floyd's stoic face. "Alright, last I saw him, he was standing among the horses. Now help me, please."

Floyd turned away from Akers and walked toward the horses, stopping beside Leotie and Mary Grace. "How is she?"

Leotie had just finished examining the young woman, whose blank dark eyes stared at the racing clouds above. She looked up at Floyd and shook her head. "Page?"

"I'm checking now. Akers said he was with the horses when we came over the bank."

Floyd examined the horses. They had been tied along a rope stretched between two trees. There was a space between two of them. He checked the area and found where a horse had been led away. Following the tracks, he found where a man had mounted, no saddle, and headed north. Stepping to the edge of the grove, Floyd gazed north and saw nothing.

Leotie stepped to his side. "Do we follow him?"

He shook his head. "He has no supplies, no water, nothing besides what's on his back. To top it off, there's nothing out there to help him survive. In fact, he's headed directly for where the Pawnees were hunting. If he's lucky, he'll die, if not, the Pawnees will find him. They've got to be pretty upset at the loss of so many braves. I'd hate to be a white man who falls into their grasp. It won't be pretty."

Leotie stared at the northern prairie. She broke the silence with one word. "Good." Then she looked up at Floyd. "The girl is dead."

"Too bad she went for that shotgun."

"But if she had been unharmed, what would we have done with her? She's been with them throughout all the killings and the beating of Salty."

Floyd's long arm encompassed her waist. He held her close, feeling the warmth of her body. "Fortunately, we don't have to make that decision." He leaned down and kissed the top of her head.

Shorty called from behind them, "The old man's asking for you."

"I want to talk to him."

He dropped his arm from her waist and headed for Akers. Reaching him, he knelt.

Akers grimaced in pain. "What are you gonna do with me?"

"You're dying, Akers. What does it matter?"

Akers's lips pulled back, showing broken teeth, and he gasped. "It hurts almighty bad."

"You won't hurt much longer. What do you want?"

"My brothers will come after you."

Floyd shook his head. "No, they won't. Your brothers will never hear about you or your brood. We're going to dump you in a big hole in the middle of the prairie with no marker. There won't be anyone who'll know or care what happened."

Akers fought through the pain, his teeth unclenched. "Page knows. Gent knows."

Floyd gave a short laugh. "Page is riding bareback in the middle of the prairie, with no supplies, surrounded by angry Pawnees. If he makes it a day, it'll surprise me. As far as your son, he's in jail at

Fort John. The trappers have probably already hanged him, but if he survives, I don't think he'll ever mention your name again. If he's still alive, he has probably already changed his name."

The old man, still filled with hate, grabbed Floyd's forearm in a viselike grip and, through broken gasps, said, "I hope someone sends you straight to . . ." His eyes widened, and his body went rigid, his heels bounced on the ground like he was running, and then his hand relaxed on Floyd's arm. He, like his daughter, stared unseeingly at the racing clouds above.

Floyd pried the hand from his arm and stood, looking at the very angry and very dead man.

Leotie slid her arm through his. "His was a furious spirit. It is good he is gone."

Floyd, for the first time, became conscious of the wind having changed. It was out of the northwest and cooler. He saw Jeb and Morg on horseback, ropes looped over several of the bodies, dragging them away from the waterhole and into the prairie.

Shorty was standing over the girl, staring down at her. "She was a pretty girl. It's hard to believe she could've been as bad as Gideon said."

Leotie placed her hand on Shorty's thick forearm. "She was like the coral snake, Shorty, pretty but deadly."

He patted her hand. "Yeah, you're right, ma'am." He bent down and lifted the dead girl. "Guess she'll get to sleep with those who brung her." He tossed her body over his horse, climbed into the saddle, and followed Jeb and Morg.

It took a good part of the remaining daylight to get the hole dug and the bodies buried. Besides being hard, the ground was filled with rocks, and they had only one shovel, but were thankful for it. They had found it at the Akers camp, probably part of Gideon's goods. They placed no markers.

Before leaving, Floyd said a brief prayer. "Lord, you know these fellas. Thy will be done. Amen."

Shorty spit. "Reckon you're a lot nicer than I would've been."

"My ma's influence."

Leotie stepped close to Floyd and slipped her hand in his. "I do not want to spend the night here. It is full of evil spirits. Let's go home. Mika is waiting."

Floyd looked down at his wife. *Home,* he thought. *I have Leotie, Mika, and my friends. I am a blessed man.* "Yes, my wife, let's go see our son."

AUTHOR'S NOTE

I hope you've enjoyed reading *Burden of a Mountain Man,* the fourth book in the Logan Mountain Man series.

If you have any comments, what you like or what you don't, please let me know. You can email me at: Don@DonaldLRobertson.com, or fill in the contact form on my website.

www.DonaldLRobertson.com

I'm looking forward to hearing from you.

Reviews on Amazon are also appreciated.

Also, if you enjoyed the *Burden of a Mountain Man* and haven't read the first book in the series, *Soul of a Mountain,* you can pick it up on Amazon.

Have a terrific day.

BOOKS
A Jack Sage Western Series
STRANGER WITH A STAR
WITHOUT THE STAR
RETURN OF THE STAR
THE HANGING STAR
FIVE WOMEN AND THE STAR
THE LOYAL STAR
JUSTICE OF THE STAR
HONOR OF THE STAR

Logan Mountain Man Series
(Prequel to Logan Family Series)
SOUL OF A MOUNTAIN MAN
TRIALS OF A MOUNTAIN MAN
METTLE OF A MOUNTAIN MAN
BURDEN OF A MOUNTAIN MAN

Logan Family Series
LOGAN'S WORD
THE SAVAGE VALLEY
CALLUM'S MISSION
FORGOTTEN SEASON
TROUBLED SEASON
TORTURED SEASON

Clay Barlow - Texas Ranger Justice Series
FORTY-FOUR CALIBER JUSTICE
LAW AND JUSTICE
LONESOME JUSTICE

NOVELLAS AND SHORT STORIES

RUSTLERS IN THE SAGE
BECAUSE OF A DOG
THE OLD RANGER